AMNESTIC

Milena Nikolova

Cover art by Brady Vencill

Printed in the United States of America.

Contents

Prologue

Ten years ago, the European Alliance attacked and invaded the United States. They struck without warning. Out of nowhere, the first EMP was detonated. It was fast, silent, and final. The cities fell into darkness. The grid collapsed. That was an unexpected attack from a former ally. China or Russia, maybe, but never Western Europe.

By the time anyone realized what was happening, it was over.

Without the grid, all operations ceased. The Americans attempted to resist, but eventually, all major cities fell. The American government was disbanded, and Alliance collaborators were installed.

Dark years followed. Those who didn't conform were imprisoned or executed.

The only ones who dared to fight back were the American Resistance. Small cells were scattered throughout the country, mainly in the mountains and the swampy lands of Louisiana, where it was difficult for the enemy to search.

Still, Alliance patrols circled daily, looking for insurgents. Those who refused to cooperate retreated to Resistance locations and lived frugally, barely managing to secure food and shelter.

Even though everything seemed final and hopeless, small sparks of the old fire still burned in the souls of the people, who vividly remembered freedom. Hidden in barely survivable lands, they waited and prepared to reclaim their lives and take revenge for all the souls lost since the invasion. There was no light at the end of the tunnel, but there was hope. It was weak and battered, but still there, clinging to life. As long as there was hope, nothing was fully lost, even if it seemed that way.

Chapter 1

Tahoma Jensen was thirty years old when everything started. He was born and raised in Wyoming, half Cheyenne, half everything else. Not that it mattered anymore. He had fought against the invasion since day one. At the beginning, he had hopes. He had fire. Now he wasn't sure if he even cared anymore.

All his friends and loved ones were gone, extinguished by the merciless war machine called the Alliance. He'd nearly died more times than he could count, but for some unknown reason, he was still here.

He ran his hand along the old scar on the left side of his face. He carried the scars of war on his body and the pain of countless losses in his heart.

Frustrated, he shook his head.

He could swear the wind had razor blades tonight. It whistled between the needles of the pine trees as if it were warning him to get off the road and stay put. His truck struggled to gain traction. The engine was choking on its last breath. It was snowing, and the headlights were more of a distraction than help. It was like driving in a warp-speed tunnel.

He hadn't planned to be out that late, but one of the widows in Ravenville needed firewood. He also had to put some more work into the building he had outfitted for a health clinic. He had learned that a physician was coming from Denver. Even though the town desperately needed medical help, he didn't trust this type of generosity from the Alliance.

No one had ever cared for the well-being of the people in Ravenville. Getting a physician all of a sudden was suspicious, to say the least. Either way, he wasn't about to deny medical care to anybody. He was going to watch every move of the supposed doctor whenever he decided to show up.

Tahoma had lived in the mountains around Ravenville for the last five years. The people in town knew him as Ash. He had carried this name since the early resistance days when he was the only survivor who rose from the ashes of burned-down cities and battlefields.

He frowned. There wasn't much he cared about anymore. If the Resistance were to decide to go into action, he was ready to follow. Fighting was the only thing that had any meaning for him.

His own life wasn't worth much.

There was a time he could still get excited and feel his heart flutter. It was right before he came to the mountains. He was the host of an online forum named "Amnestic." It was an encrypted site where he posted news and photos from America for the world to see. He needed others to remember that the American people were still human and that they were suffering under the boot of the Alliance.

Ash had chosen the name "Amnestic" to highlight how the world had forgotten what the United States had done for everybody, and now that Americans needed help, the world had turned a blind eye.

There was a girl named Tina. He loved talking to her. He always jokingly called her Tinker Bell or just Tink. She was young and naïve, but there was fire in her heart. Ash wasn't sure where she was from, but they spent many days talking, arguing, and laughing together. He would sign in to Amnestic every day with the sole reason to talk to her. Tina always called him "an insufferable grump" and did her best to lift his spirits.

"Hey, Ash, why are you such an insufferable grump?" Her voice echoed in his head. *"Look outside. The sun is shining, and the flowers smell so sweet. Not all is lost."*

She was so full of light.

Ash felt a sharp pain right down to his soul.

Tink had told him that she planned to join the Resistance. Ash brushed that off as just a crazy idea. He was planning to ask her to meet him, but suddenly, she disappeared.

I should've found her before...

He was sure she had spoken to the wrong people, and the Alliance had eliminated her. He blamed himself and carried this guilt for years. After he lost Tink, his heart closed up. He lived from one day to the next, waiting for the fight to start.

Ash sighed heavily. He had a bad feeling. The Alliance had been closing in on the last operational Resistance cells, and the arrival of that doctor reeked of a setup. For the last several years, his gut feelings had been his best friend and had saved his life countless times.

He wasn't going to allow anything bad to happen to his people. Whoever that imposter pretending to be a physician was, he wouldn't leave Ravenville alive. Ash knew that much. He clenched his jaw. So it was decided.

A suspicious sight jolted him out of his thoughts. His headlights flickered across something that wasn't there earlier. Right around the bend, where the road met the solid rock of the mountain, there was a vehicle sitting still on the side of the road. He pulled over, switched off the engine, and jumped out of the truck. He heard the sharp squeak of the snow under his boots and silently swore. If that was an ambush, he was already dead meat.

Ash dropped down behind a rock and quietly surveyed the area.

No movement.

The only thing that disturbed the silence was the sick idling of the wrecked vehicle's engine. Staying in the shadows, he cautiously approached the car. It was a black sedan, European make. The front end was smashed against the side of the mountain. He saw smoke coming from underneath the hood and heard the fuel hissing. The vehicle was going to ignite at any moment.

Ash gripped his rifle and pulled the driver's door open. The mangled metal screeched. He pointed his rifle at the dark mass inside. The silhouette was still. He poked it with the muzzle of the rifle.

Nothing.

Ash grunted, pulled a flashlight out of his pocket, and shined the light at the person. Long dark hair, fancy coat, a woman. She had slumped over, half on the driver's seat, half on the passenger's.

With growing frustration, Ash turned her over. There was a wound on the left side of her forehead. The blood was soaking her hair and dripping down her face. He could see her breath steaming in the freezing night. He pointed the light at the shattered window on the driver's side and saw a bloody stain on the glass. That must be where her head had hit after bouncing off the airbag.

He shrugged, turned around, and walked toward his truck. Either the cold or the fire was going to take care of the situation. Whoever that woman in the wreckage was, she didn't belong. The Alliance was getting bold, openly sending people into Resistance territory. Ash was already reaching for the door of the truck when he hesitated. The woman was still alive...

"Goddammit!" he swore, abruptly turned around, and walked back to the car.

He picked up the traveling bags from the backseat and put them on his shoulder. Then he carefully took the woman in his arms. She was cold and limp, but lighter than he expected. There was a fleeting scent of jasmine radiating from her. That detail annoyed him for reasons he didn't understand. Ash laid her on the back seat of his truck, threw her bags in the bed, and jumped behind the wheel. He drove off, knowing that he'd regret that.

The woman moved around and opened her eyes. Ash looked at her through the rearview mirror. She tried to raise her head, but suddenly retched and vomited on the floor. Then she drifted into unconsciousness again.

"Great!" Ash looked over his shoulder. "I knew I should've left her behind."

He wrinkled his nose.

"Just what I've always wanted, a vomit-infused truck. Damn it!"

He hit the gas harder. The truck struggled to climb up the steep mountain road but made it. Ash parked it at the end of the trail and switched off the engine. He slung the rifle across his back and the bags on his shoulder. Then he picked up the woman and hiked up the mountain. About a mile later, he reached a small cabin. He walked in, unloaded the woman on the small cot, and locked the door. Then he pulled the blackout curtains over the windows.

Ash squatted by the wood stove and started a fire. He warmed up his hands, lit up an oil lamp, and put a kettle of water on. He patiently waited for it to heat up. Ash took the lamp and set it by the woman, who was still lying unconscious on the bed.

He pressed his lips together, looking at her for a minute. She was beautiful; he had to give her that. Soft skin, thick dark eyelashes, full lips...

He shook his head and proceeded to remove her coat and check for more injuries. It appeared that the wound on her forehead was the only one. Still, more than enough. He was hoping that she wasn't bleeding in her head, or he would end up with a corpse he wouldn't know how to get rid of.

"Seatbelts are not optional," he muttered under his breath.

Ash took a clean towel, brought the kettle by the bed, and started cleaning her face. When he was satisfied with his work, he pulled an old, rusted-out metal trunk from under the bed and dug out a suture kit. He put a couple of stitches in the still bleeding wound and slapped on a bandage.

"There, no more bloody mess on my bed." He cleaned up the blood-stained tissues.

Then he sat in his chair with the rifle across his lap, and gazed at the woman, who still lay motionless in his bed.

What did I get myself into?

He sighed heavily.

Chapter 2

The woman stirred in the bed, and her eyelids fluttered. She stared at the ceiling, trying to break through the confusion.

A strange, dingy room, hard bed under her back...

Then she turned and saw him.

A tall, grim-looking man. Long black hair. A vertical scar on the left side of his face, and a rifle resting on his lap. He was gazing at her with an expression that didn't promise mercy.

Her heart seized. She bolted upright and tried to run. She barely took two steps when her legs gave out. She collapsed, hitting the floor hard.

Ash jumped to his feet. The rifle clattered to the ground. He reached and grabbed the woman before her head could hit the ground. She thrashed weakly, swinging her arm at him.

"Easy," he said, his raspy voice brushing against her ears. "You were in a wreck. I found you bleeding on the side of the road. You're in my cabin. Just calm down."

Slowly, she stopped fighting and let him put her back into bed. She sat up and continued to stare at him. He looked like one of those mountain men who shot foreigners on sight. He reached for her, and she pulled back, shivering.

"I just want to check the wound on the side of your head," he said, exhaling sharply. "I patched you up earlier. You were bleeding all over the place."

She just sat silently with her arms wrapped around her knees.

"I could've left you in your car to freeze to death," the man said with audible regret in his voice. "Thinking about it now, I should have. You puked in my truck. What were you doing so far up the mountain?"

She hunched her shoulders as if to protect herself and buried her face in her knees.

"My patience is wearing thin. Start talking, lady. I don't keep liabilities around long." His voice was colder than the night outside.

"My name is Celestine Beaumont," she whispered.

Ash pursed his lips. The only thing more French than her name was her accent. He silently cursed. He knew it was a mistake bringing her up to his cabin.

"What were you doing so far up the mountain?" There was an open threat in his voice.

"I was on my way to Ravenville when my GPS told me to turn onto the side of the mountain."

"Well, that was your first clue that you don't belong," Ash laughed coldly. "What is your business here?" He gazed at her with contempt.

"I'm the physician assigned to that town."

"The physician..." Ash frowned.

A damn woman?

That was going to complicate things. He intently gazed at her. Her big brown eyes made her look like a deer in headlights. He wasn't sure whether she was scared or if it was the concussion.

Shit!

He knew he wouldn't be able to shoot her in cold blood.

"So, you are the doctor," he said slowly. "Care to explain why you chose this town?"

"I volunteer. Here is where they sent me."

"They?" His face became stone-cold in an instant. "Who are they?

"I'm with Doctors Without Borders."

"Yeah, right," he laughed cynically. "I haven't seen one of those in years. You need to come up with a better lie."

"I'm not lying." There was some stubbornness in her voice.

"Prove it." He locked his eyes with hers.

"You can look at my ID badge. It's in my coat, whatever you might've done with it."

He quickly walked to the stove, where her coat was hanging to dry, and searched the pockets. He pulled out a passport and an ID badge.

"*Celestine Beauwhatever,*" he mumbled. "Okay, Celeste, don't expect me to pronounce that French nonsense."

"Celeste's fine. What is your name?"

"Tahoma Jensen." He noticed that her eyes slightly widened.

Ash's eyes darkened. She had heard his name before. That was bad news for him and especially for her.

"You've heard my name before."

There was danger in his eyes.

"Well, yeah, you were the one I was told to contact about the location of my office."

"Who told you?"

"Doctors Without..."

"Forget it!" He cut her off.

"Is this your home?" she asked.

"Yes, that's my *'ome*." He mocked her accent.

"Why are you so mean?" Her lip quivered.

"Don't tell me you're gonna start bawling now. Get some sleep." He grimaced.

Then he got up, shrugged on his coat, grabbed the rifle, and walked outside.

Standing by the door, Ash gritted his teeth. The European woman in the cabin stirred the worst memories buried deep in his heart. People like her had taken away all his family and friends. They had taken Tink...

Ash took a deep breath in an attempt to suppress the pain that was rising in his heart. He cherished no illusions that she was just a volunteer. He could smell a setup from a mile away. He was facing a lose-lose situation. Ash rubbed his forehead. For now, he would let her be and watch her. He walked back in and crouched by the stove to warm his hands.

He looked over his shoulder. The woman had covered her head with the blanket and appeared to be sleeping. Ash slowly stood up, pulled his chair close to the bed, sat down with the rifle across his lap, and watched the woman sleep. The morning found him in the same position, gripping his rifle with his eyes fixed on the intruder in his bed.

She stirred under the blanket, mumbling something unintelligible. Finally, she emerged, holding her head in her hands.

"Do you have some headache medicine?" she whined.

Ash abruptly stood up.

"Do you *'ave* some *'eadache* medicine?" he mocked her, walking toward the cabinet above the sink.

He pulled out some acetaminophen and handed it to her.

"Is there a restroom in this..." she looked around.

"You can call it a shack," he said. "Down the hall to the right." He pointed toward the opposite end of the cabin.

She slowly stood up, staggering all over the floor and, holding on to the wall, walked to the restroom. Once inside, she locked the door, reached down her shirt, and pulled out a government-issued phone. She quickly typed in code:

"I have contacted the subject. So far, no suspicious activity. He may not be the same person. Will continue to monitor."

She tapped "send" and slipped the phone back inside her shirt. Then she used the restroom, washed her hands, and walked back to the bed.

"You took too long in there." Ash took a second to study her face. "What were you doing?"

"Are you for real?" She looked at him with apprehension. "You're timing my bathroom breaks now? This is outrageous!"

Her exaggerated anger couldn't fool him. He didn't know what she did in the bathroom, but it was definitely not bathroom business.

Ash decided not to argue about that for the moment. He had plenty of time to figure her out. He stood up and stirred the pot of soup he had started on the stove. Ash threw another look at Celeste, but she had covered her head with the blanket. He put his coat on and went outside to make sure no one had followed them up the mountain.

As soon as the door closed behind him, Celeste tiptoed to the window and looked. The man was nowhere in sight. She reached down her shirt, pulled out a different phone, and quickly started to write:

"Dave, this is going to be harder than I thought. Your guy, Tahoma, is meaner than a snake. He's going to kill me before I manage to save his ass. I already started my disinformation campaign with the Alliance, but someone might have to help me."

She cautiously looked at the door, then continued to type:

"I think he already suspects that I'm a spy. Unfortunately for me, he thinks I'm the wrong kind of spy. I can't tell him the truth because I'll blow my cover. He scares the living hell out of me."

She put the phone away and lay her head on the pillow. She had joined the Resistance about five years earlier. The Alliance thought she was their spy. In reality, she was feeding intel to the Resistance. She had been good at her job up until now.

The Alliance had recently begun hunting several individuals suspected of organizing Resistance activities. Tahoma Jensen was high on that list. And judging by the way he carried himself, they were right.

This man was going to be the death of her.

She knew it.

Chapter 3

Celeste sat on the bed with her stomach churning. She was scared of the man who stared at her, holding a gun. He could decide to put a bullet in her head at any moment. No one from the Resistance could help her here, certainly not in this secluded cabin. Jensen had saved her life, but that could change the second his suspicion deepened.

If he found the government-issued phone, she was dead. She pressed a hand to her chest. Both phones were in hidden pockets in her padded bra. If her captor wanted to find them, he had to strip her clothes off. Somehow, she didn't think that he'd ever do that, so she exhaled with relief. Either way, she had to find a way out of this cabin. She felt like a prisoner. She wasn't even sure if Jensen would let her leave.

She went to the window and looked outside. The man was nowhere in sight.

This is my only chance.

Celeste hurriedly put her boots and coat on. There had to be a path leading down the mountain. She stepped onto the porch and scanned the woods.

Good. There is no one.

Celeste looked at the tree line. If she made it there, she could try to find her way to the nearest town.

She stepped off the porch and, in that split second, realized that there was no solid ground under the snow. She lost her breath when her back hit the ground, and then the world spun around her in a wild, snowy blur as she rolled down the slope.

She felt her insides turn over, and then the panic gripped her. She felt something slam into her shoulder. The pain exploded, then everything went black.

Ash was stacking wood in the shed when he heard the thud.

He ran around the cabin to the porch, quickly chambering a round in his rifle. The first thing he saw was the open door, and then, Celeste tumbling down the hill.

He swore.

He saw her hit the trunk of a pine tree. Her body bounced off and continued to roll down like a rag doll.

He sprinted down after her. If she fell into the ravine, it would be over.

He continued running, even though he knew that he was too far to catch her. He saw her body hit a patch of dense bushes and come to a stop. He quickly reached her. She wasn't moving. He dropped to his knees and put his fingers on her neck. She was alive. He scooped her up and carried her to the cabin. One of her boots was missing.

"Stupid idiot!" he muttered, shaking his head.

He took her coat off, and she cried in pain.

"What the hell did you think you were doing?" he snapped.

"I thought there was a path off your porch," she mumbled, avoiding his eyes.

"Want the bad news or the worse news first?" His voice was flat.

She just stared back.

"The bad news is, you dislocated your right shoulder," he paused. "And the worst news is that I don't have anything stronger than acetaminophen for what I'm about to do."

Ash got up, went to the stove, and poured soup into a metal bowl.

"This is all I can offer you for after." He set the bowl on the stand next to the bed. "Elk meat, potatoes, and carrots. It's a feast if you ask me."

He handed her a couple of pills.

"Here, take that. You will need them."

She took the pain medicine with a trembling hand. Celeste knew exactly what she was about to endure.

"Hurry up and do it," she whispered, biting her lip.

"Okay, on three," he said, placing one of his hands on her right shoulder and the other on her upper arm.

Celeste winced, feeling his cold hands against her bare skin.

"Ready?" Ash looked at her. "One, two..."

He popped her shoulder back in place.

Celeste gasped. A powerful wave of nausea rose in her throat. She grabbed the soup bowl from the stand and vomited into it.

"Great!" Ash wrinkled his nose, grabbed the bowl, and threw it out the door.

"You said 'on three,'" Celeste whined.

"Well, I lied," Ash smiled coldly.

He tore up an old sheet and fashioned a sling, securing her arm against her chest.

"Let me check for more injuries." He pressed against her joints and ribs, but there was no pain. "You're lucky. You could've killed yourself," he muttered. "Not that I care. But I'd probably be accused of pushing you. Where were you trying to go?"

She looked away. "Just wanted to leave."

"Leave?" He raised an eyebrow in a mocking grimace. "If you walk out of here alone, you'd be dead before sunrise. I'll take you to town, just be patient."

"You're not going to shoot me?" She timidly raised her eyes to meet his.

"That's all up to you," he said flatly.

"What do people call you?" she asked. "Tahoma Jensen doesn't exactly roll off the tongue."

"Like Celestine Beaumont does?"

He shot her an angry look.

"Well, I told you that you can call me Celeste. It's only fair for you to return the favor."

"I don't think fair has anything to do with anything," he muttered. "But okay. People just call me Ash."

"Ash!" Celeste stared at him.

She knew that name.

Years ago, she had an online friend named Ash. They met on an encrypted forum called "Amnestic." Ash was the one who had inspired her to join the Resistance. She went under the name Tina, but he called her Tinker Bell or just Tink. She had asked him why, and he'd said that she was full of light just like her.

Was this gruff, broken man her Ash?

She thought he was dead. After joining the Resistance, she searched for him, but he had vanished without a trace. She assumed the Alliance had executed him.

Her heart fluttered. Was Tahoma Jensen her Ash? He had to be.

She studied his face.

This is exactly how she had always pictured Ash, hardened and tired of life. He was such an insufferable grump!

She smiled.

Ash caught her smile at the corner of his eye.

Why the hell is she smiling?

"What's so funny?" He frowned, stood up, and headed to the stove.

"Why do you hate me, Ash?" she asked softly.

"Why do I hate you?" He abruptly turned around, towered over her, and locked his eyes with hers.

"I'll tell you why." His voice was low and full of hate. "Your people killed mine. My family. My friends... You killed my Tink."

He turned on his heel and stormed out of the cabin.

My Tink...

Celeste smiled through tears.

He is my Ash!

She wanted to tell him she was Tink, but she couldn't. She had to protect her cover. Celeste felt the tears rolling down her face.

Ash was alive!

He hated her, but it didn't matter. He was alive. And if someone was going to kill her, she preferred it to be him.

She knew how much he had suffered.

In this moment, she forgave him every harsh word, every cold glare, every sharp remark. She understood, and she loved him for surviving.

After a few minutes, he came back in. Ash looked at her face and sighed.

"So, you are going to whine after all," he grumbled. "Lie down and get some sleep."

He pulled the blanket over her shoulders and sat in his chair, not moving his eyes away from her.

"Now, I have to guard you, so you don't try to run again," he muttered. "In case you try another brilliant escape... And ... sorry about earlier." He looked away. "You touched a nerve."

"It's okay, Ash," she said, covering her head with the blanket.

He frowned.

It's okay, Ash?

That was new.

There was something off about her. Something had changed in the way she looked at him. The fear was gone from her eyes. Perhaps the concussion had worsened after her fall.

He grunted and put his rifle on the side of his chair.

He noticed that Celeste was looking at him from under the blanket.

"If you have something to say, say it," he snapped.

"I have to open the clinic in Ravenville."

She threw the blanket off and sat up.

"Fine." He nodded. "We'll go tomorrow. I have already prepared the building. I guess I have to do everything since you decided to fling yourself down a cliff."

"I'd be grateful for your help," she said.

"Stop looking at me with that weird glow in your eyes," he grimaced. "It makes me think you're planning to stab me."

"Sorry," she whispered, looking down. "I just feel... dizzy."

"Get some sleep." He grabbed his rifle, threw on his coat, and went outside.

Ash leaned against the cabin wall and pressed his hand to his forehead.

She knows who I am.

He shouldn't have mentioned the name Ash. That was the name everybody in the Resistance knew him by. He'd just handed her everything she needed to report him.

He had to stay alert. He still didn't know why she'd really come to Ravenville. He could only hope she was at least a real doctor and would help the town.

"I'll let her help," he muttered, "and then we'll see."

He walked back inside.

Chapter 4

Celeste woke up and smiled. This was the best sleep she'd had in years.

Ash was alive.

My Ash!

She still couldn't believe it. After everything, after giving up hope, he was right here in front of her. He was angry; he hated her, but none of that mattered.

He was alive.

Just now, she realized that he was still sitting in the chair, gazing at her.

"I think that fall knocked a screw loose in your head," he said.

There was no humor in his voice, just an observation.

"Maybe it did," she replied, smiling again.

He shook his head.

"Did you get the medical supplies from my car?" she asked. "Please, tell me you did!"

"I don't know. I found two duffel bags on the back seat. I brought them with me."

"You mean you didn't look inside?" Her eyes widened.

"What kind of person do you think I am?" His voice sharpened. "Why would I go through your bags?"

"Sorry," Celeste mumbled, lowering her eyes. "I thought..."

"Well, you thought wrong." He cut her off. "Now hurry up. We need to get going."

She sat up, slipped one boot on, then looked around.

"Where's my other one?" she asked.

"Ask the mountain." He smirked. "When I dragged you up the slope, it was already gone."

"So, what am I supposed to do now?"

"That's a problem, isn't it?" He eyed her feet, then sighed. "I was going to lend you a pair of my boots, but now I realize that they wouldn't even stay on your feet. Guess I have to carry you. Again."

"You don't have to," she mumbled.

"So, what's your plan? Walk barefoot and freeze your toes off? Then what, amputate? You make no sense."

"I'm sorry," she sighed.

Ash slung his gun across his back and grabbed her bags, heaving them over his shoulder.

"Let's go." He picked her up and stepped outside. "Don't worry. Downhill's easier."

She wrapped her good arm around his neck.

"Thank you for taking care of me," she whispered.

He glanced at her but said nothing.

For the rest of the way, he walked in silence.

Once they reached the truck, he settled her into the front seat and tried the ignition several times before the engine caught.

"This truck's on its last breath," he muttered. "But it's got a few more miles in it."

The drive to Ravenville was about an hour. Celeste spent it in silence, staring out of the window. Everything was buried under heavy snow. She had noticed the chains wrapped around the wheels of the truck. That was probably the only reason the truck could handle the icy mountain roads.

Ash was right. If she'd tried to leave alone, she wouldn't have made it.

When they drove into Ravenville, Ash parked the truck in front of an old building that looked like it used to be a shop of some sort.

"Welcome to your doctor's office," he said. "It's not as fancy as what you're used to, but no one here lives in luxury."

His voice was colder than the snow outside.

Celeste opened the door and tried to climb out, but before her feet could touch the ground, Ash scooped her up and carried her inside.

"I'll stoke the wood stove," he said, placing her in a chair. "I'll also look for boots. Stay off the cold floors until then. You need to start learning how to survive in the mountains. Whoever sent you here had no idea what the hell they were doing."

Without waiting for a response, he stocked the stove. Once the fire caught, he moved the chair closer to the heat.

"Warm up," he ordered. "Don't move until I get back."

Then he left.

Celeste smiled to herself.

No matter how rude he tried to be, Ash was still a good man. She always knew that. She looked around. The room appeared to be an old kitchen, but it was clean. Ash must've done the work himself before she arrived.

While she waited, she used the time to send another false update to the Alliance. She reported that she'd be staying in Ravenville for several weeks to provide medical care and gather intel.

She smiled again. Everything was finally going according to plan. The Alliance was being misled, and Ash no longer wanted to kill her. She was glad he had mellowed out because the Resistance phone had shattered during her fall down the hill, so she had no means to check in with them.

Yes. Everything was good.

She moved her right shoulder. It no longer hurt. Ash had done a great job, despite not having any medical background. The war had probably forced him to learn.

Celeste's smile faded.

She was ashamed of her European connection. That made her complicit in the suffering inflicted on all those people here. Ash had every reason to hate her.

She understood why.

He didn't know she was Tink. And maybe that was for the best. She wanted him to remember Tink as someone bright, someone worth missing. Not...her. If he knew who Tink was, he would be sorely disappointed. Celeste needed to hold on to their shared memories as they were in the past.

Ash returned in a couple of hours with a pair of old boots.

"Try these," he said, handing them over.

They fit surprisingly well. Ash definitely had a good eye.

He waved her forward. "Come on, I'll show you around."

The building had four rooms: two for patients, a small bedroom for Celeste, and the kitchen. Each room had a wood stove.

She was impressed. Given how scarce resources were, Ash had done a remarkable job.

"I'll stay here with you," he said. "You can have the bedroom. I'll sleep in the kitchen."

"But... you hate me," she said, bewildered.

"Hate has nothing to do with it," he said flatly. "If I leave you here alone, you won't last a day. Someone will shoot you before you ever realize what's happening. You're only useful to us alive. That is why I'm staying, to protect that usefulness. Not because I care. I'm doing it for my people."

Her heart tightened, but she said nothing.

Celeste sighed.

Ash had every right to feel the way he did. The irony wasn't lost on her. To the Alliance, she was a traitor. To Americans, she was the enemy.

She shook her head.

She was fighting for the right side. That was all that mattered. Personal happiness didn't factor in. She had no regrets.

Celeste gradually established her practice. At first, people were wary, but eventually, they started coming in with complaints. Supplies were limited, but she did what she could.

Days blurred into weeks. The snow thinned.

The townspeople warmed up to her. Some even stopped by just to talk.

When Ash thought it was safe enough, he took her to the mountain cabins to visit people who needed help. He never introduced her by name, just "the Doctor."

Celeste's heart ached. The people out there lived in brutal conditions. There was barely any food. Their clothes were worn out. The houses lacked insulation. Sometimes she cried alone afterward. She hated that there was so much suffering, and so little she could do.

Ash had stopped mocking her.

He noticed her compassion and her hard work.

He had not heard or seen any agents of the Alliance, so maybe, just maybe, he was wrong about her. And maybe she really was here to help.

He wanted to believe it, but still, he didn't let his guard down. Ash had seen enough people perish because of complacency.

Celeste grew to love the town and the people. Their honesty and kindness were heartwarming. Even though she was different, they accepted her and trusted her.

She didn't need fancy clothes or a big house. What she had here was enough.

She didn't want to go back to Denver.

She had managed to convince the Alliance that she needed to stay longer to investigate "possible resistance activity." It was a lie, but one they were happy to believe.

Celeste stepped outside and took a deep breath of the crisp, mountain air. The scent of pine and moss filled her lungs. The mountains no longer felt like a prison.

They felt like home.

It was the end of March. Snow still clung to the ground, but spring was coming. She could almost smell it in the air.

"What are you doing, sitting outside in the cold?"

Ash's voice cut through the air.

She looked up.

"Come inside before you freeze," he said. "I've made tea. Old Mary gave me some of her dried thyme and elderflower."

Celeste smiled and followed him in.

Yes, things were better, much better.

Chapter 5

Celeste closed her eyes and turned her face toward the sunlight. It was May, and spring was in full bloom. The air was rich with the scent of herbs and tree blossoms. The days were warming up, and for a few hours at a time, she could even go outside without a coat.

Celeste smiled, genuinely happy.

In this small mountain town, she found the peace she hadn't known in five years. She still communicated with the Alliance. They had told her to continue her work in Ravenville. They expected Resistance activity to increase as the weather warmed. Celeste didn't mind.

Ash returned from his morning supply run and saw her sitting on the grass in front of the clinic, enjoying the sun. He stopped and stared. Sunlight danced in the strands of her hair, setting off mahogany sparks.

He grimaced and looked away. He hadn't looked at a woman that way since Tink disappeared. He'd never seen Tink's face, but still, it felt like a betrayal, especially with this woman. He quickly carried the medical supplies inside.

When Celeste came back in, she stopped at the doorway. The rooms were filled with a scent almost forgotten to her senses.

Wait...is that coffee?

She ran into the kitchen to check if she was right.

No, her nose didn't deceive her. Ash was making coffee.

"You brought coffee!" she exclaimed. "Where did you find coffee?"

Ash looked at her and nearly laughed. There was some childish glow in her face, a kind of joy he hadn't seen in years.

"I got ahold of some contraband," he said with a shrug. "You want some?"

"Yes, please!"

Her face lit up.

Amused, he handed her a cup. How could she just walk into a room and make everything look brighter? The only other person who'd ever done that...

Tink.

Ash stood up abruptly and headed to the door.

"Where are you going?" Celeste said, looking at him with surprise. "Your coffee..."

"You can have it," he snapped as he walked out.

Celeste shook her head. What was wrong with him? Lately, his mood had been unpredictable.

Celeste pursed her lips.

She'd lived with him for months, yet he was still a mystery. It was easier when he was just a face behind the computer screen.

Still, he was the reason for her happiness. She could forgive his strange behavior.

Celeste took her coffee mug and went outside to look for him. She heard a noise behind the building and followed the sound. In the backyard, Ash stood shirtless, splitting wood.

She leaned against the wall, quietly watching him. He was tall, muscular. His dark hair fell to his back, and the scar across his face somehow made him more attractive.

Celeste had spent years trying to imagine how Ash looked but never expected this.

As if sensing her, Ash turned around. He tilted his head, surprised to see Celeste.

She looked away so he wouldn't see her face blush.

I should've known he'd catch me gawking.

"You coming inside to drink your coffee?" she asked, trying to sound casual.

Ash didn't respond. He just turned and continued splitting wood.

Celeste sighed and went back into the house.

Over the next several days, Ash avoided her. He was gone from dawn till dusk and barely spoke to her.

Celeste tried to figure out what she'd done to upset him, but nothing came to mind. Perhaps, he had never stopped hating her.

Sometimes, she dreamed she was someone else, someone who didn't carry the weight of war, someone not marked by betrayal. But she was a European woman in an American mountain town.

She deserved to be hated.

That morning, Celeste pulled out the government-issued phone and sent her scheduled message to the Alliance. She winced when Ash barged into her office. She quickly shoved the phone into her desk drawer.

Celeste looked at Ash and raised an eyebrow. He didn't usually bother her while she worked.

"I need your help," he said.

His voice was pressured.

"What's wrong?"

Worried, she stood up from her chair.

"One of the kids up in the cabins is sick."

"What are the symptoms?"

"Fever, abdominal pain. His mother said it's been going on for days. I think it's appendicitis. Do you do surgeries?"

"I have to examine him," she said. "But yes, I can operate."

Celeste quickly gathered antibiotics, a surgical kit, and sterile gloves.

"Let's go," she ran out the door.

Ash drove them high into the mountain. They had to hike the rest of the way. Celeste put a mask on. She'd been coughing all week and didn't want to infect anyone.

A young woman opened the door.

"Thank God, the doctor's here," she exclaimed. "Come in, I'm Rose."

Celeste frowned, walking in. The house was dark and cold. The child, a boy no older than six, lay on a small cot. His face was flushed, and he was quietly moaning.

Celeste touched his forehead. He was burning up. As soon as she touched his right lower abdomen, he cried in pain.

"You were right," she said to Ash. "It's appendicitis. I have to operate right away. I will need help. Scrub up."

"Me?" he looked staggered. "I'm not..."

"You know enough," she interrupted. "Get ready."

"Yes, ma'am," he muttered as he went to wash his hands.

Celeste started intravenous antibiotics and fluids, then administered an anesthetic.

When the boy fell asleep, she began.

Ash followed her instructions, handing her instruments quickly and calmly. Celeste's hands trembled at first. She had never done surgery in the field, but the boy's vitals held. She finished the procedure and sutured the incision.

"I'm glad you came to get me when you did." She looked at Ash. "If we were a few hours late, the appendix would've ruptured. Thank you for your help."

"No, thank you! You are an amazing physician."

Celeste turned, expecting sarcasm, but there was none. His eyes sparkled with honest admiration.

She smiled. For the first time, he looked at her without contempt.

She felt her heart flutter.

Celeste looked in her bag for the thermometer but couldn't find it.

"Ash, I forgot to bring a thermometer. Can you drive to town and get it for me? It should be somewhere in one of the patient's rooms. I have to stay here and monitor the patient."

Ash turned without a word and left.

Celeste checked on the child. He was sleeping peacefully.

She finally sighed with relief.

The surgery was a success. She was grateful for the help Ash gave her. Without him, the outcome might not have been as good.

Celeste looked around the room. There were two small cots and a worn rug on the floor.

She stared at the rug. It was slightly shifted.

Beneath it was a trapdoor, probably to a hidden passage.

That wasn't a surprise. Everyone in these mountains had an escape route. It was the only way to stay alive.

About an hour and a half later, Ash returned, tossed the thermometer on the table, and walked out without a word.

Celeste shook her head.

Here we go again.

However, now wasn't the time to worry about his mood.

She spent the night monitoring the child. He woke up and appeared to be fine. Celeste kept checking his temperature and administering antibiotics and fluids. By morning, he was better.

She instructed the mother on post-operative care and prepared to head back. Probably other patients were already waiting.

Ash wasn't outside.

Probably waiting down by the truck, she thought.

Celeste looked up. The sky was heavy and gray. A storm was coming. She hurried down the slope.

The truck was gone.

Where is Ash?

She sighed in frustration and started walking.

Then the storm hit.

Rain soaked her clothes. Mud dragged at her feet. She slipped and fell. Cursing, she got up and kept going. Her fingers and toes felt numb from the cold. She couldn't stop shivering.

She wondered what had happened to Ash. She was only hoping that he hadn't run into armed patrols.

Celeste rubbed her hands together, trying to warm herself up.

After walking in the freezing rain for several hours, right when she thought she would freeze to death, Celeste finally reached Ravenville. Ash's truck wasn't there.

She didn't care.

Shivering, she hurried inside, changed into dry clothes, and lit the stove. As her hands warmed, she opened the drawer at her desk.

The phone was gone.

Her heart stopped.

Ash had found it while looking for the thermometer. That's why he'd left her in the mountains. That's why he hadn't come back.

She knew it.

Celeste closed her eyes.

There was nothing she could say to fix that. She grabbed her head in her hands and just sat like that.

How could I be so stupid?

Ash was going to kill her!

She was scared, and there was nowhere to run. She had no means to call for help.

Every creak of the floor made her flinch.

Maybe Ash was letting her suffer first.

When night fell, and he still hadn't returned, she went to bed. Her heart was racing. Celeste tossed and turned, haunted by dread. Finally, she fell into a restless sleep.

A pulsating headache woke her. She stood and collapsed. The room spun. Cold sweat dripped down her back.

It was so cold!

Shivering, Celeste covered up with the blanket. Soon, she drifted off to sleep again.

Then she started coughing. Her lungs seared. Her breath caught in her chest. She touched her forehead. Her skin was burning hot.

The cold rain had pushed her over the edge.

Suddenly, the blanket ripped off.

A hand grabbed her arm.

A gun muzzle pressed against her forehead.

Ash!

She didn't even scream.

Ash was furious. He'd opened the drawer, looking for the thermometer, and found the government phone. The slick black casing was too familiar.

She was a spy.

He was enraged by his stupidity. He was the one who brought her to Ravenville, and if anyone got hurt, it would be his fault.

Ash had hurried to evacuate the entire town. He sent everyone to the

Resistance camp deeper in the mountains. People who had their own vehicles drove, and the rest, he transported with his truck.

Then he had come back to serve justice.

He pressed the muzzle harder against her forehead. His chest was rising fast with each ragged breath.

He had almost liked her. He had trusted her.

He should've known better.

No one, especially a woman, would volunteer to come to some godforsaken town in the mountains to do charity work.

"Any last words, spy?" he hissed between his teeth.

"I have nothing to say."

She didn't plead or fight.

She just looked at him. Her face was flushed from the fever. Her hair was stuck to her forehead. Her eyes were empty.

She wanted him to shoot her.

His hand trembled.

Shit!

He couldn't do it, not like this.

"Pack your stuff," he barked. "You're coming with me to the Resistance headquarters. You'll stand trial."

He lowered the gun and pushed her away.

Celeste tried to pack a bag, but a coughing fit dropped her to her knees. Her head swam. She tried to reach the wall but collapsed to the floor.

Ash swore.

He thought about pulling the trigger and walking away, but he couldn't.

He touched her forehead. She was burning up.

He swore again, packed a bag for her, and carried her to his truck.

She stirred, barely conscious.

"Don't take the phone," she whispered. "It has a tracker."

Ash pulled the phone out of his pocket, stared at it for a second, and smashed it against the ground. Then he jumped behind the wheel and peeled out of town.

Chapter 6

Celeste lay in the back seat, unable to stop her tears. She'd always known that Ash would eventually figure out her connection to the Alliance, but she wasn't ready for the fallout.

The hatred in Ash's eyes hurt more than a bullet ever could. He should've just shot her, so she didn't have to suffer his contempt.

I deserve that for being careless.

With the phone gone, the Alliance would think she'd defected.

David was going to be furious.

David Hayes was a ruthless, sharp-edged Resistance leader who helped her build her cover. What would she even tell him? Then again... he had set her up. If he had told her that Tahoma Jensen was Ash...

"Stop bawling already," Ash snapped. "Learn to take your failure with dignity."

He inhaled sharply. At that moment, he *wished* Celeste were a man, so he wouldn't hesitate to shoot her. He hated himself for falling for her act, for letting her manipulate him for so long. He should've trusted his initial gut feeling about her.

It was sheer luck that Alliance drones hadn't hit Ravenville.

He looked back at her. She was shivering and coughing violently. She probably had pneumonia.

It didn't matter.

She wasn't going to be around much longer. Taking her to the stronghold of the Resistance would guarantee a swift execution.

"Don't you dare puke in my truck again," he muttered.

She didn't answer, just pulled her knees up, shaking.

Ash gritted his teeth. He *knew* she had to die. But the sickness in his gut refused to ease.

Why did she have to be a spy?

He had never felt more conflicted in his life. He knew he couldn't let her loose, but he also knew he didn't want her to die.

"Goddammit!" he slammed a fist against the steering wheel.

He looked at the back seat again. Celeste was curled into herself, trembling like a leaf in a storm.

With a groan, he peeled off his coat and tossed it at her.

"Cover up. I'm sick of listening to your whining."

Without making a sound, Celeste pulled the coat around her shoulders.

The rest of the ride was silent.

As soon as he entered the camp of the Resistance, he hauled her out of the truck and dragged her to a tent. He tied her wrists and ankles, then walked off to report to David Hayes.

He found Hayes in the camp's command building.

"Why did you bring the spy here?" Hayes asked, frowning. "Are you trying to compromise our location?"

"I thought she should stand trial," Ash muttered.

"Trial? Nah." Hayes shook his head. "Take her into the woods and shoot her."

"Me? You want me to do that?"

Ash's eyes widened.

"Who else?" David shrugged. "You brought her here. Clean up your mess."

"Fine!" Ash growled and stormed out.

Celeste lay on the cold ground of the tent, shivering violently. She prayed Hayes was in camp. If he wasn't... she was done. The leadership of the resistance had protected her identity to keep her cover intact, so there weren't too many people who knew her.

She sighed.

It was her fault. She'd been careless.

The tent flap opened. Celeste winced and turned her head.

Ash!

"Come on." He cut the rope off her ankles. "Let's go. Your time's up."

"Wait! What are you doing?" She tensed up. "You said I would stand trial..."

"You don't get a trial. Let's go!"

His voice was low and bitter.

Celeste tried to catch his eye. He wouldn't look at her. He just yanked her to her feet and dragged her toward the trees.

Celeste struggled to keep up with him. She stumbled and fell in the mud. Ash didn't speak, just grabbed her arm and hauled her up again.

When they reached the woods, he shoved her to her knees.

The cold muzzle of the gun touched the back of her head.

Her heartbeat roared in her ears.

Ash was going to kill her after all.

She closed her eyes, waiting for him to pull the trigger.

She could tell him the truth, but it wouldn't matter, not even if she told him she was Tink.

"I'm sorry, Ash," she whispered, struggling to breathe.

His hand trembled. Her voice hit something deep inside him.

"I'm sorry, Ash!"

Her words echoed in his head. He had heard pain greater than simple regret in her voice.

Shit!

"I'm not doing that," he holstered his gun. "You're gonna be somebody else's problem. Let's go!"

He dragged her back to the tent, tied her ankles, and left.

Celeste couldn't stop shivering.

She was sure Ash was going to shoot her. Now someone else would, and that somehow felt worse.

Her breathing quickened. Her vision narrowed. She was on the verge of a panic attack. She tried to steady her breathing.

You signed up for this. You knew the risks.

But logic wasn't helping.

She flinched as the tent opened again.

"Oh, you look like shit!"

Celeste turned her head and saw Hayes.

"What the hell, Dave!" she rasped. "Why did you let Ash drag me into the woods and put a gun to my head?"

"I told him to," Hayes said, completely unapologetic.

"Have you lost your mind?" she snapped, squirming against the ropes. "Why would you do that?"

"Just testing a theory," he smirked.

"Let me out of these ropes right now, or I swear, I'll punch your lights out."

She managed to yank her arm halfway loose before he calmly unknotted the bindings.

"I *could've* been killed."

"Nah," David shook his head, dismissing it with a shrug, "I knew he wasn't gonna do it. You were with him for months and survived. So far, he's killed every European he's come across. For some unknown reason, he spared you. So no, I didn't think he'd shoot you."

He shrugged and smiled.

"Anyway, I wasn't going to take a chance on your life, so I followed him, and I watched him. He never released the safety. If he did, I would've stopped him. But now, he thinks he made the choice. So, when I let you live, he won't question it. His guilt will make sure of that."

"You almost gave me a heart attack," Celeste muttered, pouting. "Besides, I think I have pneumonia."

"Yes, I can see that," Hayes said, and his smile faded. "Let's get you to the hospital."

He picked her up and carried her to a bunker-like structure, built into the side of the mountain. Hayes shrugged on a white coat and quickly started barking orders.

"You know I won't let you die, right?" He smiled and ran his hand through Celeste's hair.

"I don't know, Dave," she said with a crooked smile. "You tested that theory pretty hard today."

"I'm sorry about that, but I have to balance between protecting your cover and keeping you alive. I wanted to be sure Ash isn't going to snap and kill you. He's quite unpredictable. I had to put him to the test."

"Speaking of Ash," Celeste frowned. "Why would you do that to me? Why would you send me to him without telling me? You know, I looked for him high and low."

"The fewer people who know about you, the better. I was hoping you wouldn't find out. Now I realize I was wrong. Get some rest now. Doctor's orders."

"Yes, sir." Celeste closed her eyes and let the nurses hook her up to IV fluids and antibiotics.

Finally, the exhaustion from the anxiety took its toll, and she fell into a deep, feverish sleep.

David Hayes stood by her bed, making sure she received the appropriate care. He felt guilty for putting her through all this. She was one of his best operatives and a close friend. He regretted not telling her about Ash, but if he had done that, she would've run straight to Ravenville and blown her cover.

"Get better, girl," he patted her shoulder and walked out of the hospital.

Hayes walked through the camp looking for Ash. He saw him sitting outside of Celeste's tent, holding his head in his hands.

When Ash saw him, he jumped to his feet.

"Where is she? Did you kill her?"

There were mad sparks in his eyes.

"Well, you failed," Hayes smirked.

Ash's expression crumbled. He remembered the light in her eyes and her childish smile when he made coffee...

What have I done!

I should've never brought her to this camp!

He tried unsuccessfully to slow his breathing.

"Did she... was it fast?"

He clenched his trembling hands in fists and bit his lip.

"Jesus! Ash, are you into her?" Hayes said, looking at him in disbelief. "Chill! I didn't kill her. She's at the hospital, getting her pneumonia taken care of."

"I'm not into her," Ash barked and quickly walked away.

Chapter 7

Ash walked through the camp with his head spinning. What was wrong with him? Why was he obsessed with that woman? She was the enemy. People like her had killed Tink.

He felt his mind spiral. Never, in his entire life, had he imagined that he would be that weak.

Damn it!

Now Hayes would think he was a traitor.

The devil himself must've sent that woman to ruin him.

He hiked up the mountain and sat on the cold ground to clear his mind.

The next morning, Celeste woke up feeling much better. The antibiotics had taken hold. She turned her head and saw Hayes sitting by her bed.

"You and Ash, huh?" He smirked.

"There is no me and Ash." She shook her head. "He hates my guts. He was going to shoot me, for God's sake."

"Ahem... my observations say otherwise."

Celeste looked at him in confusion.

"Okay." He shrugged. "I won't pick on you anymore."

"So, what's the plan now?" She sat up in her bed. "How are you going to justify sparing my life?"

"You're an asset at the least. If someone asks, I'll tell them that you've agreed to give us intel; although, I don't think anyone would."

"So, now I'm a traitor."

"Well, what do you prefer, to shoot you, so you can keep your good name? And I'm using the term loosely."

Celeste shot him an angry look.

"Calm down, spy girl." He laughed. "I'm talking about your covert personality. You know I love you."

"You have an interesting way of showing it," she mumbled. "So, where's my prison cell?"

"I'll prepare a room for you in my office building."

"Your office shack, you mean." She gave a half-smile. "Okay, that's acceptable. Are you sure that Ash isn't going to reconsider and gun me down?"

"I'm sure," Hayes smiled. "Try to get some rest for now. I'll get you out of this hospital tomorrow."

Celeste closed her eyes. What did Hayes mean, implying something was going on between her and Ash? Well, Hayes knew that she had feelings for Ash; she always had, but Ash? He hated her guts. She could tell him that she was Tink, but he would either not believe her or start hating Tink's guts too. No, she would rather keep it a secret. That way, there would be at least one version of her that Ash didn't hate.

Celeste thought about David Hayes. They had known each other for a long time. She met him when she started residency in New York. He was a surgeon at the same hospital. They dated for about a month but realized that they wouldn't work out as a couple and decided to remain friends.

Celeste was a year into her residency when the first bombs fell. She was terrified. For a while, she leaned on her French origin, but then hated herself for it. She finished her training as a surgeon and worked in New York. She was deeply ashamed of what the Alliance had done to Americans.

That was when she got the invitation to Amnestic.

She spent a couple of years on Amnestic, talking to Ash every day. He was always angry. Celeste tried to cheer him up and always called him "an insufferable grump."

Learning from him about all the atrocities committed by the Alliance inspired her to join the Resistance. She wasn't sure how to contact them until she ran into David Hayes. She was happy to see that he had survived. She told him that she wanted to fight on the American side. He had doubts at first, but eventually, he chose to trust her. Then, she had to drop out of Amnestic.

Two years went by.

Celeste missed Ash. Finally, unable to resist, she tried to log in, but the forum was no longer there. That scared her. She was sure the authorities had probably arrested and executed Ash. She tried everything she could to find him, but to no avail.

Celeste closed her eyes, weighing in her mind every choice she had made since the beginning of the war. Even though her actions came with consequences, she couldn't see any other path she could've taken. At least, she had finally found Ash.

And now he hated her. She'd never told Hayes how she really knew Ash. She had only said that she had heard tales about him. Celeste kept the secret of Amnestic to herself. The time spent with Ash on Amnestic was her most precious memory.

The next morning, Hayes came and took Celeste to her "jail" cell. She didn't protest. Being locked up in there was safer than trying to figure out who wanted her dead on the outside. She sat in the room for a couple of days but then started to become anxious. That wasn't a good fit for her.

"Can you figure something out, Dave? I'm going insane here." She impatiently shifted from foot to foot.

"Fine, you can walk around outside. I don't think anybody here really knows who you are. Ravenville people are here, but I don't think Ash told them anything about you."

"Thank you!" Celeste smiled. "You have no idea how much I needed that."

Ash sat on a rock near the edge of camp, staring at the dirt. He was shocked by how much the thought of Celeste being dead terrified him. That wasn't supposed to happen. He hated her.

Who am I kidding!

That damned woman was everywhere, in his head, his gut, his goddamn bloodstream!

In fact, he thought about her all the time.

It felt like a betrayal of his Tink. He hated himself for it. How had he let that happen?

"Ash?"

He looked up.

Celeste was standing in front of him. She looked better, cleaned up, and rested. For some reason, Hayes was protecting her. That was very strange since Hayes had no sympathy for Europeans. Maybe she had bewitched him too. Ash felt a jab at his heart, which only made him angrier.

Am I jealous now too?

"You didn't shoot me. Why?" Celeste asked, looking at him.

Those big brown eyes... At one time, he thought they were innocent. It was almost as if she cared... Now he knew better.

Ash shook his head.

"Get out of my face," he blurted out. "I can't even look at you."

Celeste quickly turned around and walked away before he saw her tears. Why did he have to be so mean?

He looked in the direction she had gone. He wanted to hate her, but seeing her walking and breathing was like sunshine on a stormy day.

What is wrong with me?

Ash exhaled harshly and walked out of the camp. His head was splitting. He wanted to hop in his truck and drive away from this place, but Hayes had told him that there was an important assignment for him. At least it was something to occupy his mind with.

Celeste stormed into Hayes's building and was heading to her room when he stopped her.

"How bored are you?" he asked.

"Very." She turned to look at him. "Do you have a cure?"

"Yes, ride with me for a supply run tomorrow. Be ready at six in the morning."

"Perfect!" She smiled and then went into her room.

Finally, a break from this place!

Celeste lay in her bed and closed her eyes. She felt better physically, but mentally, she was falling apart. She'd replayed last week's events countless times in her mind. It was her fault for everything that happened. Her carelessness had uprooted the people of an entire town from their homes. They had to stay in tents when it was still cold outside. This was unforgivable. Ash had the right to hate her. She was surprised that he didn't put a bullet in her. The way he reacted earlier made her wonder if he was reconsidering.

Hayes, on the other hand, was acting like a total jerk. He had always been mischievous, but now it was on another level.

What the hell is wrong with those men?

When she took this assignment a few months ago, she never thought that there would be such severe complications. The only upside to all that mess was that she found out that Ash was alive.

She sighed and got out of bed. There was no way she could go to sleep with all those thoughts in her head.

Celeste walked out of her room and sat at the table across from Hayes.

"Dave," she said, looking at him. "Why are you acting so weird?"

"What do you mean?" He raised his eyebrow.

"What you did the other day was wrong. I was scared."

"I had to do it, and you're a spy. You should be able to deal with those types of situations."

"Yeah, but that was Ash..."

"I've always wanted to ask you, why are you obsessed with him? He's unstable and unpredictable."

"I don't know. I admire him, I guess."

"You've been chasing him for years."

"And you spent years lying to me. That's not what friends do."

"You're forgetting that we're always just a moment away from being discovered and executed by the Alliance. We didn't survive by cross-contaminating our agents."

Celeste laughed. "'Cross-contaminating,' I guess you can call it that. Okay, I'll leave you alone. See you first thing in the morning."

Celeste couldn't fall asleep for most of the night, analyzing everything and everybody. She could swear her life was easier when she was just stealing information from the Alliance. This here was a whole other level of convoluted nonsense. Finally, she fell into a restless sleep.

Chapter 8

Celeste got up early in the morning. After washing up, she looked in the bag of clothes that Hayes had given her. She found a pair of black tactical pants with multiple pockets on the pant legs, a gray T-shirt, a hooded jacket, and a pair of military boots. She put the clothes on and frowned.

Goddamn Dave!

The clothes were too damn tight.

Ash would've never picked the wrong size.

"I have to find clothes that fit," she muttered with frustration.

However, today was not the day. It was almost time to go. She put her hair up in a messy bun, grabbed the jacket in her hand, and went outside. Hayes was already standing by his truck. She was about to climb in when she noticed that someone was sitting in the passenger seat.

"Sorry," Dave answered her silent question. "The spot in my truck's taken. You'll go with the other vehicle."

As soon as he spoke, Celeste saw a truck whip around the corner. It was Ash behind the steering wheel. He was driving one of Hayes's vehicles. Ash left the engine running and jumped out.

"Your ride." Hayes gestured toward Ash and smirked.

"What the hell, Dave!" Celeste looked at him with murder in her eyes.

"You two have unfinished business." Hayes pointed at her and Ash. "Make sure you finish it today. I can't have this type of tension in my camp."

Furious, she yanked the door of Ash's truck open and sat inside.

Ash hesitated. The clothes she wore...

He was able to see every curve of her perfect figure. It was almost as if she had planned it.

Shit!

She was the most wicked woman he had ever met. How was he going to collect himself with her sitting next to him, looking like that? He cursed one more time, sat behind the wheel, and peeled out of camp. Hayes followed right behind.

"Where are we going?" Celeste broke the silence.

Ash shot her an angry look and grunted.

"Well," Celeste didn't leave him alone, "you heard Hayes."

"Dave, you mean?" he mumbled under his breath. "Since when is an Alliance spy on a first-name basis with Resistance leaders?"

Celeste silently swore. Of course, Ash would hear her.

"Maybe we made friends," she said sarcastically.

"You must have. Why else would he allow a spy to go on a supply run? You must've made pretty good friends... You know what, I don't really care," he muttered and continued driving without saying anything.

"Why aren't you driving your own truck?"

"Hayes's orders. He thinks my truck's trash. Anyway, why would you care what I'm driving?"

"Just curious, that's all. Since we are asking questions," Celeste said with a mischievous sparkle in her eyes, "who is Tink?"

Ash whipped his head and shot her a freezing look.

"Well, you accused me of killing her." Celeste tilted her head and narrowed her eyes. "So, I deserve as much as an explanation."

"Tink is someone whose name you have no right to say."

"How did she die?"

"I don't know how she died. I just know that if she were alive, she would've never dropped off the face of the Earth without letting me know."

Yes, she would've, and she did.

Celeste sighed.

Poor Ash! He had way too much faith in her.

"So, you don't know for sure that she's dead." Celeste shrugged.

"If she were still breathing, she would've found me."

She did...

Celeste took a deep breath, so she wouldn't start crying.

"So, where are we going?" she asked again.

"Ravenville," he said dryly. "We are going to collect everything usable. You wiped the entire town off the map."

Celeste looked at him and saw condemnation in his eyes.

She turned her head. She knew he was right, and it hurt.

"I'm sorry," she whispered.

"Somehow I don't think you're sorry at all," he muttered. "Be quiet now, your voice is drilling a hole in my brain."

Celeste shook her head and let her eyes wander out of the window. There was no way she would ever reach any kind of understanding with Ash. He hated her.

After they had traveled several hours, Hayes's vehicle veered and took a different route.

Celeste looked at Ash with a question in her eyes.

"They'll approach the town from a different direction," he explained without taking his eyes off the road.

The landscape started to look familiar. Celeste realized that they had almost reached Ravenville. They were just coming around the bend where she had wrecked her car when they found themselves at a checkpoint.

"Shit!" Ash swore. "This is your fault too," he said, looking at her with contempt. "I'm not planning on letting myself be captured."

He floored the accelerator and flew through the checkpoint. Gunfire erupted. The truck skidded and came to a stop. She could smell burned rubber. They must've shot the tires.

Soldiers swarmed the truck. Ash reached for his rifle. Celeste knew that if he touched the weapon, that would be the end.

"No!" She jumped on his lap, so he wouldn't be able to grab his rifle. "You are not doing that!"

"Get off me, bitch!"

He tried unsuccessfully to throw her off. She had wrapped her arms around his neck, not letting him shake her off.

Within seconds, Alliance soldiers with loaded rifles surrounded the truck.

"Get out with your hands up," she heard a soldier speaking with a French accent.

"'*Hé, doucement! Ne tirez pas!*' (Hey, don't shoot!)" She raised her arms. "'*C'est Célestine Beaumont. L'une des vôtres.*' (I'm Celestine Beaumont. I'm one of yours)."

Then she pointed to Ash.

"Make sure you tie him up tight. Denver will be interested in him." Her voice was sharp, but she felt the guilt from the betrayal piercing her heart.

She looked away, so the soldiers wouldn't see the regret in her eyes.

"You'll die for that." Ash's voice could cut steel.

Celeste climbed off his lap and watched the soldiers hog-tie him and drag him to a vehicle.

"Why are you with this terrorist?" the French soldier asked her.

"He kidnapped me several months ago. I wasn't able to escape. I have to call my family. They probably think I'm dead."

"Go with them to town, they'll take care of you," he waved at the soldiers, who had grabbed Ash and told them to wait.

Celeste ran toward their vehicle and jumped in, trying to ease her breath. Her determination to save Ash's life battled the pain of betraying him.

I have to pull myself together.

She sat by Ash, who was tied up in the back seat, and smiled at him.

She knew her betrayal would infuriate him, but he'd expect that from her. Still, she felt her heart tighten. He would hate her even more.

It didn't matter as long as he got to live.

Ash gritted his teeth.

I knew I should've shot her. Now she'll have me executed.

Again, he knew he would never be able to hurt her. He sighed heavily. He would never have, not in his wildest dreams, thought that his downfall would be a woman from the enemy camp.

Tahoma Jensen, a soldier with a special forces background, hardened by the horrors of war, ended up being finished off by a female Alliance spy.

I'm a pathetic son of a bitch.

Even worse, after they locked him up in jail, he continued thinking about her. Ash shook his head. He had to figure out how to provoke those soldiers to shoot him. He wasn't going to allow them to ship him off to Denver. He walked back and forth in the narrow cell.

Maybe I'll meet Tink on the other side.

He smiled and nodded his head. Yes, it was time.

Celeste followed a soldier to the military office. She let out a crooked smile when she saw that they had taken over the building of her old clinic. The officer directed her to the telephone.

"Is the line secure?" she asked. "I don't want the Resistance finding out that their operative and the prisoner have been apprehended."

"Don't worry, the line is secure," the officer nodded.

She quickly dialed the number of the Alliance intelligence agency in Denver.

"I need to speak with Gabriel Clement," she said after the office in Denver answered.

"Right away," the secretary responded.

"Celeste!" Clement exclaimed when he heard her voice. "I thought you were dead. What happened?"

"I was able to infiltrate a Resistance stronghold. They trust me. There is something big coming, so I will keep you updated. I had to destroy my phone, but I will find a way to notify you when the time comes."

"That is exceptional." Clement's voice sounded satisfied. "Where are you now?"

"We were captured by a patrol in Ravenville. I told them that I was a prisoner in the Resistance camp. The terrorist who was with me is locked up. I'm planning to break him out. That way, I will cement their trust."

"That's good planning. Would you like me to order the soldiers to stand down?"

"Absolutely not. A Resistance operative could sniff out a setup from a mile away. I'll figure a way to do that on my own."

Her voice didn't falter, but her heart twisted in doubt. Was she about to risk everything, her cover, her dedication to the Resistance cause, for a man who couldn't stand the sight of her?

Her training screamed to leave Ash and walk away, but her heart tore at the thought of him being hurt.

"Well, if someone can pull that off, it's you." Clement laughed. "But if you get shot in the process, remember, I offered to help."

"I'll figure it out." Her hand tightened around the receiver for a second, and then she hung up.

Celeste stared at the phone with her heart beating in her ears.

Now I have to find a way to break Ash out.

Chapter 9

As soon as she got off the phone, Celeste ran to the medicine cabinet. She looked at the bottles and found the one with "midazolam" written on it. She quickly slipped it into her pocket and walked out of the room.

"Thank you!" she said, smiling at the soldier who had let her in. "Who's in charge of your patrol?"

"Captain Jacques Rognon," the soldier said.

"Where can I find him?" Celeste smiled. "I would like to properly thank him for saving me from the terrorists."

"He's at the jailhouse down the road."

"Thanks." Celeste ran out of the building and headed in that direction.

The makeshift jail looked like an old barn from the outside, but inside, the walls were reinforced with steel.

She asked the soldier, standing guard at the door, to check if the captain would speak with her.

The soldier disappeared inside but returned shortly after.

"Follow me." He waved his hand at her.

Celeste hurried after him. He walked her into a room, which appeared to be adjacent to the cells. She immediately spotted Ash. As soon as he saw her, he grabbed the bars of the cell. There was darkness in his eyes that she had never seen before.

She took a deep breath and ignored him.

Celeste needed every bit of strength she had left to ensure that her voice didn't tremble. Every word she was about to say would drive the dagger of betrayal straight into Ash's soul. Celeste hated what she had to do to him, but it was the only option that would end with him being alive.

She looked at the officer. Captain Rognon was a short, stocky, bald man. He had beady, dark brown eyes that gave him the look of someone who had just rolled out of bed.

"Captain Rognon," she addressed the officer in French. "I cannot express how grateful I am to you and your men. I had lost hope that I'd ever be free again."

"I'm happy to be of service, madam." He nodded. "Were you treated fairly at the terrorists' camp?"

"No, they starved me and threatened to shoot me. That animal right here," she said, pointing at Ash, "dragged me to the woods and put a gun to the back of my head. Mind you, I was sick with pneumonia at the time. The whole experience was a nightmare."

"That's to be expected from the Resistance terrorists," the officer muttered. "I'd enjoy blowing this one's brains out myself if Denver isn't interested in him. What's his name?"

"This is Ash," she said, throwing a look back at him.

The knuckles of his fingers had turned white from squeezing the bars. Celeste was sure he wanted to rip her head off with his bare hands.

"Great." The officer grinned. "I'll inquire about him. By the way, I would like to treat you to a good dinner. What would you say?"

"Oh, that would be marvelous!" She clapped her hands. "I haven't had a good meal for months."

"Okay, come back here at nine tonight. We will feast in front of this animal to show him that we can."

Celeste turned away, hiding her disgust. On her way out, she walked by the cell where Ash was locked up.

"'*Je parle français, tu sais*' (I speak French, you know)," he whispered as she passed by him.

Her eyes widened for a second, but she ignored him and walked out of the room.

Ash felt like his head was going to explode. Celeste had given them his name. He wished he could put his hands on her.

Beautiful and deadly. That Jezebel!

She was the enemy, one whom he hated, but still, some part, deep inside him, wished she hadn't betrayed him.

Once outside, Celeste leaned against the jailhouse wall and covered her face with her hands. The fact that Ash understood everything she said made her sick to her stomach. The last thing she wanted was to hurt him, but there was no other way.

Celeste knew that if she failed to free Ash, they were both dead. She was terrified, but still, she'd do anything to save him, even if it meant losing her life.

At exactly nine, she showed up at the jail house. The soldier up front, again, led her to the prison section. She walked in and sighed. There was so much food! She thought of the American people she had lived with for the last few months and felt her throat tighten. This wasn't fair.

"That looks great, Captain Rognon." She clapped her hands and smiled. "My mouth is watering. It feels like forever since I had a real meal."

"Dig in." The officer smiled smugly.

Celeste sat at the table. Rognon poured whiskey into two glasses.

"To us!" He raised a toast.

"Check out the terrorist." Celeste pointed at Ash. "He looks like he'd kill for a shot of that. Poor bastard!"

Ash's eyes shot lightning her way.

As soon as the officer turned his head to look at Ash, Celeste pulled the bottle of medication out of her pocket. Her hand shook briefly, but then she quickly dumped the medicine into his glass.

"I'm sure he'd like some of this, but guess what?" The officer laughed cynically. "He gets nothing."

Celeste stared at the table. There was roasted chicken, ham, vegetables, bread, and fruit. That amount of food was obscene. Such a feast could put a smile on the faces of so many of Ravenville's children. She took a deep breath. She couldn't allow the officer to become suspicious.

"So, tell me, Mademoiselle Beaumont," the officer said, looking at her lustfully. "Is there a Monsieur Beaumont?"

"Yes." Celeste felt nauseous. "I have family in New York. They are probably looking for me."

"That's too bad," the officer said, curving his mouth in disappointment. "Would you like another shot of whiskey?"

"No thanks," Celeste smiled. "You know what I'd like?"

"I'm listening."

"I would love a cup of strong black coffee."

"Don't we all," he sighed. "Coffee is a rare commodity these days. I haven't had any since I arrived in this godforsaken place."

"I know where we can get some."

"You do?" the officer asked, clearly intrigued.

"When I was at your office building, I saw a box of coffee in the cabinet above the sink in the kitchen. You can send the guy who's standing by your door to go and get it."

"Right away. I'd do anything for a cup of coffee."

He jumped out of his chair, opened the door, and quickly ordered the soldier.

Celeste glanced at Ash. He appeared so furious, she feared he might kill her as soon as he was free. She looked at the officer. He was visibly drunk and dizzy from the medication but still awake. Celeste knew she had only a small window to act. It didn't seem that the captain was going to fall asleep anytime soon. Nervous, she looked around. The bottle of whiskey was half full. That should do.

"Mademoiselle Celeste." The officer slurred his speech. "Come, sit on my lap."

"I doubt that she'd be satisfied by your nonexistent manhood." Ash laughed at him.

What is Ash doing? He'll have himself killed.

Celeste shot a look at him. Then it hit her. He wanted the officer to kill him.

She saw Rognon reaching for his pistol.

Without wasting a second, Celeste grabbed the whiskey bottle. For a split second, she felt the weight of it in her hand and then broke it over the officer's head. He immediately collapsed to the ground.

Celeste searched his pockets, grabbed the jail cell keys, and threw them to Ash. Then she took the keys for the officer's vehicle.

"Come awn, sha!" Celeste waved at Ash, who was standing frozen with the keys in his hand. "Snap owtuh it. We gotta make haste."

Ash unlocked the cell but hesitated.

Why the hell is she talking with this southern accent?

"Let's go, yeah! We're runnin' outta time, sha." Celeste waved her hand at him and ran outside.

Ash still couldn't process what was happening and why she was talking like that, but he shook his head and quickly followed her.

The officer's truck was parked in front of the building. Celeste threw the keys to Ash and jumped in the vehicle. Ash hopped behind the wheel and peeled out.

"I'll kill you, Celeste," he muttered, but a light smile flickered at the corner of his mouth.

Ash tore down the road, pushing the vehicle as fast as it would go. Celeste thought that they were home free when she suddenly spotted a blockade on the road right in front of them.

"Shit," Ash swore. "Hold tight!"

The truck blew through the barricade. Gunshots immediately erupted. Celeste heard the windows of the truck break; the metal screeched as the bullets pierced the frame. Ash grabbed the back of her head and shoved her under the dashboard. She covered her ears with her hands. They were going to die for sure.

"Sons of bitches are right behind us," she heard Ash swear. "You stay down." His hand pushed her head under the dashboard again.

"I won't be able to shake them," he said. "I'll dump the truck in the ravine. Prepare to jump when I tell you."

Celeste felt her heartbeat in her ears. He wanted her to jump out of a moving car...

"Get ready," Ash pulled her up into her seat. "Now!"

Celeste opened her door and flung herself out of the car. She rolled a few times on the ground and lay until she heard the explosion of the truck, after it hit the bottom of the ravine. She tasted the grit of dirt in her mouth. She spat and raised her head.

Did Ash make it?

Panicked, she stood up, but before she realized what was going on, his hand grabbed hers and pulled her after him.

"Hurry up," she heard his voice. "We have to get into the woods before they see us."

She ran as fast as she could. Finally, they took cover behind the trees. From there, they watched the soldiers lining up by the ravine, looking at the burning vehicle at the bottom.

"They think we're dead," Celeste whispered.

"Good. Let's go now," Ash pulled on her arm.

She grabbed his sleeve and felt something wet and sticky.

Blood!

"Ash, you are bleeding!" She panicked.

"Yeah, they might've clipped me. I'm not dead yet. Let's move."

Chapter 10

Celeste followed Ash up the mountain with her heart pounding out of her chest. The thought of him being shot and the inability to assess the severity of his wounds was throwing her into panic.

"Are you sure you'll be okay?" Her voice trembled.

"Yes." He laughed. "It's not my first rodeo."

After walking for about two hours, Ash sat on the ground.

"I need a minute," he said, trying to catch his breath.

"Ash, where are you shot?" Celeste felt the panic creep in.

"My left arm and right side, I think," he groaned.

"That has to hurt." She felt her heart tighten.

"It does," he said, standing up. "Let's go."

Celeste followed him up the mountain, silently cursing his stubbornness.

Finally, they reached a cabin tucked deep behind tall pine trees.

"That's your cabin!" Celeste exclaimed.

"Of course it is. Where do you think I was heading?"

He opened the door, pulled the blackout curtains over the windows, and collapsed on the bed.

"Ash!"

Terrified, Celeste lit the oil lamp and ran to him. She pulled off his shirt and looked at the wounds. There was one bullet wound in his left biceps and one on his right chest wall. She checked the chest wound first. Her stomach twisted at the sight of the bullet hole on his chest. She felt a wave of panic ripple through her. She fought to keep her hands from shaking. She was simultaneously running multiple worst-case scenarios in her head. Then she saw the exit wound and sighed with relief. It was just a graze. The bullet had slid over his ribs without entering his chest. The wound on his arm was more serious. The bullet was lodged inside.

"Are you still with me, Ash?" she asked.

"Yes, I'm still conscious, if that's what you're asking."

"You have a bullet in your left arm. I have to remove it."

Celeste looked around. "Do you have any medical instruments here?"

"Yes, there's a trunk under the bed. I have a bottle of whiskey in one of the cabinets."

Celeste brought the alcohol and prepared the instruments.

"I have nothing for pain," she said, squeezing his hand.

"That'll have to do," he said, tipping the bottle back. "What are you waiting for? Come on, mademoiselle Doctor, do it."

Celeste shook her head and started. She tried everything she could to work fast, but she knew that he was in pain. She could hear him grinding his teeth. As soon as she pulled out the bullet, she irrigated the wound with saline and tightly bandaged it. She also disinfected and bandaged the flesh wound on his side. Celeste wet a clean rag and gently wiped the sweat from Ash's face and the blood from his body. There were old bullet scars on his arms, chest, and back.

So many of them!

Surely, he had been to hell and back. She closed her eyes and took a deep breath. Exhausted, Ash had fallen asleep. Celeste pulled up a chair and sat by his bed to make sure no complications developed.

Ash opened his eyes. A thin shaft of sunlight was streaming from the side of the curtain. Across from his bed, he saw Celeste. She was sitting in the chair, gazing at him. It suddenly dawned on him. She had saved him. He remembered what she did last night in the jailhouse and then here. She wasn't a rookie. She was a seasoned operative. But why did she go against her own people to save him?

"Why did you break me out?" he asked.

"I didn't want you to die. I owe you after all. You didn't leave me to die in the car wreck either."

"After everything that transpired, I think that I should've," he muttered.

"But you didn't, so..."

"Why did you give them my name?" His eyes sparked angrily.

"They already knew your name. That made no difference."

"I've been trying to figure you out for months now." Ash rubbed his forehead. "You are unpredictable. Why were you speaking with that crazy Southern accent?"

"What Southern accent?" She raised her eyebrow. "You're delusional."

"Yeah, Southern accent, I heard you. And what happened to your French accent? I haven't heard it since I brought you to the camp. I still don't know what game you're playing. Any normal person in your place would've let me burn. I don't understand."

"Why don't you let me take care of you first? When you get better, you can try to figure me out again."

She sat on the edge of the bed and dabbed the sweat from his face. Then she walked to the kitchen cabinet and found the bottle of acetaminophen.

"Here, take some pain medicine," she said, handing him a couple of tablets.

"You know, I'm not that bad off," he said, taking the medicine. "I'll be okay."

"Tell me something about yourself," she asked with curiosity. "What did you do before the war?"

"Why would you think that I'd give you more information about myself?"

"I'm just curious."

"Fine," he muttered. "It no longer matters anyway. I was a Navy SEAL. I fought the war. I saw all my friends die. Then I lost my family and everybody I ever knew or cared about. After it was all over, I joined the Resistance."

"You've gone through hell," she said, tracing the scar on his face with her finger. "I'm sorry."

He looked into her eyes, and his heart picked up pace. He felt a storm rage inside his soul. How could he want someone he was supposed to despise? Her betrayal still burned, but so did the memories of every moment they had spent together. He hated her, but some part of him was drawn to her in a way that he was unable to fight. He sat up and stared at her for a second with a feverish glow in his eyes.

Without warning, Ash's hand slid behind Celeste's neck. For a breath, he hesitated, questioning his sanity, but the pull toward her was stronger than reason, rooted deeper than logic, something primal and unresolved. He drew her closer. His lips desperately crushed against hers, a kiss that was equal parts anger and aching need. He hesitated for a second but kissed her again. His breath was ragged, heart beating out of his chest. Ash pulled her closer, his fingers tangled in her hair.

Celeste gasped. Her hands pressed against his chest, feeling the beat of his heart, rapid and frantic. His scars were rough under her fingers, each one a story he hadn't told.

She rested her forehead against his.

"Ash," she whispered, her voice trembling.

"I should've killed you." His breath burned against her lips.

"But you didn't," she said, her words brushing his face.

"I couldn't."

Their mouths met again, soft and desperate.

Ash buried his face in Celeste's hair. He inhaled deeply. The scent of jasmine was so light, it felt like it was in a dream.

After that, Ash's guard and walls that he had diligently built around his feelings crumbled.

Their clothes flew off, and they made love like their lives depended on it. For a moment, war, prejudices, and hate evaporated like they'd never existed. It was just Ash and Celeste, holding each other in the dim room of a mountain cabin.

"What the hell did I just do?" Ash said to himself, still holding Celeste in his arms.

I just slept with a spy. I'm losing my mind!

Even though Ash knew it was a mistake, he continued to hold on to Celeste. Finally, he released her from his arms, slipped his clothes on, and rushed out the door.

Celeste lay in bed a little longer, smiling. Lying in Ash's arms was something she had dreamed about for years. Still smiling, she got dressed and sat at the table. Soon, Ash returned inside, slamming the door behind him.

"That... what we did..." He clenched his jaw.

"It was great." Celeste laughed.

"It was insanity." He shook his head. "Now, I want to know what game you are playing?"

"Okay." She sighed. "Hayes wanted us to solve our issues. I see only one possible way to do that, whether he likes it or not. Since we are going to be working together, I might as well tell you."

"You just made everything more convoluted than it was."

"It's not that complicated, really," Celeste said, sighing. "You think I'm an Alliance spy. Well, I am, but not really."

Ash raised his eyebrow, waiting for further explanation.

"Actually, I'm a Resistance spy. I infiltrated the Alliance about five years ago. The Alliance sent me to Ravenville to spy on you. However, I was providing them with disinformation. I had convinced them that there were no Resistance activities in Ravenville and that you weren't an operative. Then you found the phone and...well, you know the rest."

"Jesus! I almost killed you. Why didn't you tell me?"

"Hayes doesn't like to 'cross-contaminate his agents,' as he says."

"He told me to shoot you. What if I..."

"He wasn't going to let you. I confronted him about that too. He said that he followed you and watched you. He said that he would've stopped you if you had released the safety. We can both agree that Hayes is a jerk."

"That's why you are so casual with him. You are his operative. That's too much!"

"So, Ash, what did we have a few minutes ago, a moment of stress-induced sex?" she said with a crooked smile, trying to sound playful, but her voice trembled, betraying her uncertainty.

"I should've never allowed that," he frowned. "For some reason, I can't stop thinking about you. It feels like a betrayal."

"You are really obsessed with a woman whom you've never met. For all you know, she could've been a spy." Celeste smirked.

"Don't talk about her." Ash's face darkened like a storm cloud. "You know nothing about that."

"I know that you are an insufferable grump. That's what I know." She laughed.

"What did you just say?" Ash's eyes widened.

"An insufferable grump," she repeated. "You've always been one, even when you didn't hate me."

Ash froze.

"She could've been a spy..."

"Tink?"

He stared at her.

"Yes, you found me."

"No." Ash's face went from pale to red to pale.

He stayed frozen, staring at her for a moment. Then, tears rolled from his eyes. He grabbed the corner of the table to steady himself and sat down, continuing to stare at Celeste.

"There is no way..."

"Yes, my name is Celestine, Tina."

"Why didn't you tell me?"

"You hated me as myself. I didn't want you to hate Tink too."

"I'm sorry, Celeste. I can't imagine how you felt... The way I treated you... I'll never forgive myself."

"Ash, you thought I was a spy for the Alliance, and I couldn't tell you because I had to protect my cover."

"Why did you drop out of Amnestic?"

"I had to because of the nature of my work. I did try to log in a couple of years later, but the forum was gone. I thought that the Alliance had arrested and executed you. I've been looking for you ever since... until you became my assignment."

Ash sat in silence. A stunned smile started spreading across his face like a forgotten sunrise after a long night. The realization flooded his mind, dragging with it the scent of jasmine and laughter he had only imagined.

"I have never seen you smile like that," Celeste said.

She sat on his lap and wrapped her arms around his neck.

"I love you, Ash," she whispered in his ear. "I loved you long before I even saw your face."

"I love you, Tink!" He moved a strand of hair away from her face. "I guess my soul can recognize you anywhere. That was why I loved you as Celeste, too. I hated you, but I also loved you despite everything."

He kissed her, and she laid her head on his chest, listening to his madly beating heart.

Chapter 11

sh stirred in bed.

Is someone singing?

A voice so light and pure, it caressed his soul.

A voice of an angel...

Ash sat up in bed and saw Celeste dancing around the stove.

"What are you doing, Tink?"

He sat up on the side of the bed, still gazing at her.

"I woke you up. Sorry!" She covered her mouth with her hand.

"I love your voice," he said with a smile. "It's a perfect way to start the day. What are you doing?"

"'*Le petit-dejeuner*' (breakfast)." She spun around and stirred something in the pot that was simmering on the stove.

"Breakfast?" Ash raised his eyebrows. "What could you possibly muster from the nothingness in my cabin?"

"Try it." She dipped her finger in the pot, walked to him, and traced his lips with her finger.

"Strawberry jam," Ash exclaimed after licking his lips. "How..."

"I got up early in the morning and went out to pick strawberries. You had sugar and some flour. So, we are having strawberry crepes. *Voilà!*"

She threw her arms in the air and smiled.

Ash put his hands around her waist and pulled her onto his lap.

"Tink, you are amazing!" He gazed into her eyes. "I love you!"

"Would you love me if I weren't Tink?"

Her voice trembled.

"I was getting there against my will at that." He sighed.

"Is the real Tink all that you pictured in your mind?" She looked into his eyes.

"Not even close." He shook his head. "I pictured that fragile, smiley girl. You turned out to be that and so much more."

"The reason I didn't tell you I was Tink was because I was terrified that you would hate her too. Were you disappointed?" she asked.

"Celeste," Ash said, caressing her face, "I wasn't disappointed. I was overwhelmed. You're a complicated person. I was starting to realize that I was in love with the real woman rather than the imaginary fairy. I tried to fight my feelings, but to no avail. You, turning out to be the real Tink saved me from feeling unfaithful."

"I'm sorry that I lied to you, Ash, but I'm a spy." She smiled and shrugged. "Before you say anything, remember, you were the one who inspired me to do that."

"Great, blame the victim." He shook his head but couldn't hold back his smile.

"Okay, let's eat." Celeste gave him a peck on the lips and dashed back to the stove.

The feeling of her lips on his went through his body like an electric shock.

He realized he'd loved her long before he knew who she was.

"The spy can cook," Ash said while stuffing his mouth with crepes. "I'm shocked. If that's one of your tactics, I've got to say that you're a pro at your business."

After they finished breakfast, Celeste cleaned the dishes and went outside. She sat on the grass and let the warmth of the sun caress her face. Spring in the mountains was magical. The air carried the scent of flowers and herbs, creating an enchanted potion of happiness.

"Do you care if I join?"

Ash slipped his arm around Celeste's shoulders. She leaned in, feeling as if her missing half had fallen into place.

Ash pulled her close to his chest and smiled. Who would've thought that his Tink was this amazing woman, who was able to infuriate and elevate him all at once? He felt like any moment now, he'd wake up and realize that all this was just a dream.

"Ash, I have never seen you smile."

Celeste raised her eyes to meet his.

"You gave me my life back, Tink." He kissed her on the top of the head.

"I am truly sorry for hurting you, Ash." She looked down. "If I knew how much you cared about Tink, I would've found a way to let you know that I was okay. I thought that I was the only one infatuated with you."

"And I am sorry for trying to kill you. You have no idea how much the memory of that terrifies me. What if I..." He tightened his hold on her.

"Let's not talk about that." She wrapped her arms around him and kissed him.

"I don't know what lies ahead of us." Ash caressed her face. "But I live for this moment right now."

"And I live for your smile." Celeste's eyes sparkled. "I will remember you exactly like this, sitting by me on the spring grass, smiling like you own the world."

They sat on the ground, holding each other for hours.

"I have to check the area." Ash finally stood up. "We're still fugitives. My cabin isn't easy to find, but letting my guard down would be catastrophic if something is about to happen." He walked into the cabin, grabbed his rifle, and then came back out.

"No one can reach us through the ravine." He pointed at the steep hill below the cabin. "The only way up here is through the woods. I will patrol that area. Get inside and lock the door."

Celeste nodded and followed his order. She was just finishing cleaning the room and the kitchen when Ash returned.

"Everything looks calm out there," he said, putting his rifle on the table. "I think we are safe for now. No Alliance patrol has ever come anywhere near this place. Pretty much, one has to know where it is to find it. Now, I'll get us some dinner."

He pulled a bow and a quiver of arrows from underneath the bed. Celeste arched her eyebrows.

"Well, I'm not gonna invite the Alliance by shooting." He smirked. "I'm just as good with the bow."

"I'm sold." She tiptoed and kissed him.

In a few hours, he returned with a couple of rabbits.

"Are you up for some rabbit stew?" he asked.

"I figured that you'd want to cook something like that, so I decided to help. I found some potatoes and carrots, so I got them ready for you."

"So, I'm cooking dinner?"

"I made breakfast, so it's only fair," she said sheepishly.

"Good decision. I can make a killer stew. Just maybe, don't throw up in my bowl, yeah?"

"I'll do my best not to," she said with a guilty smile. "I know that was nasty."

"I was actually impressed that you didn't faint."

"I wanted to..."

"Shhhh! Be quiet!" Ash grabbed his rifle. "Someone's here. Get down on the side of the bed."

He chambered a round with a sharp metallic click and leveled the rifle at the door.

"Do you have a spare gun?" Celeste asked.

"Under the bed," he whispered.

She reached underneath the cot and pulled out a revolver. Celeste quickly checked the chamber and clicked off the safety. Then, she ran and stood right by the door.

Ash looked at her with admiration. She wasn't helpless. Watching her carry herself with confidence, holding a gun, and the questionable clothes that she still wore made him feel flushed. Ash shook his head. What was wrong with him? They were about to be attacked, and he thought about...

I'm losing my goddamn mind!

"Finally, there's the cabin," a voice came from outside the door.

"Don't shoot; it's Hayes!" Celeste tucked the revolver in her belt and waved her hands at Ash.

He lowered the rifle.

Hayes and two other men entered the cabin and found themselves face-to-face with Ash and Celeste.

"Jesus! Celeste," Hayes gasped. "I thought you were dead." He ran, took her in his arms, and held her tight. "You gave me such a big scare. We thought you were in the truck that exploded in the ravine."

Ash watched Hayes with a frown. The way he embraced Celeste looked like he had done it before. Ash tightened his grip around the stock of the rifle.

The possessive flicker in his chest caught him off guard.

Now I'm jealous.

Ash gave Hayes a stone-cold look. Were Hayes and Celeste more than friends? They surely knew each other for years.

"Why are you in my cabin?" Ash grumbled.

"Well, we thought you were dead, so I came to retrieve any potential information that could compromise us."

"I have nothing like that here," Ash said curtly. "This is my home. Don't come here again."

"Chill, man." Hayes raised his hands. "I'm happy that you two are alive."

Ash narrowed his eyes. *I know there's only one of us you're happy is alive.*

"Pack it up." Hayes waved his hand. "We'll take you back to camp. There is more work to do."

"I'll miss staying here." Celeste sighed. "I guess we have to make the stew at camp."

"I guess," Ash huffed as he gathered the meat and vegetables.

Chapter 12

Celeste sat by Ash in the vehicle's back seat, found his hand, and took it in hers. He didn't react. His shoulders were tense, and his look was focused on the passing scenery outside the window.

Celeste was too familiar with his ability to erect a silent wall between them.

But why? What did I do?

Why was he so withdrawn? Was he starting again with the moodiness? Why was he always so difficult?

"Ash?" Celeste whispered. "What's wrong?"

"Nothing," he said tightly. His eyes darted away, and the muscle in his cheek twitched.

Celeste sighed heavily and pulled away from him. Perhaps he had reconsidered his affections for her. She closed her eyes and leaned against the window. She was going to talk to him when they arrived at the camp. There had to be something she said or did.

Ash looked at her. He hated himself for pushing her away, but he couldn't shake the image of Hayes holding her in his arms. Ash exhaled sharply. He hadn't known he was capable of that type of jealousy.

"Tink?" He reached for Celeste's hand. "I'm sorry!"

"We'll talk when we arrive at the camp." She lightly squeezed his hand.

When they arrived, Celeste walked out of the camp and paused just beyond the tree line. Ash quickly followed her.

"What's your problem with me now?" she asked and looked at him with tension in her eyes.

"Hayes. He groped you like you belonged to him. Do you?" Ash asked with a frown.

"I find this question incredibly offensive, Ash." Anger sparked in her eyes. "What kind of woman do you think I am to have business with two men?"

"Well, I didn't know what to think. He genuinely looked like he would've been heartbroken if you died."

"Dave and I have been friends for ten years. We worked together in New York. We dated briefly for about a month, but I realized that it wasn't going to work out, so I broke it off. We've been friends since. Just friends."

Ash's eyes darkened, and he gritted his teeth.

"It didn't look to me like Hayes has gotten the memo," he muttered.

"Oh my god! Ash! You're jealous," Celeste exclaimed.

"Well, yeah, I'm jealous."

"So, none of what I told you at the cabin mattered." Celeste swallowed hard. "When you decide that you can trust me, come and find me."

She turned around and walked away.

Ash raised his fist and punched a tree. The regret was so immediate and sharp that he barely registered the stinging pain in his knuckles from the impact. His breath was fast and shallow.

Stupid, pathetic son of a bitch!

He sat on the ground and grabbed his head in his hands. He should've known that Celeste wasn't a woman who would entertain that type of insecure behavior. He sighed heavily. He had to apologize to her and beg her to forgive him. But first, the dinner, he had promised to cook for her. He stood up and headed to the kitchenette.

Celeste rushed into Hayes's office. He raised his head from his papers with a question in his eyes.

"Nothing." She snapped at him.

"That doesn't look like nothing." Hayes sighed. "Are you and Ash still trying to kill each other? Didn't I tell you to solve your unfinished business?"

"Well, we had, until you showed up and stirred up his jealous streak."

"Jealous... you and Ash... are you for real? The other day, he was trying to kill you."

"Well, I had to tell him who I was. There was no other way to make up."

"I guess...but you and him?"

"I've known him for a while," Celeste shrugged and smiled. "We were online friends for a couple of years before I joined you. We weren't complete strangers."

"Why did he try to kill you then?" Hayes looked at her in confusion.

"He didn't know it was me."

"So, you and him..." He winked at her. "I wonder how long before you show him the door too?"

"I might've already done that." She let out a guilty smile.

"You're awful." He shook his head. "But I still love you."

"Please, don't antagonize Ash!" Celeste clasped her hands. "He deserves a breather."

"I guess you do care about him." Hayes sighed. "Okay, I'll stop being a jerk."

"Thank you!"

"Anyway," his face became serious, "I have an assignment for you."

"I'm listening." Celeste dropped into the chair across from him.

"I need you to meet with some of our potential allies from Mexico and Canada. You speak Spanish, right?"

"Sí," she smiled, "muy bien."

"Okay, the meeting is scheduled for tomorrow evening. You will meet them in Dubois. You have to leave now. There is at least a two-hour drive."

"You want me to travel alone?"

"It would be best. If you're stopped by a patrol, your active cover will hold. Of course, if you don't feel comfortable..."

"No, I'll go. I'm okay. Do you have clothes that actually fit this time?"

"Yes, I already placed a bag of clothes in your room."

"Okay, I'll be on my way shortly. I guess being away will give Ash time to cool down."

She quickly washed and changed. Then she returned to Hayes's office.

"Here, take my vehicle," he tossed the keys to her.

Celeste ran outside, climbed in the truck, and drove away.

Hayes sighed. He hated sending Celeste off alone. His heart tightened. If something happened to her...

It was the same every time she went on assignment. He sent her, but then he nearly lost his mind until she returned, every single time.

He couldn't lose her, yet there was no other way.

The Resistance has been working slowly toward securing support from Mexico and Canada. America's neighbors saw the Alliance as a threat to their own borders as well. However, they needed to have people on the inside of America to build a strong offensive when the time came. Stakes were high, and Celeste understood that. As always, she didn't hesitate to put her own life on the line in the name of freedom. Hayes respected her. She had always been faithful to America.

After the invasion, many Americans just accepted the new reality and conformed. They never considered fighting for their old world. David Hayes had joined the Resistance from the very beginning. He was a physician, but he was also an excellent strategist, so he planned and executed many of the operations of the Resistance, as well as providing medical care between the different camps and towns.

When Celeste asked him to enroll her in the Resistance, he was skeptical at first, but she managed to convince him. There was a fire in her that he had rarely seen in others. He had to admit he still had feelings for Celeste, but he respected her too much to impose.

He was shocked when he realized that Celeste and Ash had clicked, but now he could see it. Ash was as explosive as Celeste was. It all made sense. He smiled and shrugged. As long as she was happy, he was content.

Startled, Hayes raised his head. Someone had entered his office.

Ash.

"Where's Celeste?" he asked sharply. "Tell her that dinner is ready."

"Celeste's not here," Hayes prepared himself to face Ash's anger.

"What do you mean by 'she's not here'?"

"She left for an assignment."

"What?"

What? The bastard sent her off alone.

"Where the hell did you send her?" Ash's eyes dangerously sparked.

"I'm sorry, Ash, it was an important assignment, and she was the best person for it."

"You sent her off hungry. You didn't give her a chance to say goodbye..."

"She didn't look like she wanted to."

"It's all your fault, Hayes."

"Yes, I know. Sit." Hayes waved his hand. "You need to hear this."

Reluctantly, Ash sat in a chair at the desk.

"Celeste is a very good friend of mine, and I deeply care about her." Hayes sighed. "Yes, we briefly dated a long time ago, but we weren't a good match. We are great as friends. You have no reason to be jealous. Celeste truly cares about you. Please, don't hurt her!"

"I'm sorry," Ash muttered. "I realize I was a jerk to you and her. I have to make amends when she comes back. When is she coming back?"

"She should be back tomorrow or the day after."

"You should've let me go with her. Now I will be worried sick..."

"No," Hayes shook his head, "she has an active cover. If she is stopped by the Alliance patrol, she can handle it. You would get her killed."

"I guess you have a point," Ash said, standing up. "I'll just go and feed some of the kids. I'm no longer hungry."

Ash walked out the door with a stiff posture. He paused for a moment at the threshold. His eyes clouded with regret before he stepped into the fading light outside.

Hayes looked after him.

What did Celeste see in him?

Chapter 13

Celeste drove, unable to stop her tears.

Why was Ash such an insufferable grump?

The things he had said to her were so hurtful. Was Hayes right when he said that Ash was unpredictable and unstable? Maybe so, but still, she knew that Ash had a good heart. Hayes's behavior wasn't exactly innocent either. Celeste sighed and wiped her eyes. She should have talked to Ash before she left. Now he probably thinks that she no longer cares. She bit her bottom lip. It was too late now. At this point, the assignment came first. After she completed her work, she'd attempt to talk to Ash if he was still willing to hear her.

Well, it's not like I've had a stellar relationship track record.

Celeste turned the radio on and took a deep breath. An upbeat German song played. The Alliance no longer allowed American songs on the radio. She shut off the radio and frowned. Instead of a helpful distraction, the radio just infuriated her.

Perhaps being away for several days will let all emotions settle. Maybe not all was lost. Hopefully, Ash wasn't completely disappointed in her. Celeste shook her head. Now wasn't the time to get distracted. She had to focus and do her job.

When she arrived in Dubois, Celeste went to the hotel and checked in. Hayes had reserved a room for her there. The first thing she did was take a hot shower. Washing up with cold water at the camp wasn't her favorite. Then she relaxed in bed. She enjoyed the soft mattress and warm blankets caressing her skin. Celeste sighed. Most Americans didn't have that luxury. That reminded her how important her work was. Celeste closed her eyes and slowly drifted off to sleep.

She woke up early. Her meeting wasn't until the evening, so she had breakfast and walked to the location where she had to meet the Mexican and Canadian representatives. It was a small, dingy bar on the outskirts of town, with a flickering neon light casting a sickly purple glow on the cracked sidewalk. She stepped in and wrinkled her nose. The air was thick with the obnoxious smell of stale ashtrays and cheap beer. Celeste frowned. Who had chosen that location? That was the best way to raise suspicions.

"It's not like I have any say-so in the matter," she muttered and walked back to her hotel.

Before she left for the meeting in the evening, she put on a pair of jeans, a T-shirt, and a hooded sweatshirt. She parked her truck in the parking lot of a public building and walked to the bar on foot.

She walked into the bar, squinting to adjust to the dim lighting. The air inside was cloaked in hazy cigarette smoke, lit by the weak flickers of dying neon lights. The sticky floors and chipped wooden tables fit right in. A bartender wiped a glass with a worn-out rag while the old jukebox played old French music. A few apathetic patrons sat, hunched over their drinks. Their eyes flickered toward her, but then returned to their glasses. She saw two men sitting at the corner table. They matched the description provided to her by Hayes.

She approached the table.

"Can I share the table with you? I need a good drink," she said, the code phrase.

"Sit," one of the men said, pointing to the chair.

She followed his gesture, sat in the chair, and looked at the men. Something wasn't right. The way they were dressed and their body language just didn't fit. Everything screamed "setup."

Celeste started to stand up when she saw one of the men shake his head. "No."

"If I were you, I wouldn't try," he said in a low voice. "I have a gun pointed at you."

Celeste pressed her lips together and sat back down. Hayes must've received bad intel. She closed her eyes. Those men were Alliance agents. That was going to be a problem.

"Get up and walk," the man with the gun ordered her. "If you try to run, I'll shoot you."

Celeste did as she was told. The agents walked her to a black SUV and pushed her inside. They drove for about an hour and pulled up to a concrete building. One of the agents grabbed Celeste by her elbow and dragged her inside. There, they forced her to sit in a chair and cuffed her wrists to the table. One of them held her by the hair and lifted her face, while the other agent snapped a picture of her face.

"Let's see if the Denver office is interested in this one."

They left her in the room and walked out. Celeste knew that the director at the Denver office would refuse to get her shipped there, so her cover wouldn't be compromised with the Resistance. She was on her own. Celeste knew she was in trouble. She had no idea where they had taken her.

I think my luck finally ran out.

She had to figure out how to interest the agents in herself, or they were going to shoot her as soon as Denver told them that she was of no value. She winced; the two agents had just walked back in.

"What is your name?" one of them asked.

Celeste looked at him with a sinking feeling in her heart. He was stocky with sharp facial features and cold gray eyes that pierced through her like ice. In her mind, she called him Darian. She felt a shiver down her spine. He had the look of someone who enjoyed cruelty. The other agent appeared more mellow, with dirty-blond hair and hazel eyes. She called him Felix.

"I advise you to cooperate," Darian said coldly. "You just drew the short straw. Denver has no idea who you are. You have no value to them. It's in your best interest to speak. That would prolong your life by a day or so."

"What do you want to know from me?"

"For starters, where's the camp of the Resistance?"

"I'll think about it. I'd like some food and water first."

"You are in no position to make demands," the man said, huffing. "Okay, we'll feed you."

"Thanks," she muttered.

"You have an accent," Felix said. "French?"

"French Canadian," Celeste lied.

"No wonder they sent you. Your leadership isn't very smart," he said, laughing. "Our operative said they took the bait without any second thoughts."

Celeste didn't answer, but she had to agree with the agent. Hayes had really messed up this time. In an hour, they brought her a sandwich and a glass of water. She wasn't hungry but forced herself to eat the food since she had asked for it.

"Are you ready to talk now?" Darian asked, standing in front of her.

"I changed my mind," Celeste said defiantly.

"You, bitch!" His cold gray eyes sparked with hatred, and he punched her in the face.

She felt blood in her mouth. He had broken her nose. Without another word, the agent dragged her to a cell and locked the door.

"I'll let you think about your options tonight. If you are still stubborn in the morning, I assure you we have more methods to extract information from you."

Celeste sat on the cold, moist ground in the cell and wrapped her arms around her knees. The floor was hard. The moisture in the cell seeped through her clothes, chilling her to the bone. The metal cuffs were cutting through her skin, and her face hurt from the earlier assault. She shivered from pain and fear but tried to keep her shoulders tight. She wasn't going to show fear in front of her torturers.

It didn't seem that there was a way out. She sighed. Risks were a part of her job. Then she thought of Ash. She wished she had talked to him before she left. Now she was going to die, and the last thing he would remember would be her walking away from him.

She wiped the tears from her eyes. For the rest of the night, she thought of every moment she had spent with him. Despite his hurtful words, she loved him, and it hurt knowing that she'd never see him again. She remembered his strong arms wrapped around her shoulders and silently cried. She should've never told him that she was Tink. Now he'd be hurt all over again. Celeste also thought of Hayes. He would be devastated because this failure was ultimately his mistake. She sighed heavily. She should've checked the intel herself, but she was too busy arguing with Ash. She should've known that relationships are not good for her type of work.

Early in the morning, the agents returned to her cell.

"So, did you reconsider?" the stocky one that she called Darian asked.

"You are out of your mind if you think I'd talk," Celeste's eyes narrowed.

He tried to kick her, but she swiftly moved away, causing him to strike the wall.

"You, little bitch!" He grabbed her by the hair and slammed her face into the wall.

Celeste collapsed to the floor. The room was spinning.

"Don't hit her anymore or her face would be unrecognizable. I have an idea," Felix said. "Hold her up for a picture."

He snapped another photo of her.

"Let's have our contact post this on the resistance encrypted networks. Her friends are about to come looking for her. We might be able to catch one that would talk."

"That doesn't sound like a bad idea."

Darian kicked Celeste and walked out. She lay on the ground, trying to fight off the headache and nausea. Soon, exhausted, she fell asleep.

A sharp pain in the ribs woke her up. She saw the Alliance agents standing in her cell.

"Did you come to your senses?" Darian asked. "You've outlived your purpose with two days already."

"I told you I'm not telling you anything."

"I commend your stoicism, but it's time to face the consequences of your bad choices," the agent she called Felix said. "Last chance, are you going to talk?"

Celeste just closed her eyes.

I wish I could see Ash one last time.

Darian cuffed her wrists behind her back, grabbed her by the elbow, and dragged her outside.

Celeste moved in a daze. Her steps were uneven, and her knees were threatening to buckle. Her head was pounding, and everything was floating around her. She lost balance and stumbled, but the agent pulled her up by her elbow. She felt as if reality was losing its grip.

The only constant thought in her mind was Ash. She thought of his smile. He had a beautiful smile when he was happy. She felt guilty for dragging him into her convoluted world. She should've left him hating her. Then this wouldn't have hurt him much.

Darian stopped dragging her and pulled his revolver out. Celeste felt the cold muzzle against her temple.

"Last chance," he said coldly.

Celeste turned her head and closed her eyes. She took a deep breath of air. The scent of flowers and herbs filled her lungs. The morning breeze caressed her face.

She heard the safety click off.

She clenched her jaw in an attempt to ease her breathing. Her mind spun wildly, but then she latched onto a single image: Ash. His face, his voice, the way he looked at her, like she was the only thing in the world he could see. Her thoughts flew back to him as if he could anchor her one last time.

She almost felt his arms' embrace and his body's heat.

The sound of her own heart drummed in her ears…

"Ash…"

The name slipped from her lips in a trembling breath.

A single shot echoed.

Chapter 14

Ash sat on the grass at the edge of camp, holding his head in his hands.

"When you decide that you can trust me, come and find me."

Celeste's words burned into his mind. He was such an idiot! He didn't deserve a woman like Celeste. He had insulted her and wounded her.

He had hurt Tink!

Ash sharply exhaled. When she returns, he must apologize. He prayed that she'd forgive him. He hated himself.

Ash remembered the day he and Celeste spent in his cabin. They had cooked together, laughed, and fallen asleep, holding each other. That was the happiest time in his life, a brief moment when the outside world had ceased to exist and only the warmth shared between them mattered.

Then he had to go and ruin it. Celeste was more incredible than he'd ever imagined. His Tinker Bell had grown up and morphed into a self-confident, courageous, beautiful woman. A woman, who saved his life, nursed him back to health, and told him she loved him.

And what did he do? He attacked her character in the worst possible way. Now she had gone who knows where, without even saying goodbye. All because of his stupidity. His chest was tight with regret, but there was nothing he could do. He had to wait for Celeste to return.

Over the next two days, Ash paced back and forth. He couldn't eat or sleep. The thought of Celeste being in danger was eating him up inside. Hayes had said she would return in a couple of days. Ash counted the minutes, driving the road in both directions, hoping to spot her truck.

Ash woke up in a panic. It had been three days, and Celeste still wasn't back. There was something wrong. He knew it. He walked to Hayes's building.

Ash was standing in Hayes's office, nervously tapping his fingers on the desk.

"It's been three days." Ash's voice was tense. "Celeste should've been back by now."

"I know." Hayes looked on edge. "I'll check the chatter..."

He took his phone out and scrolled through it for several minutes. Suddenly, his face drained of color.

"What?" Ash clenched his jaw.

"We got bad intel. Celeste was ambushed and captured by the Alliance."

Captured by the Alliance!

"You said she has cover."

The panic gripped Ash's heart with steel nails.

"I thought she did... We have to go." Hayes jumped up from his desk. "They are torturing her."

He threw his phone down. Ash looked at the screen and saw a photo of Celeste. Her face was bloodied and bruised.

Goddammit!

His hand gripped the rifle.

"Do you know where they're holding her?" he grumbled, already heading outside.

"I'll figure it out."

Hayes ran outside.

Ash stepped out of the door and waited.

"Come on, get in." Hayes pulled up in a truck.

"Move over." Ash opened the driver's door. "I'm driving. You're navigating."

Hayes moved over to the passenger seat without protest.

Ash jumped behind the wheel and peeled out of camp.

Hayes should've never sent her alone!

Ash slammed the steering wheel with his hand.

"Hayes, if something happens to Celeste, I'll kill you." His voice was ice cold. "How could you send her off alone without checking your sources? I will never forgive you."

"I'll never forgive myself," Hayes muttered. "I care about Celeste."

Ash snapped his head, and his eyes narrowed to slits as they locked onto Hayes. His body tensed, radiating fury.

"Our relationship is strictly platonic," Hayes added quickly. "You can tone down your murderous temper at any time."

Ash just clenched his jaw. They drove the rest of the way in silence, arriving in Dubois around noon. Hayes directed Ash to the hotel where Celeste had a room. They quickly climbed up to her floor and checked the room. The only thing they found there was the bag that she had packed with her.

They returned to the truck. Hayes sat behind the wheel this time and drove to the bar where Celeste was supposed to have the meeting. He drove around the area and finally found his truck parked down the road. He checked inside and found the keys under the sun visor.

"Wait for me here," he told Ash and drove away.

Ash closed his eyes. He was only hoping that they'd find Celeste on time. If her cover was blown, they were going to kill her.

He knew it!

His heart was pounding so loudly that it echoed in his head. Now he fully realized that being in love with a spy wasn't romantic; it was horrifying. But still, he loved her. Right now, he would gladly trade his life for hers. At this moment, he didn't care that she was upset with him. He'd accept her hatred of him; he'd be okay if she never looked at him again, if she could just be safe.

I'm spiraling.

Ash gripped the steering wheel until his knuckles turned white. His palms were sticky with sweat. His heart was pounding with every breath, escalating into panic.

I have to pull myself together. Celeste is counting on me.

He winced. Somebody was knocking on the window. Ash gripped his rifle. Then he saw Hayes. Ash rolled the window down.

"What the hell are you doing?" Hayes's voice was irritated. "Come on, follow me. We've got no time to waste."

Ash cursed at himself and started the engine. Hayes jumped behind the wheel and floored his truck.

He must really care about Celeste.

Ash followed right behind him, this time feeling no anger toward him. Given that Hayes cared about Celeste, he must've felt guilty about what had happened. God only knew what was going through his head. Ash had never seen him so panicked before. Besides, he was driving like he had a death wish.

I don't care if he still has feelings for her, as long as she survives.

At that moment, Ash forgot his jealousy, anger, everything. He just silently prayed that they weren't too late.

The drive lasted about forty minutes. Hayes abruptly turned onto a dirt road going into the woods. Then, he pulled over and switched off the engine. Ash grabbed his rifle and jumped out of his truck.

"What now?" He looked at Hayes.

"Now we continue on foot. There is a black site about two miles from here. My informants told me that Celeste was taken there. They also said that Denver didn't put protection on her. I just hope her cover isn't blown. If that's the case, she is already... let's hurry up." Hayes ran.

Ash sprinted after him. A suffocating feeling squeezed his throat. Never, in his entire life, did he feel so scared. What Hayes said had extinguished all possibilities of a favorable outcome. But still deep down in his heart, there was a flicker of weak, stubborn hope refusing to let go.

Soon, the two men reached a large clearing in the woods. They crouched behind the trees to assess the area. There was a small concrete building. The entire clearing was surrounded by a barbed wire fence.

"I don't think anyone is here," Ash whispered. "There are no vehicles."

"Let's go in and check."

Ash took off his jacket and threw it over the barbed wire. The men quickly climbed over the fence. They ran to the building. The door was unlocked. They quietly sneaked inside. The agents' office was empty. There was only one cell in the holding area. The door of the cell was open, and there was no one inside.

Ash went in there, crouched down, and touched the floor.

"There is fresh blood."

He looked at the red stains on his fingers and felt his blood boiling.

Celeste's blood!

"She was here," Ash said, standing up. "Where could they have taken her?"

The color drained from Hayes's face.

"We were too late," he whispered and sagged into one of the chairs.

"What do you mean by 'too late'?"

Ash intently looked at him.

"If she's not here, she's already dead." Tears welled in Hayes's eyes.

"No. I can't accept that," Ash said sharply.

He turned around and left the building. He walked to the middle of the yard and froze. He stood over a dark pool of blood.

Ash collapsed to his knees and just stared. The metallic scent hit him like a jolt, turning his stomach and tightening his throat with rage and an unbearable ache. His mind was refusing to accept what logic was dictating.

No, that is not possible!

Not Celeste!

Not my Tink!

With trembling hands, he touched the blood. It was still warm. His throat closed up.

If they had left earlier. If they had driven faster...

Ash turned his head and saw Hayes standing by him. He looked like he had been crying.

"Do you think that's her blood?" Ash asked, grasping at straws.

"Who else would it be?" Hayes whispered.

"I have to find her." Ash clenched his jaw. "They had to bury her here somewhere."

"They wouldn't give her that much respect," Hayes shook his head. "At this site, they usually throw the executed insurgents in the ravine."

Without saying anything, Ash sprang to his feet and ran toward the ravine. He fell to his knees and looked down at the edge.

"Celeste!" he called her name.

The only answer that returned was the echo of his own voice.

Chapter 15

Ash squinted and gazed toward the bottom of the ravine. There were trees and bushes in the way. It appeared that there was some dark mass down by the creek. With trembling hands, he lifted his rifle and looked through the scope. It was definitely a human body. Motionless...

Celeste!

Ash felt like the entire air was instantly sucked out of his lungs. His heart was beating in his chest like a caged bird. He felt cold sweat break through his skin. A wave of panic surged through him, leaving him dizzy. Without saying a word, he jumped off the edge and started sliding down the slope, slowing his descent by grabbing onto the grass and bushes. When he reached the bottom, he ran toward the creek.

Please, God, let her be alive!

As soon as Ash looked at the body, he felt as if someone had kicked him in the chest. It was Celeste. She lay half on the bank, half in the water. The right side of her head and her face were soaked in blood.

He rushed to her and wrapped his arms around her.

"Oh, no, Tink!"

He pulled her against his chest, his sobs strangling his breath.

Hayes, who had just caught up with Ash, put his fingers on Celeste's neck.

"Let go of her." Hayes pried her off Ash's grip. "She's alive."

She's alive?

Speechless, Ash stared at him.

Hayes quickly started checking Celeste's body for wounds.

Ash was silently watching every move he made.

"She only has a flesh wound on her right temple," Hayes said. "I'm not sure if she hit her head when she fell down the ravine. I'm not detecting any abnormality of her cervical spine. Let's go."

Ash put Celeste over his shoulder and started climbing back up. The weight of her limp body didn't even faze him. All he thought about was getting her up to his truck. Once they reached the top, the two men ran back to their vehicles.

"Let me have her," Hayes said, carefully taking Celeste off Ash's arms. "In case she takes a turn for the worse. I'm not sure if she has any internal injuries."

Ash just nodded and climbed into his truck. Hayes drove off at mad speed. Ash followed right behind him. If someone tried to stop them, Ash was going to deal with them. The only thing on his mind was the woman lying in the truck in front of him.

He didn't feel the tears roll down his face. He prayed with everything he had that she would be okay. It didn't matter whether she was upset with him or if she even talked to him again. As long as she lived, he didn't care. She was his Tink. He would do anything to see her well.

They reached the Resistance camp late in the afternoon. Hayes rushed Celeste to the hospital. Ash paced nervously in front of the treatment room. He continued to see her pale, bloodied face. He wanted to kill Hayes for sending her on that mission, but he knew that assignment was Celeste's job.

Finally, after what seemed like an eternity, Hayes came out.

"It's not as bad as it looked," Hayes said before Ash asked anything. "She's dehydrated and beat up from falling down the ravine, but she'll recover just fine. The wound on her head is just a graze; I sutured it. Right now, she is getting fluids. She will be okay, Ash."

"Can I see her?" he asked, still trying to slow his breathing.

"Yes, give us a minute to move her to one of the rooms."

Ash nodded.

Ash sat by Celeste's bed, gazing at her. She was pale, but they had cleaned the blood from her hair and face and changed her dirty clothes into a hospital gown. He closed his eyes. The past several hours slowly replayed in his mind. He was so close to losing her before he even got to tell her how much he regretted the words he had said to her.

"Ash?" Celeste whispered.

"Tink." He touched her face. "How are you feeling?"

"Like a used-up dirt rag." She smiled crookedly. "I should've known that you'd come looking for me."

"I thought I was too late... How did you survive? I saw a big puddle of blood in the yard of that building."

"It wasn't my blood. I, too, thought I was a goner. The agent put a gun to my head. I braced for the bullet. Then I heard a shot. I waited to die, but it was he who collapsed on the ground. The other agent shot him dead. Apparently, my trusted position in the Resistance was worth the life of one of their agents. I guess the poor sap didn't have enough clearance."

"Why were you shot and at the bottom of the ravine then?" Ash looked at her in confusion.

"I was told it has to look like I escaped. He made me run and shot at me. He was supposed to graze my arm, but his poor aim almost blew my brains out. I survived by sheer luck. I thought he killed me, so I tripped and fell headfirst down the slope. I must've hit my head or was so spooked that I just checked out. Anyway, where's Hayes? I have to talk to him."

"I'll find him for you," Ash sighed.

She asked for Hayes.

The sound of the name felt like a slap across his face. His stomach wrenched. If he hadn't insulted her...

It didn't matter. Nothing mattered except that Celeste was alive and well. He stood up and went looking for Hayes.

"Dave, we have to talk," she said as soon as Hayes walked in. "I've managed to ensure that we will no longer be ambushed if we attempt negotiations with Mexico and Canada. I told them that in order to get intel, those meetings must happen, and I must attend them. I assured them that the negotiation would fail. That way, the Alliance will want those meetings to happen."

"Celeste, I don't think I want you to do this anymore." Hayes frowned. "What we just went through almost gave me a heart attack. I can't have anything happening to you."

"Dave," Celeste said, sitting up in bed. "Let's not allow emotions to dictate our actions. We have the opportunity to negotiate in peace. We have to take it. There are high stakes at play. Is there a chance I'd get killed? Absolutely. However, we all knew the risks when we signed up for this. Why do I have to explain that to you? You are the leader, not me."

"I don't like that, but you have a point," he said, shaking his head. "Okay, we will proceed. Just, please, don't die."

"You think I want to die? I don't, but are we fighting for our freedom or just playing around?"

"You know how to put me on a guilt trip, don't you?" he muttered.

"I need to get out of this bed," Celeste started to get up.

"Don't you dare." Hayes put his hand on her shoulder. "I swear, if you stand up, I'll tie you down myself. You are staying in this bed at least until tomorrow."

"I need to talk to Ash."

"He's not going anywhere. Speaking of Ash. Give him a break, would you? He was ready to fight a bear for you out there. But seriously, I've never seen somebody fall apart faster than he did when we thought that you were dead. That man loves you. Give him a break."

"Wow, I see you two are bros now. Don't worry, I'm not going to stomp his heart. I promise."

Celeste relaxed in her bed, waiting for Ash, but he never came. She sighed and covered her head with the blanket. Obviously, Hayes had lost his mind. If Ash wanted to talk to her, he would've come. She knew she was too short with him before she left for her assignment, but there was no way she would entertain accusations questioning her honor, even if it did come from Ash. She sighed and closed her eyes. They can sort that out tomorrow. Now she needed rest.

The next morning, Celeste woke up feeling much better. She saw clothes hanging on the back of the chair and figured that Hayes had brought them for her. She dressed and walked out of the hospital.

She looked around, but Ash was nowhere in sight. He was probably in one of his moods again.

"Have you seen Ash?" Celeste asked Hayes.

"No, he bolted out of here yesterday. He's probably back home."

"Can you drive me there?"

"I guess. You two need to stop your nonsense." Hayes mumbled but got in his truck and drove Celeste to the foot of Ash's Mountain.

Ash's truck was parked at its usual place.

"I'll go up there alone," Celeste said. "You can go back. Come and get me when you have work lined up for me."

"Alright, just don't kill each other."

Hayes shook his head and drove away.

Celeste sat on the ground and sighed. The air was warm, and the faint breeze rustled the dry grass around her. She wasn't sure that this was the right decision. What if Ash didn't want to see her? What if he no longer cared? The real Celeste was surely a step down from his shiny idea of Tink. She was afraid of that. There was no way that he wasn't disappointed. First of all, Celeste was European. Second, there was Hayes.

Hayes!

Suddenly, she realized what had happened yesterday. She had asked for Hayes without talking to Ash. He probably thought...

Damnit! Of course, he thought that.

She closed her eyes.

I need to think before I speak.

She thought of what Hayes had told her about Ash, and felt her heart tighten. Ash must've been truly hurt by her indifference yesterday.

She wanted to slap herself upside the head. Ash had every right to be upset with her.

Tink would've never done that to him.

Celeste sighed. She was aware that the girl she was when Ash called her Tink was gone. The war had changed her, and not for the better.

Celeste stood up, took her jacket off, and tied it around her waist. It was a warm day, and hiking was easier in just a T-shirt.

Chapter 16

Celeste winced. There were muffled voices not too far from her. Someone was here. She quickly took cover between the trees. Soon, she spotted two Alliance soldiers walking up to Ash's truck. That must be one of the patrols, probably the soldiers who had taken over Ravenville. They must be looking for Ash and her. It would've been too good to be true that they would just give up. They must've realized that there were no bodies in the truck that exploded in the ravine.

Dammit!

Celeste couldn't allow them to return to town. They would bring a whole party of soldiers, and Ash would be history. She bit her bottom lip and pulled her knife from the sheath tied to her leg. Celeste approached the truck and crouched on the opposite side, still following the soldiers with her eyes. They split up. One of them entered the truck, and the other one circled the vehicle and approached Celeste. As soon as he passed her, she jumped onto his back, covered his mouth, and slit his throat.

Celeste quickly ran to the truck. The other soldier was digging in the glove box, not paying attention. She sneaked close to him and sliced his carotid on the side of his neck. Terrified, he looked at her while holding his neck. He tried to pull his pistol out of the holster, but he fell over on the ground before he managed to.

Celeste collapsed to her knees and vomited. The heavy metallic smell of the blood was stuck in her nose. Shaking, Celeste frantically started wiping the blood from her trembling hands into the grass. She could still see the terrified face of the soldier, the question "Why?" in his eyes. She had never killed a man before. A feeling of suffocation squeezed her throat. Murder was the last thing on her to-do list today.

With her stomach rolling, she dragged the bodies of the soldiers into the woods and then went back to the truck. She had to move it away from here. Celeste looked for the keys, but they weren't there. Of course, Ash must have taken them with him. Celeste immediately ran up the mountain. She had to tell Ash that Alliance patrols were snooping around.

She was halfway up the hill when she heard a sharp whistling sound and almost immediately felt a burning pain through her left side. She took cover behind a tree and looked down. There was an arrow sticking out of her body.

Ash!

Oh, great! My head hasn't even healed yet, and now I'm rabbit stew.

She tried to look from behind the tree but immediately saw another arrow whizz past her face, close enough to make her flinch. In this instant, she realized that Ash was going to kill her before she managed to tell him it was her. Celeste thought for a second, then bit her lip and moved her arm out of the cover. She felt an arrow pierce her upper arm. With a painful sigh, she threw herself on the ground and lay motionless, hoping that Ash wouldn't loose another arrow for good measure.

Celeste tried to lie still, which was close to impossible. The pain was unbearable. She realized that when she fell, the arrow in her side jammed further into her body. She bit her lip until it bled. This was all her fault. If she hadn't upset Ash, he would have never left, and...

I'm ridiculous...

She opened her eyes and saw Ash running toward her.

"Jesus, Celeste... what the hell," he gasped, panicking.

He lifted her from the ground.

"Well, finally, you shot me."

She let out a crooked smile.

"Goddammit! What are you doing here? This is bad!"

He broke the arrows at their shafts.

"I have to take you to Hayes's hospital now."

"You can't!" She grabbed his arm. "The mountain is crawling with patrols."

"You think I don't know that?" he grumbled.

"Take me up to your cabin. We'll deal with this ourselves."

"Ourselves?" He gave her a staggering look. "I shot you in the gut. You'll die."

Celeste touched the blood seeping around the arrow in her side and looked at it.

"I don't think you perforated my intestines. I'll be alright."

"You, stupid idiot, you! Why would you come here?"

"Hurry up, let's go to your cabin. I'll take care of that. You have to come back down here. There are two dead soldiers in the woods by your truck. You've got to get rid of them. Also, move your truck away from here."

"You killed them?" he exclaimed in disbelief. "I didn't hear any shots."

"I used my knife," she said between her teeth. "Let's hurry up."

Ash helped her stand up, but she lost her balance.

He took her in his arms and quickly scaled the mountain.

Once in the cabin, he sat her on the bed and carefully looked at her. She looked pale and in pain.

"Go now. I'll be okay. When you're back, we'll deal with the arrows." She gritted her teeth and waved her hand, telling him to go.

"Here, take this," he said, handing her a revolver. "I'll be back shortly."

Ash ran out of the door and down the path. His heart was beating in his ears. He couldn't shake the image of the painful expression on her pale face. How could he have been so careless! He should've assessed the situation before he shot that arrow. Now, because of that, Celeste's life was on the line. He was still trying to process the fact that he had shot the woman he loved. The thought of her alone and bleeding out made him run faster. He was terrified, but he had to admit that she had a point. If more soldiers showed up, they would eventually find his cabin.

Ash drove his truck about a mile away from his mountain and then quickly ran back. He found the dead soldiers. He stared at them for a second.

Damn! That's one dangerous woman.

He was terrified, amazed, and stupidly proud.

That's my Tink.

He dragged the bodies up the hill to a shallow cave and covered the entrance with branches. Then he sprinted toward his cabin. His stomach was in knots, and his lungs burned every time he took a breath.

I can't believe I shot Tink.

If something happened to her...

Barely catching his breath, Ash ran into his cabin, and his blood ran cold.

Celeste was lying on the floor. Both arrows were out—blood everywhere.

She lay motionless, her face deathly pale.

Shit!

"Tink!" He knelt next to her and shook her. "Please, don't do that. Please, wake up!"

He felt the panic rising in his heart.

"Ash..." Her eyelids flickered. "Calm down. I'm not dead. I don't die easily. I think we've established that already. I just fainted a little bit."

"Fainted a little bit." Ash laughed as he took her in his arms. "I thought you died. There's blood everywhere..."

"It looks worse than it is," Celeste mumbled.

"And what are you lying on? Did you put plastic on the floor?"

"I didn't want to make a mess."

"Jesus! Celeste, you'll be the death of me."

"Don't cry, Ash." Celeste touched his tear-streaked face. "I'll be okay."

"I almost killed you..."

He moved a strand of hair from her face.

"I will never forgive myself."

"I can't say I didn't deserve it," she sighed. "I'm sorry I hurt your feelings yesterday."

Ash blinked, feeling his stomach twist. He took a breath he didn't know he was holding. Celeste had come all the way here to apologize to him, and he had… The guilt pressed heavier on his shoulders.

"Forget about that." Ash shook his head. "Let's take care of your wounds first."

He took the kettle with warm water from the stove, lifted her T-shirt, and started cleaning the wound on her side. She was still bleeding.

"This one could be trouble," he muttered with a frown.

"Let's hope not."

"I ruined your clothes."

"I brought several shirts, don't worry."

Ash picked her up and laid her on the bed. After he finished cleaning the wounds on her side and her arm, he prepared his suture supplies. He paused for a second to steady his trembling hands.

"It will be okay." Celeste smiled and put her hand on the top of his. "I'll be okay."

Ash took a deep breath. Then, trying to keep his hands steady, he sutured the wounds on her side and her arm.

"Why didn't you wait for me?" he asked while running his fingers through her hair.

"I thought I'd save some time and remove the arrows, but I didn't factor in the pain. It wasn't nice."

"I can't believe I almost killed you." Ash closed his eyes. "I was scouting the woods when I noticed the patrol. I ran back to the cabin and took my bow. I had no idea you were here. I thought it was one of them."

"It was just a misunderstanding, Ash." She caressed his face. "Please, don't torment yourself. I'm alive."

"Barely," he grumbled. "I'm glad you aren't angry with me. I saw what you did to those men."

"I didn't want to, but I had to stop them before they discovered you or told someone about it."

"You did that for me, and look how I repaid you for it."

"Please, Ash." She sat up with a painful grimace, "I'm okay. I came to apologize to you. I know I hurt you when I asked to speak to Hayes yesterday. I'm sorry. I had to brief him on the intel that I had collected. There were no personal feelings involved. I'm sorry. I should've thought about you before I did that."

"Tink." He lifted her chin with his fingers, "I'm sorry too for overreacting. Because of my insecurities, you almost died. I promise, I will never doubt you again."

"I love you, Ash!"

She whispered with her voice trembling from pain. As she leaned in and kissed him, Ash felt a rush of guilt, relief, and overwhelming love. Her lips were soft and warm. He kissed her back with a quiet desperation as if this kiss could undo the horror that had unfolded earlier.

"I love you, Tink," he murmured, pulling her up to his chest.

He came so close to losing her today.

He buried his face in her hair. At that moment, nothing mattered, not the war, not the danger. It was just Celeste and Ash, holding each other as if it were the last day on Earth.

Chapter 17

sh stirred in bed. Someone was crying.

Celeste!

"Tink, are you okay?"

He hovered over her. She was holding her side, quietly crying.

"Hold on." He quickly got out of bed. "I'll give you something for pain."

He handed her some acetaminophen.

She took the medication and looked at Ash.

There was so much pain in his eyes!

"I'm sorry," she wiped her tears, "I didn't mean to wake you up. I feel better now."

Ash clenched his jaw. Of course, she was lying. She claimed she felt better, but her pale, exhausted face said the opposite.

This is all my fault.

"Tink, please, tell me how to help you. I can't bear watching you suffer."

"Lie next to me and hold me. It will help."

She reached for him.

"Yes, my love," he wrapped his arms around her, trying not to touch her wounded side.

She laid her head on his chest and fell asleep.

Ash sighed heavily. His heart was breaking, seeing her like that. He stayed awake all night, holding her in his arms. He knew he would do anything to trade places with her right now.

She's paying for my jealousy and insecurity.

"I am so sorry, Tink." He laid a kiss on her forehead and winced. She was burning up.

Ash sprinted out of bed and grabbed acetaminophen from the cabinet.

"Celeste, wake up! You have to take medication. You have a fever."

She mumbled something incoherent.

Panicked, Ash dipped a rag in cold water and wiped her skin down. Then, he turned his fan on and put it on her.

Soon, Celeste started shivering uncontrollably. Ash touched her forehead and startled, pulled back. She was hotter than before.

What do I do?

Please, God, help me!

Ash ran to the cabinet, grabbed the medication, and crushed it into powder. He mixed it in some water and forced it down Celeste's throat while holding her head up. His mind was on fire.

He grabbed Celeste's bag and emptied it on the table. The medication bottles clattered across the table.

Which one?

"Which one do I use?" he repeated, feeling the panic taking hold of him again.

"Ash..."

He abruptly turned around. Celeste was awake.

"Tink! Thank God!"

He ran to her.

"How are you feeling?"

"Not great," she whispered weakly. "Do you have IV fluids?"

"Let me check my supplies."

He went to the small closet in the hallway and pulled out a duffel bag. He looked through it and found several small bags of saline.

"Would that work?" He showed them to Celeste. "I don't know if they are still good."

"It doesn't matter." She tried, unsuccessfully, to sit up. "Let me see the medications."

Ash scooped up all the vials from the table quickly and brought them to the bed.

"Use those." Celeste pointed to the bottles. "You have to inject some of the fluid in the vial with the antibiotic and shake it until it's diluted. Then transfer it to the bag with fluids and... Do you have an intravenous catheter?"

"Yeah, I've stocked the basics. Just in case."

"Can you start a line?"

"Yes. I've learned that much during the war."

He quickly followed her directions, started an IV line, and connected the antibiotic to it.

"You were burning up," Ash said, almost to himself. "I tried to cool you down with cold water, but you started shivering, and everything got worse."

"It's the shivering," she said with a crooked smile. "It raises the temperature..."

"Tell me this medication is going to be enough... Celeste!"

She didn't answer.

Ash ran to the bed. She had fallen asleep. He touched her forehead. The fever was going down. He sighed with relief. The acetaminophen had kicked in. Ash watched her for a few more minutes, then stood up and grabbed his bow and his rifle.

Those woods aren't going to patrol themselves.

Once outside, Ash took a deep breath of the clean mountain air. He was going to deal with his guilt later. Now, he had to ensure that they were safe. He completed his usual round but didn't see anybody. That was good.

He hurried back to the cabin. Celeste was still sleeping.

Ash quietly left the cabin.

Celeste moved around in her bed and opened her eyes. The room smelled good. She looked over and saw Ash stirring something in a pot on the stove.

"Are you cooking?" Her voice was scratchy from sleeping.

"I believe I owe you rabbit stew." He smiled and stirred the pot again.

"You went hunting?" Celeste's eyes widened, and she lifted herself on her elbows.

"Of course I did. After I almost killed you, the least I can do is feed you."

"Please, Ash, don't torment yourself about it."

She stood up, holding her side.

"What are you doing?" Ash ran to her and wrapped his arm around her shoulders.

"I need to get to the restroom."

He walked her down to the bathroom.

"Yell if you need help."

Once he helped her back to bed, he tucked her in and pulled up a chair.

"There are only two vials of the antibiotic left," he said, looking at Celeste. "I have to go and get some medication from Hayes."

"Hand me my bag."

Ash grabbed the bag from the floor and brought it to the bed. Celeste started looking through the bottles with pills.

"There are oral antibiotics I can take when the intravenous is gone. You don't need to go back to camp."

"Are you sure?"

Is she lying to me?

"I won't allow you to die from infection, Celeste."

"I'll be okay, Ash. Trust me."

"You scared me to death." His voice broke as he traced her lips with his thumb.

"It was an unfortunate situation." She sighed. "You didn't know it was me. Bad luck, I guess. Please, don't blame yourself!"

"I don't think I can," he muttered.

"How about we try some of your famous rabbit stew?"

"Coming right up."

Ash smiled and got up. Soon, he brought two bowls of food.

"This is amazing!" Celeste exclaimed while quickly emptying the bowl. "I was starved."

"I'm glad you like it."

"You weren't kidding when you said you made good stew."

"I guess that's one way to redeem myself."

Ash cleaned the bowls, pulled down the blackout curtains, and lit the lamp. He sat on the chair by the bed and gazed at Celeste.

"Come and lie by me." She waved her hand.

"Last time I did that, you almost died."

"Don't be ridiculous," she laughed. "I need you. Right now, you're the only one who could make me feel better."

Ash moved to the bed and put his arm under her shoulders.

"I'm sorry for all the times that I disappointed you." Celeste caressed his face. "You never doubted Tink, and she intentionally abandoned you. If I had known how much that would hurt you, I would have never done it. Please, forgive me!" Her voice cracked under the crushing weight of regret.

"You had your reasons. You are in my arms now. That's all I care about. I found my Tink. Just get better. My heart breaks when you hurt."

Ash lowered his head and kissed her.

Celeste nestled against him and closed her eyes. The warmth of his body felt like home. The memories of the horrors of the past ten years melted away every time she was in his arms. She smiled and fell asleep with her head lying on his chest.

Chapter 18

In the following days, Celeste watched Ash change into a completely different person. He was caring and loving, and he also smiled. Even though she was in pain, Celeste was happy. Every ache reminded her of the nightmare she'd endured, and of the miracle that she was still alive.

The warmth of Ash's presence, the comforting silence of the cabin, and the sunrays trickling between the curtains wrapped around her like a safety blanket. For the first time in years, she had been able to stop and breathe. She knew this peaceful state was an illusion, but she didn't care. The war had taught her to enjoy the moment, as tomorrow wasn't promised.

"How are you feeling today?" Ash put his hand on her forehead.

"I'm getting better," she assured him. "The pain isn't as bad, and I haven't had any fever for the last two days."

"Thank God! I was losing my mind."

"I know." She sat up and wrapped her arms around his neck. "I need you to know that I'm still alive, only thanks to you. You saved my life."

"Yes, after I shot you," he said with a sigh.

"You won't let that go, will you?" Celeste shook her head.

"Absolutely not."

"Ash, I need a shower or a bath or something."

"There is a tub in the bathroom. I can warm up water on the stove for you."

"Where are you getting the water from?" Celeste was curious.

"I have a well and a small pump to pull water to containers connected to the cabin. I also have some electricity available from a solar panel on my roof. However, I keep that for emergencies and to power my water pump."

"Wow, you are a jack of all trades, aren't you?"

"Well," Ash smiled, "at one time, I was trained to be just that. I might look dumb, but I speak multiple languages and have a degree in software and mechanical engineering. Well, when any of that mattered anyway."

"I never called you dumb, Ash. You're the smartest man I've ever known. Don't forget that I've known you for years."

"I'm not forgetting. I thank my stars for finding you every day. Although what I found wasn't exactly the Tink I had imagined. What I found was this amazing woman, who surpassed any of my illusions about Tink."

"Were you disappointed?"

"Disappointed?" Ash raised his eyebrow. "I'm still in awe."

"Can you help me outside?" Celeste asked after she was done with her bath. "I need some fresh air."

Ash walked her behind the cabin, and they sat in the tall grass. Celeste closed her eyes and leaned on his chest. The light summer breeze caressed her face, bringing with it the light hint of pine resin and wildflowers. The fresh scent of mountain herbs and the song of the birds completed her bliss. This was all she needed in her life: Ash, the cabin, and the mountains.

"You make me happy." She opened her eyes and looked at him.

"You are my happiness, Tink." Ash laid a kiss on her forehead.

"So, what do we do from now on?"

"Once you're strong enough, we can walk to some of the cabins throughout the area and warn everybody about the patrols."

"That sounds like a plan."

Celeste and Ash spent the next two weeks in the cabin. She felt better every day, and soon, the pain was completely gone. Celeste often laughed about the predicament with Ash's arrows. He didn't think it was funny, but his guilt was slowly dissipating. He was finally at peace with himself.

"Tell me something about you that I don't know," he asked her one night while they were having dinner under the dim light of the lamp.

"I was born and spent half of my childhood in Paris. My mother was a Louisiana Cajun. I'm French on my father's side. I was ten when my parents separated. My mom and I moved to America."

Celeste knitted her brows.

"We lived in a suburb of New Orleans, Louisiana, my mom's home state."

"The southern accent," Ash smirked.

"Well, I was nervous. What do you want from me? Anyway, after graduating from high school, I went to med school in Boston... I can see the question in your eyes. Yes, I have dual citizenship, American and French. My French accent was an act."

"Obviously, you were born a spy," Ash laughed. "That answers the question about the whereabouts of your French accent. So, tell me more."

"I was doing my residency in New York when the war started. I didn't know what to think until I met you on Amnestic. You opened my eyes to the atrocities committed by the Alliance. Then Hayes recruited me for the Resistance, and the rest you know. How about you?"

"I'm local. I was born in Dayton. I joined the Navy right after high school. I got my engineering degrees in the military. Later, I was recruited to the Navy SEALS. I was on active duty when the war started. After it was all over, I came home to look for my family, but they were gone. My parents and my two younger brothers were killed trying to evacuate. Most of my friends were gone too. I lost everybody who ever mattered to me."

"I'm sorry, Ash." Celeste squeezed his hand. "Now I realize that you have every right to hate me."

"You've done more for us than most of my compatriots. Besides, you aren't really French. If anything, I'm grateful for you. After the war was over, I joined the Resistance immediately. At the beginning, we did raids and sabotaged the Alliance, but after taking heavy losses, we realized that we needed to play the long game. That was when I created Amnestic. I was naïve to think that it would change anything."

"It changed everything for me." Celeste smiled. "I'm sure your truth reached many people, probably in Europe as well. Your Amnestic is the reason Mexico and Canada are ready to support us when the time comes. They see the danger the Alliance poses for them too. You were the face of Amnestic and of all Americans. People saw that. None of what you did was lost."

"I never knew that my voice was heard. I thought that you were the only one who listened. After you disappeared, I was crushed. I thought that you had gotten yourself killed. Then the Alliance got a word about Amnestic and came after me. I shut the forum down and ran to Ravenville. I built this cabin and lived here for the last five years. Of course, I often traveled to Ravenville to help people with different chores. Hunted for food and sometimes drove to Dubois for medical supplies and other items."

"And I ruined all that with my recklessness. If you hadn't found that phone..."

"No, Celeste, I think the Alliance had already marked Ravenville for capture. You might've saved everyone's lives by blowing your cover."

"When you put it that way..."

"I don't even want to remember those days. I almost killed you. If only you'd told me..."

"Hayes wouldn't let me. He is guarding my cover with the Alliance more than his own life. To be honest, he has a point. We were able to save many lives by collecting intel from them. What I do is vital to the Resistance. I know, it makes me look bad, but it has to be that way."

"You are amazing," Ash said, looking at her with admiration. "You have risked so much for us."

"I am one of you, Ash. I have been for the last ten years. I just speak very good French."

"You're funny," he laughed.

"Are you a Native American?" Celeste asked. "You look like you are."

"I'm mixed blood. My dad was Cheyenne, and my mom was white. Does that change anything for you?"

"It makes you hotter if that's even possible. I hope you know you're very handsome."

"Well, I don't believe anybody has ever said that about me before. I think you're delusional."

She just shrugged and smiled.

"Since we are exchanging compliments, I have to say that you are perfect in every way. You're the full package. The fact that your beautiful eyes are looking at me like that must be a pure miracle."

"Then, let's enjoy our miracles."

Celeste wrapped her arms around him and kissed him. Then they made love under the dying light of the kerosene lamp as shadows flickered on the walls. At that moment, time stood still. Ash and Celeste were the only beings in the entire world, and nothing else mattered.

Celeste opened her eyes with the feeling of Ash's touch against her skin, sending warm sensations throughout her entire body. A light scent from the woodstove lingered in the air. Her muscles ached, as she remembered the pleasure from the closeness they had shared. When her gaze adjusted to the dim morning light, she saw Ash sitting on the bed, looking at her.

"Are you feeling okay?" he asked.

"I'm fine, why?"

"I was afraid that I had broken you last night."

"Nope," she laughed, "not only did you not break me, but you sent me to the stars and back. It was amazing. I love you so much!"

"I love you too!"

He leaned over her and kissed her.

"I have to go and circle the area," he said, and grabbed his bow and rifle. "See what you can pack for our trip. I expect us to be gone for at least several days. We'll leave as soon as I return."

"Don't worry, I'll take care of everything."

Celeste got out of bed. She cleaned the cabin and packed a couple of duffel bags with clothes and medications. She also packed some crackers and canned food. Celeste knew that the mountain people were short on food, so bringing their own supplies would prevent additional hardship for the families they were going to visit.

Ash returned at noon. He slowly walked toward the cabin. There was something in Celeste's face that puzzled him. He could swear that while she was talking about her and her mother's life in America, there was a dark shadow in her eyes, one that he had never seen before.

She also never said what had happened to her mother. Celeste was hiding something. Ash knew it. He decided to respect the fact that she didn't want to talk about it.

"Thank God, you're okay!" Celeste ran into his arms as soon as he walked through the door.

Celeste sighed with relief. Every time he left to patrol the area, she was worried to death that he'd run into Alliance soldiers.

"Have some faith in me," he laughed. "I'm pretty good at that stuff."

"I can't help it." She gave him a quick kiss. "Are we ready to go?"

"Wait a second."

Ash opened one of his bags and took something out of it.

With eyes wide open, Celeste watched him take a knee.

"Celeste," he said with a smile. "Would you marry me?"

He opened his hand, and she saw a beautiful diamond engagement ring.

She felt her heart beating out of her chest. Ash wanted to marry her. He had chosen her despite their differences, despite the war. She never expected that. Celeste looked into his eyes and saw excitement and fear pushing against each other.

"Yes, Ash, I will marry you."

She lowered her head and kissed him. Ash slipped the ring on her finger. She raised her hand in front of her eyes and looked at it. It was a beautiful diamond ring.

"It was my mother's." Ash sighed. "She gave it to me before I enlisted in the military. She told me to give it to 'the one.' I think I found her."

"You made me very happy, Ash, but for now, you just have to trust my word."

She took the ring off and handed it back to him.

"I don't understand," he frowned.

"Ash, I'm a spy. I can't be walking around with a diamond ring on my fingers. Once the war is over, I will proudly wear it. For now, my promise has to be enough. I hope you understand."

"I do." Ash nodded. "I can see that you have a point."

"I hope you aren't disappointed." Celeste dropped her head.

"No, Celeste, I'm not disappointed."

Ash lifted her chin with his fingers and kissed her.

"Are you ready to go?"

. . .

"Yes, let's go."

They took the bags that Celeste had packed and walked out.

She looked back and smiled. The happiest moments of her life would always be in that mountain cabin.

Chapter 19

Ash led the way in the direction of Ravenville. He wanted to visit the people in the cabins above the town. They had stayed in their homes after Ravenville was evacuated. Alliance soldiers avoided disturbing the mountain people.

It was a warm summer day. The air was saturated with the scent of wild thyme. It was so strong, Celeste could almost taste it. The mixture of the different mountain scents, herbs, flowers, and moss was magical. As the sun reached its peak at noon, the air started to heat up.

Celeste was doing her best to keep up with Ash, but soon, a nagging pain gripped her left side. She didn't want to look weak in front of Ash. The last thing she wanted was for him to think that she was a burden. She tried to continue on pure willpower, but soon her head started spinning. She stumbled and fell.

"Celeste!" Ash grabbed her in his hands. "Are you okay?"

"I'm sorry, city girl here." She smiled crookedly.

"You really don't feel well." Ash frowned. "I should've thought about it. Let's sit down for a bit."

"I'm usually not that weak." Celeste sighed. "I might be anemic from blood loss."

"Also, my fault." Ash pressed his fingers to his forehead.

"Please, don't start blaming yourself again." Celeste caressed his face and kissed him. "I'll get better, just give it some time."

Without saying a word, he wrapped his arms around her and pulled her close. He wanted to shield and protect her against the cruel world that surrounded them.

Celeste smiled. Being in his arms was the only medicine she needed right now.

After she rested, they continued walking. It was evening when they reached the first cabin. Ash circled the area, making sure there were no Alliance patrols before he knocked on the door. A middle-aged woman greeted them. She smiled when she recognized Ash.

"This is Rachel, and this is Celeste," he introduced them to each other.

"Celeste..." The woman pursed her lips.

"If you feel uncomfortable, we won't stay," Ash quickly said.

"No," Rachel shook her head. "Since she's with you, I trust her. Come on in."

They sat in the small room, and Ash started to explain to Rachel the situation with the Alliance's increased patrol activities.

Celeste silently listened. She knew she wasn't welcome in this home. A subtle chill ran down her back, and her hands clenched in her lap. Her name was like a neon sign screaming, *"outsider."* She understood, but she felt her heart tighten. It didn't matter what she did; in the eyes of the American people, she would always be a European woman, an invader. She sighed heavily.

"Are you okay?" Ash asked after they left. "I'm sorry, I didn't think. From now on, you are Tina."

Celeste nodded. She didn't want to deceive anybody, but on the other hand, not antagonizing people would make their work easier. They managed to talk to several different households before nightfall.

"Let's go to a friend of mine." Ash led the way. "We can spend the night there."

"A friend?" Celeste echoed Ash's words. "I thought you had no friends."

"Well, not real friends, but I've known him for a while. His name is Bill. He was one of the first people I met when I relocated to Ravenville."

Bill's cabin was modest, not much furniture, just a cot, a table, and a couple of chairs. Celeste sighed. The misery these people lived in was breaking her heart. She knew she would do anything to put an end to their suffering.

While Ash talked to Bill, Celeste lay on the floor and covered up with the blanket she had packed. She was exhausted. She realized that Ash's arrows had done more damage than she thought. Besides the infection that she was still recovering from, the blood loss must've been significant. The exhaustion and shortness of breath with activity indicated severe anemia. Celeste would never tell Ash how serious that was because he'd spiral into self-blame. She knew that with time, her health would improve. Celeste closed her eyes and slowly fell asleep.

Ash woke her up early in the morning.

"Are you ready to go?" He shook her shoulder.

She rubbed her eyes and got up. She felt fatigued like never before in her life. She felt like her life was slowly draining away. A slight nausea was lurking in her stomach, and her heart seemed to race. Celeste straightened out her shoulders so Ash wouldn't notice. For the rest of the day, they circled the entire area. When they arrived at the last cabin, Celeste exclaimed in surprise. It was the same place where she had performed a surgery on the young child several months ago.

The child's mother, Rose, was surprised to see Ash and Celeste.

"I'm so happy to see you," she clapped her hands.

"How is your son?" Celeste said with a smile.

"He is doing great. But don't stand out there, come in," she waved her hand. I'll make dinner, and you can spend the night here."

"Here, I have food." Celeste took several cans and crackers out of her bag.

"Thank you so much," Rose said. "Food is scarce around here. By the way, I never caught your name."

"You can call me Tina." Celeste shook her hand.

After dinner, Celeste sat on the bench in front of the house, leaned against the wall, and closed her eyes. She deeply inhaled the air saturated with the smell of firewood. An owl called, and the crickets chirped. She smiled. After hiking in the mountains with Ash, she was exhausted and in pain, but she felt more alive than ever.

Suddenly, she was startled by someone grabbing her arm. She tensed and tried to free herself.

"Stop fighting. It's me," she recognized Ash's voice. "Come inside. Now!"

She quickly followed him.

"What's going on?"

"There's an Alliance patrol closing in on us. Someone must've turned us in."

"Oh, no!" Celeste's blood ran cold. "What are we going to do?"

She looked over and saw Rose clutching her son, shivering.

Guilt clawed at her heart. They had put that woman and her son in danger.

"Rose, do you know where Shadowpine Cave is?" Ash asked.

"Yes, I know where it is."

"Take your son and go there. I'll try to buy you some time. Go now. Celeste, go with her."

"I don't think so," she pulled her revolver and quickly checked it over. "I'm not leaving you here to die."

"So, you want to stay and die with me. Is that it?" he grumbled.

"I'm not planning on dying. It's already dark. We have to find a way to escape."

"How are you planning on doing it?"

"When I was here a few months ago, I saw a hidden door on the floor."

"Okay then, let's do that, but if you die, I'll kill you."

Celeste just laughed.

Ash wrapped his arms around her shoulders and kissed her. They crouched back-to-back in the corner, away from the windows, and waited. The silence was deafening. Suddenly, the owl called, and the crickets chirped.

"Come out with your hands up," a voice sounded outside the cabin. "You are surrounded."

Ash raised his rifle and shot in the direction of the voice. Immediately, the soldiers returned fire. The windows exploded, and the walls were riddled with bullets. Celeste sent several rounds in different directions through the windows. She heard them swearing in French.

"I think I hit someone," she whispered, feeling her stomach tighten.

"Good." Ash sent a round as well.

They continued to exchange fire for several minutes. Suddenly, several glass bottles flew through the windows and exploded into flames.

"Damn it! Those are Molotovs," she swore.

"We have to go, or we are going to suffocate." Ash waved his hand to move the smoke away from his face.

"Okay, let's get out of here," Celeste said, coughing.

She dropped to the floor, trying to avoid the smoke, and crawled across the floor.

Ash followed her. She lifted the rug and uncovered a door on the floor. They quickly slipped through it and found themselves in a tunnel under the house. Celeste quickly followed it away from the house. She briefly lost balance as her legs threatened to give out. She grabbed the moisture-drenched wall to steady herself. Her lungs burned with every breath. Celeste bit her lip and continued to follow Ash. They emerged somewhere in the woods.

"Follow me," Ash said, sprinting between the trees.

Celeste ran after him, her heart beating in her ears. She couldn't catch her breath, but there wasn't time to rest. As soon as they entered the cave, she fell to the ground, gasping for air.

"Celeste, are you okay?" Terrified, Ash took her in his arms.

"I'm fine, just exhausted."

Ash looked over and saw Rose and her son standing there, waiting.

"Let's go." Ash waved at them. "We have to get as far as we can from here. You are all coming to my cabin."

Rose didn't wait for a second reminder. She took her son's hand and stood up.

Ash looked at Celeste and shook his head. Then, he picked her up in his arms and hiked up the mountain at a fast pace.

Chapter 20

Celeste was warm and safe in Ash's arms. The rhythmic beat of his heart lulled her into sleep. The sunlight on her face woke her up. For a fleeting moment, she felt at peace. She was still in Ash's arms.

"Thank you, Ash," she whispered in his ear and pressed a soft kiss on his cheek.

"Do you feel better?" he asked, carefully studying her face.

"I feel okay. I was just exhausted. I've never hiked that much in my life. Are we close?"

"We have another hour before we get there."

"I can walk now."

"Are you sure?" Ash lowered her gently to her feet.

"Yes, I'm good."

Celeste slipped her hand into Ash's and followed. She was trying to figure out what was wrong with her. It couldn't be just the anemia.

There was something else. She hadn't started feeling like that until hiking up the mountain. Celeste felt dizzy, nauseous, short of breath, and her heart was pounding continuously. The pain in her left side had worsened as well. Maybe it was just exhaustion. Her wound was healing. The infection was gone, so everything should be fine.

"We're almost there." Ash lightly squeezed her hand. "One steep slope left, and you can relax for the rest of the day."

Celeste clenched her teeth, trying to keep up with Ash. Suddenly, she felt a searing pain in her left upper abdomen and left shoulder.

I must've pulled a muscle or irritated my wound.

Why was it so painful? She wondered if she had caused more damage than she thought by pulling the arrow out of her side by herself. Celeste fell to her knees, holding her side.

"Celeste! You're not okay."

Ash scooped her up and ran up the mountain. His heart was racing, causing his breathing to become ragged and shallow. The panic squeezed his chest like a vise. As soon as he entered his cabin, he abruptly stopped in the doorway. Hayes was sitting at the table.

"What are you doing here?" Ash asked as he sat Celeste on his bed. "Didn't I tell you not to come back?"

"What's wrong with Celeste?"

Ignoring Ash's protests, Hayes jumped to his feet and ran to her.

Celeste fell on the cot, writhing in pain.

"For God's sake, Celeste, what happened to you?" Hayes was starting to panic.

"I shot her," Ash muttered.

"What?" Hayes snapped his head around.

"It was an accident," Celeste said through her teeth. "He thought I was one of the patrol soldiers and sent an arrow into my side. I pulled it out. I might've caused damage..."

Hayes put his fingers on her neck to check her heart rate and immediately lifted her T-shirt. He touched her upper abdomen, and she gasped.

"Shit!" His face turned pale.

Hayes closed his eyes and took a deep breath.

"Oh, no," Celeste whispered. "Dave, it's my spleen, isn't it?"

He just nodded. She saw heartbreak in his eyes.

"That's it then... the end of the road," she said bitterly.

"Take the child outside." Hayes waved at Rose. "He doesn't need to see this."

She understood and quickly followed his order.

"What are you all talking about?"

Ash knelt by the bed and took Celeste's hand in his.

"Ash," she said, looking into his eyes, "it breaks my heart to tell you that, but I am going to die. I don't think there is anything we could do."

"Celeste, what the hell are you talking about?"

Ash looked at Hayes, hoping for a different answer.

"She's right." Hayes sighed heavily. "Her spleen has ruptured. She doesn't have much longer left."

"No!" Ash shook his head. "There is no way. Celeste, please, fight this."

"Ash," she whispered, using her elbow to lift herself from the bed. "Please, promise me that you will take care of yourself. I need to know that you will be okay."

"No, you don't get to just leave me. No! I refuse to accept that. I don't survive this without you. Do you hear me? It has always been Tink and Ash. You can't just quit."

"Please, hold me!" She was shivering uncontrollably. "I'm scared."

Ash took her in his arms, unable to stop his tears.

Barely keeping her eyes open, Celeste looked at him.

"I love you, Ash," she whispered and drifted to unconsciousness.

"Celeste, please..."

Ash put his forehead against hers, soundlessly crying.

A noise from falling objects drew his attention. Ash turned his head and saw Hayes pulling everything out of his closet.

"Where are your medical supplies?" Hayes looked at him. "Stop your whining and come to help me."

"What are you going to do?"

"I'm going to take her spleen out. What do you think? Do you want her to live, or not? Hurry up!"

Ash laid Celeste back on the bed with trembling hands and dashed to the closet. He pulled all of his supplies out, trying to control the panic that was threatening to explode in his chest.

Hayes quickly found everything he needed.

"Do you have alcohol?"

Ash opened the cabinet and handed him a bottle of whiskey.

Hayes put the surgical instruments in a bowl and dumped the alcohol on them.

"What is your blood type?" Hayes asked while stirring the tools in the bowl.

"I'm A positive."

"We're in luck. That is Celeste's blood type as well. I will need you to give blood for her. Let's start. She's running out of time."

"Are you sure you can do that here?"

"No, but the alternative is to watch her die. I'll be damned if I just stand here and watch... Let's start."

"What do you need me to do?"

"Get me a door. Put it on the table and lay Celeste on it."

Ash ran to the closet and ripped the door out. He laid it on the table and covered it with a clean bed sheet. Then he carefully carried Celeste to the makeshift operating table.

"Give me your arm, now," Hayes ordered.

Ash rolled his sleeve, and Hayes started a direct transfusion line from Ash's to Celeste's arm.

Ash looked at Celeste. Her face was ghostly pale. She was still unconscious.

"She's no longer responding." Ash felt his throat closing up.

"That's good," Hayes muttered. "We have no anesthesia."

Ash's heart tightened. He pressed a kiss on her forehead, fighting tears back.

Celeste, please, fight this!

"Get out of the way." Hayes motioned with his head.

He disinfected Celeste's side with iodine from the first aid kit.

"I will start now. Please, don't hover. The last thing I need is you vomiting on my surgical site."

Hayes made an incision in the left upper abdomen, and a copious amount of dark blood gushed out. Ash gasped and turned his head. No way that was going to work. He felt his heart sink.

I caused that. Everything is my fault!

He stumbled and reached for the table to steady himself.

"Ash!" Hayes's voice brought him back to reality. "Are you okay? I think you are past your limit for blood donation."

"I'm fine. How is she?"

"So far, so good. I'm almost done. I will apply temporary sutures. When we get to the hospital in my camp, I will finish this. Once she wakes up, she will be in excruciating pain. I hate that there's nothing I can do to help her."

In a few minutes, Hayes discontinued the blood transfusion and bandaged Celeste's abdomen.

"Can you carry her to my truck?" Hayes asked.

"That's not a problem. Did you check for Alliance patrols?"

"Yes, I have people guarding our vehicles."

"Why were you here?"

"Celeste told me to come and tell her when I need her. Well, obviously, that has to wait. I never imagined that I would walk into that type of mess, but I'm glad I came when I did."

"Thank you, Hayes!" Ash sighed. "Celeste owes you her life."

"I care about Celeste. She's like a sister to me. Part of me wants to kill you for what you did to her, but I know you didn't mean it."

Ash gazed at Celeste's pale face while carrying her down the mountain. He had almost lost her. If it wasn't for Hayes...

I was all wrong about him.

"Ash!" Celeste's voice shook him out of his thoughts.

"Celeste, how are you feeling?"

"It hurts so bad!" She bit her bottom lip.

"Sorry, my love!" Ash felt his stomach wrench. "I wish I could help you. Once we get back to camp, we'll get you something for the pain."

"What happened? I thought I was dying."

"Hayes wouldn't allow it. He removed your spleen."

"In the cabin? That's savage." She smiled through her tears.

"Well, I owe him for life now," Ash muttered.

Ash kissed her and wiped her tears with his sleeve.

She closed her eyes and faded into unconsciousness again.

Once they reached Hayes's truck, Ash put Celeste in the back seat.

"Give me the keys. I'll drive," Ash said, looking at Hayes. "You can ride on the back to watch her."

Without argument, Hayes threw the keys to Ash.

Rose and her son rode with the other vehicle.

As soon as they reached the camp, Hayes rushed Celeste into the operating room to finish the surgery.

Ash walked the floor in front of the door, trying to come to terms with what had happened. He thought that Celeste was healing. He couldn't believe that she had almost died. Even if she recovered from this surgery, she still wasn't safe. She'd never be safe, not until the war was over. At that moment, he decided that he wouldn't let her leave for an assignment alone again. He didn't care what Hayes had to say about it.

Ash winced. Hayes had come out of the operating room.

"Is she okay?" Ash's eyes were tense.

"She will be fine." Hayes smiled.

"So, what do you have planned for her?" Ash pressed his lips together.

"She has to go and negotiate our collaboration with Mexico and Canada. The Alliance won't meddle anymore."

"Okay, make sure that you include me in that assignment as well," Ash said curtly.

"But..."

"No buts. You and I both remember what happened the last time. I won't let that happen again."

"I see... Okay, have it your way. You'll go with her. That way, I'll sleep better."

"So, it's a deal."

"Yes, you will team up with Celeste. She has to sell it to the Alliance. I'm sure she will. She's good at that."

"Can I see her now?"

Hayes looked at him. Ash's face was unreadable, but his eyes were heavy with pain.

"Have a seat. I'll let you know when she's ready for you."

Ash sighed and sat down. The only thing he cared about was Celeste's well-being. He had a long road of redemption for what he had done to her.

Chapter 21

Celeste slowly opened her eyes. She saw Ash sitting on a chair by her bed.

"Ash, what happened?" Celeste's voice was hoarse. She felt her head throb. "Did I pass out?"

"You don't remember?" Ash's eyes widened.

"No," she said, knitting her brows. "The last thing I remember was us trying to escape a burning cabin. Did I get shot or something?"

"Yes, you did, by me, two weeks ago." Ash sighed heavily.

"So, what happened then?"

Ash closed his eyes and took a deep breath. Then he told her what had happened.

She stared off for a moment after he stopped talking. That was horrific.

"I'm glad I don't remember any of it," she mumbled, touching the bandage on her side.

"It was a pure miracle that you survived." He caressed her face. "I was so scared, I was losing my mind."

"I should've died of blood loss."

"I gave you my blood." Ash shrugged. "I have the same blood type as you."

"Now I will always carry you in my heart." She smiled. "I owe everything to you and Hayes."

Tears rolled down her cheeks.

"Celeste, I would've sold my soul to the devil to save you, and so would Hayes. That man would walk through fire for you."

"He's a good man. Are you two getting along *now*?"

"Not really." Ash shook his head and laughed. "That city boy and I will never get along."

"How did he end up in your cabin?"

"He was there looking for you, probably for another assignment."

"I'll be ready as soon as I can."

"No, not yet. You need to recover first."

"Hayes will be upset."

"He'll live. See, if you want to talk to him, I don't mind. Don't be afraid to ask. I promise, I wouldn't be upset."

"I'll talk to him later. Come here." She reached for him. "Lie by me. I just need to feel your arms around me."

"I don't know," Ash muttered. "I don't want to cause you pain."

"Nonsense! Come here." She pulled on his arm.

Ash took his jacket off, lay on the edge of her bed, and put his arm around her shoulders.

"Is that better?" he whispered in her ear.

"Yes, that is perfect." She felt his warm breath brush against her neck. "I love you so much!"

She laid her head on his chest and fell asleep.

Ash closed his eyes and smiled. His Tink was alive, and this time she chose him. He kissed her on the forehead and got out of bed, careful not to wake her up.

Ash looked at Celeste one more time and walked to Hayes's office. Walking in, he saw Hayes leaning back in his chair with his eyes closed. Thinking that he was sleeping, Ash turned around to leave.

"Wait!" Hayes's tired voice stopped him.

"I thought you were asleep."

"No, I was recovering from fixing your mess. You realize the fact that Celeste survived that surgery was nothing short of a miracle, right? The odds were stacked against her."

"You sounded confident at the time. I didn't detect any doubts from you."

"It was a façade. I had to make sure you didn't panic. Now I have to deal with my PTSD."

"You have no idea how much I blame myself for that. I will be eternally indebted to you."

"Don't. I didn't do that for you. I did it for Celeste. Anyway, why are you here?"

"I want to make myself useful. Tell me what you want me to do."

"Well, obviously, you're quite good with the bow. Celeste's the living proof. So why don't you go hunting? The people in the camp would appreciate it."

"Consider it done," Ash turned around and walked out.

Hayes looked at the door for a while after Ash left.

How am I going to pair this caveman with Celeste? He will blow her cover and have both of them killed.

He shook his head. There were several weeks before Celeste would do anything. She needed to recover first. By then, he would figure something out.

In a few days, Celeste was well enough to leave the hospital. Because she still had to receive intravenous antibiotics, Hayes let her stay in her old room in his office. Ash didn't protest. He was ready to agree to anything that would benefit her. Besides, Hayes didn't mind him spending most of his time with her.

Ash began hunting daily. At first, he did it to appease Hayes, but then he realized that the game he was bringing to the camp solved the food scarcity and improved everybody's life. His free time he spent with Celeste. He helped her with the daily activities as she was still very weak, and Hayes forbade her any exertion. They also spent hours in each other's arms.

"You're disgusting," Hayes would say every time he saw them together. But then he laughed.

Celeste's newest pastime was sitting in a chair in front of Hayes's office, looking at the life around her. After a couple of weeks, the pain started to fade, and she felt the weakness letting off. She knew she had a long way to go before full recovery due to the amount of blood she had lost, but she was grateful that she was alive at all. She often thought of Ash. He must be feeling guilty. He never said anything, but she knew him well.

"Are you okay, Ash?" she asked while he was tucking her into bed.

"I'm fine," he shrugged. "Why would you ask that?"

"Because I know that you still blame yourself for what happened to me. Please, don't. It was an accident."

"It's easy for you to say." Ash frowned. "You were dying in front of me, and I was to blame." He rubbed his forehead. "That image lives rent-free in my mind. I've been trying to come to terms with it, but I still can't."

"Please, Ash, let it go! It hurts my soul watching you suffer like that. Can we just enjoy our time together? You know it's not going to last. Soon, I have to go back to work, and our relative peace will be gone."

"I told Hayes that this time I'm coming with you. I'm not letting you go off alone again."

"Hayes agreed to that?" Celeste arched her eyebrows.

"I didn't give him a choice. He said you'd have to sell the arrangement to the Alliance somehow."

"We'll see. I'm grounded for several weeks, so we'll figure it out when I'm ready."

"There is nothing to figure out. I'm coming with you. Anyway, let's get some sleep now."

Ash laid a blanket on the floor by Celeste's bed and stretched out.

"Why don't you just lie in bed with me?"

"No." He cut her off. "I'll do that when we're in our own house. I can't with Hayes next door."

Celeste just shook her head. Then, gently, she ran her fingers through his hair.

The next day, while Ash was hunting, Celeste walked into Hayes's office. He was looking at some papers on the table.

"Sit down," he said, without raising his eyes. "You know you shouldn't be standing for long."

Celeste sat in one of the chairs.

"Thanks for saving my life, Dave."

"I don't want to think about it," he muttered. "You scared me so bad; I almost lost my mind."

"I'm sorry."

"None of it is your fault. That's all on your boyfriend."

"He is suffering because of it. He still hasn't forgiven himself."

"I don't know about that. He seems unfazed."

"You just don't know him. I hope you aren't constantly reminding him."

"I'm not. Celeste, you need to come up with a way to stop him from coming with you for your assignments. He will be a huge liability."

"I think you're underestimating Ash. Either way, he's coming with me. Figure it out. I just wanted to thank you for saving my life. That's all."

"I'd do anything for you. You know that."

"Dave, do you remember when our only worry was what music we were going to play at our parties?"

"Oh, do I? It seems an eternity since then. Now, most of our party buddies are dead, and a few days ago, I almost lost you, too. I'd give anything to have those old times back, but here we are."

"We'll get back there someday. Just have faith."

"Celeste, this is why you're so important to me. You are the spirit of the Resistance. Even if I lose hope and drown in doubt, you always manage to bring light to my soul. Please, never stop doing that."

"Don't worry, Dave, I will always believe that gaining our freedom back is possible, at least for as long as I am still breathing."

"And that is why you aren't allowed to die, ever."

"Well, I'm a lucky woman. I know you and Ash will fist fight Death to pull me back. You proved that."

"Not funny, but since it's you, I'll allow it." Hayes smiled.

Chapter 22

Celeste was bored. It had been four weeks since her surgery, and she felt fine. The pain was gone, and she felt strong enough to go back to her normal activities. She was itching to do something, anything except sitting in a chair all day long. However, Hayes had a different opinion. His orders for her to remain grounded were non-negotiable. She was frustrated with him, but she didn't argue. He had saved her life after all.

Ash, on the other hand, was on his best behavior. He continued to help her with everything. She caught him many times just quietly gazing at her. She had asked him why.

"I want to make sure you aren't going to just disappear in a puff of pixie dust," he said softly.

As cute as it sounded, Celeste knew it came from the trauma of him almost losing her. She wanted to hug him until all his pain dissolved, but knew it would take time.

Celeste was sitting outside, waiting for Ash to come back from his daily hunting activities. Many men from the camp had joined him, so the food situation had greatly improved. She smiled. The happiness of the people was very important to her. She spotted Hayes as he returned from his shift at the hospital.

"So, how much longer?"

She looked intently at him.

"Not long. I will check your blood and examine you tomorrow. If everything checks out, we will proceed with our initial plans. When Ash returns, tell him I need to talk to him. I have to brief him on the assignment."

"Ash? How about me?"

"One person at a time. I will talk to you tomorrow. Meet me at the hospital tomorrow at eight. We'll do your exam first."

"Good." She smiled.

Finally! Things were starting to move.

I was about to lose my mind.

Celeste saw Ash and the other men coming back. They were carrying an elk. Their heavy boots stirred the dry dirt, raising a cloud of dust around them. She waved at them. In a few minutes, Ash walked up to her. He was covered in dirt and elk blood.

"You're gross!" Celeste said, wrinkling her nose at the heavy smell of dirt and blood.

She still threw her arms around Ash and kissed him.

"I'll wash up in a minute."

"Before you do that." She stopped him. "Hayes is waiting for you. He wants to talk."

Ash shook his head with a question in his eyes.

"I don't know. It's something about the assignment."

"Okay, I'll stop by his office first."

He knocked on Hayes's door.

In a couple of hours, he returned.

"Celeste, I have to go to my cabin to gather some things. I'll be back tomorrow."

"Why?" Celeste felt her stomach wrench. "What if there are patrols in the area?"

Ash looked at her with mild exasperation.

"Have some faith in me. I've had professional training to do just that. I'll be okay... Celeste, you are shivering. I'll be okay. Trust me!"

"I'll go with him, and when I say 'I,' I mean my team. He won't be alone."

She turned her head and saw Hayes.

"We'll be back before your doctor's appointment tomorrow. Take a deep breath now. Stress isn't good for your recovery."

"Thank you, Dave!" She smiled, feeling her fear dissipating.

"Any time. Rose and a couple of the women will warm up water for you and help you take a bath. Try to relax."

Celeste smiled. Now she knew Ash was going to be safe.

After they left, she looked in the direction they had disappeared for a moment. She loved them both. Dave, she loved like a brother, and Ash was her soul and breath. She would give her life for either of them. Celeste knew they loved her too. She felt blessed.

After her bath, Celeste relaxed in her bed and closed her eyes. She knew it would be hard to fall asleep with Ash and Hayes going on a dangerous trip, even though they weren't alone. Why did they need to go to Ash's cabin anyway? What did Ash have there that was so important to retrieve? Sometimes, those men were an enigma to her.

Finally, Celeste drifted off to sleep. She woke up early in the morning. She looked around. Ash wasn't there. She got dressed and checked Hayes's office. He wasn't there either. Celeste's heart tightened. She went outside and slowly walked to the hospital.

Celeste opened the door to Hayes's office and paused on the threshold. The air was saturated with the scent of antiseptic. She saw him sitting there in his white coat, looking through papers.

"Are you okay?" He raised his eyes and gazed at her.

"Ash?" Her voice trembled.

"Calm down, Celeste." Hayes shook his head. "Ash is fine. We got back about an hour ago. He's here somewhere."

He didn't tell me he was back.

Tears welled in her eyes.

"Oh, please, don't cry now," Hayes said with annoyance in his voice. "I asked Ash to do something for me first."

"Okay, let's just do that exam."

Hayes shook his head and prepared to draw blood from Celeste's arm.

While running the blood work, he checked Celeste's surgical incision. It appeared fully healed. She was also pain-free when he pressed on her abdomen. In about an hour, he returned with the results from the blood tests.

"Everything looks great," he said. "Your hemoglobin is going up nicely, and there are no signs of infection. I have to say that you are my miracle. I didn't even think you'd survive the surgery, and now you've fully recovered. I'm happy."

"Thank you, Dave!" Celeste smiled. "I owe you my life. I apologize for all the times I wasn't nice to you."

"Please, never change. You are amazing just the way you are. Let's go back to my office now."

As soon as they entered Hayes's office, Celeste saw Ash sitting on a chair at the table. She gasped. He looked like a different person. She stared at him in disbelief. He was clean-shaven, his hair smoothed back and tied neatly. He was dressed in an elegant suit. The sight of him took her breath away, and she felt her heart race. He was the most handsome man she had ever seen.

"Close your mouth before your jaw hits the floor." Hayes laughed. "Yes, we all can see that Ash knows how to clean up nicely."

"Ash, what's going on?" Celeste continued to stare at him.

"I hope you still want to marry me." He gazed at her. "Because today I'm marrying you."

"What?" Celeste's eyes got wide, and she looked at Hayes.

"Don't look at me," Hayes said, laughing. "You're marrying him, not me."

"What is going on?" She blinked, still processing what was unfolding.

"If you don't want to marry me for real, we can have a fictitious marriage." Ash looked into her eyes. "It's all up to you."

"This is your cover," Hayes explained. "You will go to Dubois, as a married couple, and get jobs there. When the time for negotiations comes, you will proceed accordingly. I have been working on this cover since Ash told me that he is coming with you."

"Oh, I understand now." She laughed. "Okay, I'm game."

"So, what is it going to be?" Ash gazed into her eyes. "A real marriage or not?"

"Why would I want to fake marry you? We are already engaged. I'll just marry you. I love you."

She brushed her fingers along his cheek.

Ash sharply exhaled. His face glowed with relief.

"You thought I'd say no?" Celeste laughed. "There was zero chance of that happening. So, you went to the cabin to retrieve your suit?"

"Yes, and a few other things," Ash shrugged.

"You can go to your room and get ready." Hayes waved his hand at Celeste. "We'll be here waiting for you."

Celeste walked into her room and gasped. A white wedding dress lay across her bed. She put it on and stood in front of the mirror. The dress had a simple design, soft silk, short sleeves, a snug waist, and freely cascading skirts. Celeste spun around and smiled. The dress was beautiful.

She put on the matching shoes and returned to Hayes's office. Both men stared at her. Even though she was still pale and frail, she was beautiful. Her shiny brown hair cascaded down her shoulders to her back, and the wedding dress complemented every curve of her perfect figure.

"Are you going to continue staring, or are you going to tell me how you found that dress?" Celeste laughed.

"The women made it for you. Ash gave them the measurements. He has an excellent eye." Hayes shot a look at Ash. "He was planning to propose a wedding date to you anyway, but then I decided that it is a good idea for your assignment as well."

"You conspired behind my back." Celeste pursed her lips.

"Yes, we did." Ash took her hand in his and pulled her onto his lap. "I just didn't know if you'd really want to go through with it. You did return my ring."

"I'm sorry, Ash," she sighed. "I just didn't want to draw attention. Now I will take it back."

Ash pulled the engagement ring from his pocket and slipped it on her finger.

"Okay, I have prepared a marriage license and a new passport for Celeste," Hayes said, taking an envelope from his desk. "I've been working on this for weeks. From now on, you're Tina. Tina Jensen, to be exact."

"Tina Jensen." Celeste smiled. "It has a ring to it."

"The minister should be here by now. Come on, let's go."

Hayes stood up and walked out.

"We are getting an actual wedding?" Celeste looked at Ash with her eyes glowing.

"Yes, my love, we are getting a real wedding. Hayes and I arranged that for you."

"I love you so much!" She threw her arms around his neck and kissed him.

"Come on, follow me." Ash took her hand in his and led her toward the center of the camp.

When they arrived, everybody was already waiting for them.

"Come on, I will give you away," Hayes said, offering his elbow for Celeste to hold.

"Thank you, Dave!" She couldn't hold her tears back. "You are my brother."

He slowly walked her to the altar.

Celeste stood gazing into Ash's dark eyes. She still couldn't believe that this was happening.

"Tink," Ash said, taking her hand in his. "When I first met you, I was in a dark place. I had lost my entire family and most of my friends. I saw no reason for living. You were the one who showed me that there is a light at the end of the tunnel. You revived my will to fight for our freedom. When I thought that I'd lost you, my life was over. For years, I just existed without really living. I don't know who to thank for finding you again, but they gave my life back to me. You are the only woman I have ever loved. Today is the happiest moment in my entire life."

"Ash," Celeste whispered, smiling through her tears. "Before I met you, I was scared and confused. I didn't know why all this was happening to people. There was so much pain, and I didn't know how to deal with it. Then I got to know you, and I was inspired to fight for our freedom. You were like a flame that ignited in my heart. I was ready to follow you anywhere. When I lost contact with you, I thought I had lost you forever, but I never stopped looking for you. I hoped that someday we'd cross paths again, and we did. I loved you for years, even though I had never met you. You are my soul and my heart forever."

After they said their "I do's," Ash put a wedding band on her finger that perfectly matched her engagement ring and his wedding band.

"Now you can kiss the bride."

Ash wrapped his arms around Celeste's small waist, and they kissed. She felt as if she was melting. Being close to him was everything she ever needed. Ash held her close to his heart for a long time. He wished that this moment never ended. There was a war waiting for them, but he knew he'd carry this moment in his heart forever.

Chapter 23

Celeste sat on the sofa with her fingers idly tracing the throw pillow. She looked at Ash. He was at his desk, focused on his laptop.

She smiled.

It would be a lie if she said she wasn't happy. Despite being surrounded by the Alliance, for once, she felt safe. She was happy just being with Ash. They had settled in Dubois four months ago. Celeste had taken a job at the local hospital. She had always thrived in the controlled chaos of emergencies and annoying minor complaints. She had quit her last job after taking the assignment in Ravenville, and now she had settled back into her normal routine.

Well, routine was relative.

She was quietly waiting for a meeting with the representatives of Mexico and Canada. She had assured the Alliance that those negotiations would fail. That was the only way to succeed without being ambushed, as had happened the last time. Of course, she had no intention of allowing the negotiations to fail.

She looked at Ash again.

He was working as a cybersecurity expert for a local bank. All of his work was online. That way, he had access to sophisticated software, which allowed him to reopen the forum Amnestic. He was surprised by how much interest it had generated compared to the first time. That was likely due to the worsening of the political climate in Europe.

The citizens of the Alliance-adjacent countries were disillusioned with their governing style. There were many posters, especially from Europe. People were openly condemning what was happening in America. Because of the increased cloaking capabilities, the Alliance had no chance of tracing the forum. If they tried, it would appear that it was somewhere in South America.

Celeste stood up from the sofa, walked to Ash, and threw her arms over his shoulders.

"Mr. Jensen," she said, kissing him on the neck, "dinner is ready. I made some spaghetti."

"Yes, Mrs. Jensen." He looked at her and smiled, "I'll be right there. Just give me ten more minutes to finish up my conversation with my Amnestic followers."

"Of course, I'll set the table."

She went into the kitchen.

She thought about Ash. After their wedding, he'd become unrecognizable in the best way. His emotional restraints vanished. He smiled and dared to dream of better times. Celeste realized that her disappearance from Amnestic had caused him greater mental anguish than she could have ever imagined. Only God knows how many sleepless nights he spent scanning the internet looking for a trace of her, finally giving up and descending into depression. She felt guilty, but Ash assured her that he understood, and the fact that they were together now was enough.

"So, Ash, how do you feel being a married man?" Celeste asked him later, while lying in his arms on the sofa.

"How do I feel?"

He turned his head to look at her.

"I feel like all my dreams and hopes have come true. You are everything I ever wanted in my life."

"I feel the same about you, my love."

Celeste kissed him.

She didn't mind her work in the emergency room. Celeste had done her residency as a surgeon, but she preferred the ER just in case she had to leave for another assignment. That way, she wouldn't have to inconvenience patients who relied on her.

For the next several days, Ash noticed that Celeste looked tense and deep in thought.

"What is bothering you, Tink?" he asked while she lay in his arms on the sofa.

"There is a mutated strain of influenza," she muttered. "We just received the warning from the National Infection Control Agency. I haven't had any cases at the hospital, but we were told that it is raging high up in the mountain villages. I'm worried about Hayes's camp. They don't have enough antiviral medication. I have to call him and ask if they are okay."

"Isn't it just a regular flu?" Ash shrugged.

"The information we have indicates that this strain is more severe than regular influenza. I'm worried about all those children in the camp. The temperatures are falling, and they don't have warm homes. I feel guilty staying in this warm house with all the amenities while others suffer."

"I hear you, my love." Ash kissed her on the top of the head. "I wish I could undo the last ten years, but there we are. If someone is to restore our nation, it will be you. I know it."

"You have too much faith in me." She smiled crookedly.

"I do, and I believe Hayes does as well. You just need to do what you do best, and I will make sure no one touches you."

"Well, if someone can provide reliable protection, that's you."

She smiled and looked into his eyes.

"Besides, I wouldn't let anyone else but you shadow me. I'd always worked alone before you."

"Thank you for letting me in."

He caressed her face.

"I don't think I could say no. I just love you too much."

"I love you too, Tink."

Celeste relaxed. The safety of his arms cushioned her. She laid her head on his chest and slowly drifted to sleep.

Ash smiled and carried her to bed.

The next day, after she returned from work, Celeste called Hayes.

"How are you doing?" she asked. "I haven't talked to you since we left."

"You know I don't want you to call." Hayes sounded on edge. "It's an unnecessary risk."

"I know. I just wanted to know if you're safe from the flu."

"Unfortunately, no." He sighed. "It's spreading like wildfire here. We have several fatalities already."

Celeste frowned. Hayes was alone there, trying to put out a fire with his bare hands.

"I'll bring you some antivirals."

"No, Celeste, stay where you are. I don't want you coming here."

"I'm only telling you, so your people won't shoot me when I arrive. See you in a couple of days."

She disconnected the call before Hayes got a chance to protest more.

"What's going on? Where are you going?"

Ash raised his eyes from his laptop and looked at her.

"They have the flu." Her face was tense. "We have to bring some medicine to them. Hayes needs medical help. I will secure some supplies tomorrow and go to camp. You don't have to come."

"Yes, I do. You aren't traveling alone. The Alliance has increased its patrol activities."

"Okay, I won't fight you."

The next day, Celeste requested antiviral and antipyretic medication from the local public health department. She explained that the medication was needed for remote areas. At first, they argued that the Alliance wouldn't approve the treatment of possible Resistance-related areas, but after Celeste explained that if the infection were left to run unchecked, they would bring the contagion to the city, the health department buckled and provided her with everything she had requested.

Next, Celeste requested several weeks off from the ER for remote work, which the hospital granted her. One thing Celeste had noticed was that even though everybody in the city had conformed to the

Alliance rules, most people sympathized with the Resistance and were willing to help as long as there was no danger for them.

On the way home, Celeste looked at the city. The streets were clean but appeared deserted. No one liked walking or staying outside for long. People didn't want to answer questions from the Alliance agents. They would arrest someone purely based on vibes, without any probable cause. Countless Americans had vanished without a trace after an arrest like that.

People were scared and followed the rules just to survive. Celeste didn't blame them. Most of them had children. She was sure that if she had a child, she would probably live by the rules too. The thought of tiny baby fingers wrapped around hers made her feel warm.

There will be time for children after we are free.

After she had gotten together with Ash, she had asked Hayes to insert a contraceptive implant in her left upper arm. Most women actively fighting for the Resistance had done that. It effectively prevented liabilities. Ash understood.

"We will have our complete family after we win," he had said.

Celeste was glad that he supported her decision.

The more she got to know him, the more she loved him. Under the severe weight of past heartbreaks, Ash was a wonderful person. She couldn't imagine being married to anybody else.

Celeste sorted all supplies and packed them in duffel bags. She checked everything several times to ensure nothing was forgotten. She slipped a pack of antivirals into her pocket for herself and gave one to Ash as well. They had to protect themselves from getting ill. Otherwise, they wouldn't be able to help anybody. She took a deep breath to soothe her anxiety. The worry about Hayes's people had not left her mind.

"Are you ready?"

She looked at Ash, who was dressed in his tactical pants and jacket.

"Yes, let me load everything in my truck."

Before they left the house, Ash carried his rifle wrapped in a blanket to the truck and laid it on the floor under the back seat.

"I'm not getting caught defenseless," he muttered.

"Of course not."

Celeste opened her jacket, and he saw a revolver holstered on her hip.

Ash smiled. He admired her courage and compassion. Celeste was an incredible woman, and she was his wife. His heart picked up its pace.

Why does she always have to be so hot?

"I thought that you'd fight me over going back to camp," Celeste said, looking at Ash.

"Why would I fight you?"

He started the engine. "Those sick and dying people in the mountains are my people. I will always help them with everything I can. I am proud of you for offering your services. I'd be shocked if you didn't."

Chapter 24

Celeste looked out the window of the fast-moving truck, unable to hold her smile. She was happy to be going back to the Resistance camp. Those were her people, and helping them was all she ever wanted to do. Hayes would be angry with her for coming, but she didn't care. He had to get over himself. There was no way she could sit in her nice warm house, knowing that children were freezing and dying from the flu. Heavy snow covered the mountains, and she could hear the chains on the wheels squeak with every turn.

"Would you be willing to go hunting and gather some wood for the camp?" Celeste asked gently, but her voice trembled slightly under the anxiety.

"Of course I would," he grumbled. "Why do you think I don't care?"

"I know you do; I'm sorry. I just didn't want to sound like I'm giving you orders."

"Order away. I'm at your service forever."

He smiled and ruffled her hair.

Celeste leaned over and placed a kiss on his cheek.

They knew that they were close to the camp when a couple of armed men waved them down. One of them approached the truck.

"I wouldn't advise you to enter the camp," he coughed through his mask. "The situation's bad. Almost everybody's sick. People are dying left and right. If you want to live, turn around and leave."

"No way." Celeste shook her head. "I'm bringing medication and supplies. Let us through."

"It's your funeral."

The man moved out of their way.

"Drop me off at the hospital," Celeste said, rubbing her forehead. "I have to assess the situation."

As soon as they entered the camp, Celeste's heart dropped. There was an eerie silence blanketing the camp. Not a single person was outside. She could feel death hanging over the tents.

She closed her eyes. Only a few months ago, the camp was bustling with life, children playing and laughing, people going about their chores...

Celeste took a deep breath to suppress her tears.

When Ash parked in front of the hospital, Celeste jumped out of the truck, put a mask on, and grabbed two duffel bags. Ash also masked and helped her with the rest of the supplies.

Celeste carried everything into the doctor's office. Hayes wasn't there. She knew he was probably busy with patients.

"Go fetch us some grub, sha." Celeste wrapped her arms around Ash and kissed him. "I'mma see how I can pitch in 'round here."

"Sure thing! See ya 'round the bend." Ash winked at her.

"Touché!"

Celeste laughed. She loved it when Ash and she exchanged their phrases in their local dialects. That had become a running joke of theirs.

She watched him walk out of the hospital. Celeste had purposely sent him hunting. She didn't want him to spend unnecessary time with the infected, especially when the behavior of this virus was uncertain. He had antiviral medication available to him if needed, but it wasn't clear how well it would work. For herself, Celeste wasn't worried. She was a physician, and risking infection was literally within her job description.

Celeste found a pair of scrubs, quickly changed, and headed to the patient area.

She looked around and felt her heart tighten.

The sight was overwhelming. So many people were ill! Their coughs and moans were echoing off the walls. There weren't enough beds. They had given beds to the children. The adults were lying on blankets on the cold floor.

Celeste swallowed hard, holding back her tears. The last time she had seen those people, they were smiling at her wedding.

She brought the medications and distributed them to the nurses.

"Prioritize the children first for the antiviral medication," she ordered firmly. "Treat only adults who have been sick for no longer than two days. There is acetaminophen and ibuprofen in the bags too."

"Thank you!" The nurse grabbed her hand. "Thank you for helping us!"

The other nurses smiled, clasping their hands in front of their chests. Celeste was the answer to their prayers.

"Where is Hayes?" Celeste asked.

"I don't know," one of the nurses said. "I haven't seen him for a couple of days now. He might be out of camp."

Celeste's stomach wrenched. Feeling the panic rise in her chest, she ran to the medical office, threw on her jacket, and bolted toward Hayes's building. Her boots crunched in the snow, echoing through the silent camp.

She tried to open the door, but it felt as though something was stopping it from the other side. She pushed as hard as she could and squeezed in. She immediately saw Hayes lying unconscious by the door. His body was what was preventing her from opening the door.

"Jesus, Dave!" she gasped, dropping to her knees beside him.

Celeste checked for a pulse. He was alive, but his skin was burning up in fever. She felt her heart beating out of her chest.

I have to do something.

She grabbed him under the arms and dragged him to the small room she had used the last time she stayed in camp. Luckily, the bed was still in there. Celeste rolled Hayes on the bed and ran to the hospital for medication.

There was Acetaminophen left, but all antivirals were distributed already. She grabbed an inhaler and some intravenous fluids and hurried back to Hayes's office.

Celeste sat by the bed and silently gazed at Hayes. She had spoken to him just two days ago. Surely, he couldn't have been sick for long. There was still time to give him medication.

"Come on, Dave, wake up!" She slapped him across the face. "Mais, don't you go gettin' lazy on me now, you hear?"

"Oh, no, the little Cajun's here." His eyelids flickered, and he smiled.

"You scared the hell out of me." Celeste sighed with relief.

"I can tell," Hayes smirked. "You always... always slip into your Cajun lingo when you panic."

"I thought you were dying." Celeste brushed her hand across his forehead. He was burning hot.

"I feel like it."

"Here, take the medicine."

She handed him acetaminophen and the antivirals she had brought for herself.

"Give the medications to the patients first."

He pushed her hand away.

"You are the patient now, Dave. Take the medication. We need you."

"I think I'm too far gone. Don't waste resources..."

"No, you're only two days in. You still have a chance. Take the pills."

"I told you not to..."

His last words were choked out by a violent coughing spell. Celeste helped him to sit up while he was trying to take a breath.

"Take the medication. That's non-negotiable."

She forced the pills into his mouth and handed him a bottle of water. Then she started a line and hung IV fluids.

"I told you not to waste..."

Hayes fell back down, unable to finish his sentence.

"I'm not gonna let you die," Celeste said stubbornly.

She forced a puff from the inhaler into his mouth.

After a while, his fever started to lower, and he fell asleep.

Celeste sat by his bed, not taking her eyes off him. She was scared. She suddenly realized that she cared about Hayes. A lot. She imagined that she would care like that for a brother if she had one. Hayes was the closest thing to a brother she had.

"I looked for you everywhere."

Celeste raised her eyes and saw Ash.

"What's wrong with Hayes?" Ash pointed at him.

Celeste walked out of the bedroom. Ash followed her.

"He's got the flu," Celeste sighed. "Like really bad. Ash, I'm worried."

He looked at her. Celeste's face was tense, and her hands were shaking.

"You really care about him." He frowned.

"Besides you, he's the only family I have here."

Tears welled in her eyes.

"Please don't be jealous." Her voice trembled. "I don't think I can take more heartache today."

"Don't worry, love." Ash took her in his arms. "I'm not jealous."

"Can I trust you to watch Dave while I go help at the hospital? You're not going to smother him, are you?"

"No, Tink, I won't smother him." Ash shook his head. "Go do your doctor stuff. I'll take care of him."

"If he gets worse, come and get me," Celeste said as she walked out the door.

She checked on all patients and then sat in Hayes's office. She was exhausted. Celeste knew there would be several days before they saw the effect of the antivirals. She had instructed the nurses to maintain fever control and treat the breathing issues with inhalers and steroids.

Celeste thought of Hayes again. He was generally very healthy, so she never thought that the flu would get him down like that. He must've run himself into the ground working nonstop. She was glad she came when she did. Otherwise, he would've died on the floor in his office before anyone even checked on him.

Hayes was a tough leader, so most people were somewhat afraid of him and didn't seek to speak with him casually. Obviously, Hayes didn't want to appear weak, so he didn't try to get any help.

I'm glad I came.

Hayes was her only friend, and she was his.

However, while she had Ash, Hayes had no one else. From what she knew, his entire family had perished during the war. She felt tears welling in her eyes.

Why was there so much pain in this world?

She wiped her eyes with her sleeve and walked back to the hospital ward to check on the patients.

Chapter 25

Celeste sat at the desk in the doctor's office, holding her head in her hands. Yet another elderly patient had succumbed to the flu, adding to the grim tally. She had worked without rest the entire night. The patients, who had received the antivirals, were clinging to life. However, the ones who didn't qualify for the treatment were circling the drain.

Celeste couldn't understand why this influenza strain was so severe. In all her years as a physician, she had never seen a flu epidemic so devastating. She rubbed her temples, haunted by the creeping suspicion that something didn't add up.

She replayed in her mind the past couple of weeks. After the hospital in Dubois had received the notification about the mutated flu strain, the citizens were warned not to travel outside of town. Checkpoints had been set up at the city's entrance points. No one was allowed to enter.

Oh no!

In that instance, Celeste realized that this epidemic wasn't natural. Someone had released the virus into the Resistance strongholds.

This is a bioweapon!

Celeste shot to her feet with her heart pounding. The Alliance had deployed a targeted biological attack on the Resistance. She slammed her fist against the desk, rattling the clipboard beside her.

In her mind, she could see the face of every person she had declared dead since her arrival in camp. Tears rolled from her eyes. The hate for the Alliance surged through her veins like fire. She clenched her hands.

I have to pull myself together.

She winced at the sound of the door. It was Ash.

"Anything wrong with Hayes?"

She took a deep breath.

"You can say that," Ash said with a grim frown. "He's not doing well. He's refusing the medications. There might be nothing we could do to help him. I don't know what..." Ash stopped mid-sentence.

Celeste had already run out the door.

She sprinted to Hayes's office. He was lying in bed, pale and diaphoretic. She could hear him wheezing.

"Dave." She shook his shoulder. "Do you hear me?"

His eyelids flickered.

"Celeste," he whispered. "Don't waste your time on me."

"Listen, asshole!" She slapped him on the shoulder. "Pull your shit together. If you don't start taking your medications, I will intubate you. I mean it. I won't let you die."

"What for... You've moved on. You don't need me anymore."

Hayes closed his eyes.

"What the hell, Dave!" Celeste grabbed his shoulders and shook him. "Of course I need you. I did marry Ash, but besides him, you are the only family I have here. It has always been you and me in this war. You can't just walk away. Please, don't do that."

"You really mean that?" He looked at her tear-streaked face. "I didn't think you cared anymore."

"Dave, we both know that you and I would never work in a relationship, but it doesn't mean I don't care. I love you as if you were my blood brother. Please, believe me!"

"Okay." Hayes sighed. "Give me the medicine."

Celeste smiled and handed him the antivirals.

"Now that you make sense, we have to talk business."

She stood up and popped her head out of the room. Ash was sitting at the table in the office.

"Ash, come here!" She waved her hand. "I want you to hear this too."

He stood up and followed her.

"What is going on?"

Ash sat on the floor by Hayes's bed.

"Guys, I was thinking." Celeste frowned. "This influenza is only in the Resistance camps. There were no cases in Dubois."

"What are you saying?" Hayes lifted himself from the bed on his elbows.

"I think we got hit with a bioweapon."

"Shit! They won't stop at anything." Ash clenched his jaw. "We have to retaliate immediately."

"Once we recover from their attack, we will." Hayes's face tensed up.

"Now you see why I need you." Celeste squeezed Hayes's hand.

"You're always right." He smiled. "I promise, I will do my best not to die."

"Good, I'll hold you to it."

"What if this virus gets out of our camps and spreads to everybody else? It will lay waste to the entire world." Hayes rubbed his forehead.

"I believe that this is a virus designed to be self-limited. I would be shocked if it mutates. It will probably die off as fast as it started. We just have to hang on for a little longer."

"That makes sense." Hayes nodded.

"I'll go back to the hospital now."

Celeste stood up and walked out of the building. Ash quickly followed her.

"I heard everything you said to Hayes," he said. "I'm sorry for ever being jealous. I just didn't know about the type of relationship you had with him. Please forgive me!"

Celeste stopped and turned around.

"I understand, Ash." She leaned into him and kissed him. "I'm not upset. I should've told you about my history with Dave. When I met him again, after the war started, we had no family in the city. We were each other's support all those years. I guess after I married you, he thought that I'd forget about him."

"You are an amazing woman." Ash brushed a strand of hair away from her face. "Celeste, what happened to your mother?"

"That's a conversation for another time."

She turned around and quickly walked to the hospital.

Ash looked after her for a long time.

What was she hiding? There were so many questions in his head.

He shook his head and went back to see if Hayes needed anything.

Celeste spent the following days mostly taking care of patients at the hospital. Slowly, the number of infected decreased. Hayes was improving as well. By the end of the third week, there were only about ten patients left in the hospital. They were mostly people with a secondary pneumonia.

"You need to get some sleep. You look awful."

Celeste raised her eyes and saw Hayes.

"I'm glad you feel better." She smiled.

"Come on, go get some rest. I can manage now. By the way, I straightened up the bed for you. You have clean linen, so you can lie down."

"Thanks, Dave!"

She walked to Hayes's office and sagged down on the bed. Her head was splitting. Celeste wondered where Ash was, but then decided that he was probably hunting. She closed her eyes and immediately fell asleep.

Ash returned to camp at dusk. He had gotten a deer. He brought it to the kitchenette for the others to process. Then he washed up and went to the hospital. There he found Hayes.

"Where is Celeste?"

Ash looked around.

"I sent her off to get some sleep. She looked exhausted. You can find her in my office."

Ash quickly headed to Hayes's office. Spending some time alone with his wife was something he was craving right now.

He entered Celeste's bedroom and immediately sensed that something was wrong. She was thrashing around in the bed. Her hair was damp with sweat. Ash touched her forehead and winced. She was burning up. He didn't understand. She had taken antivirals...

"Celeste, can you hear me?"

He shook her shoulder.

She woke up and sat up in bed.

"My head's splitting."

She pressed her hands against her temples.

"You're burning up."

"I'm fine. I was just..." She bent over in a coughing spell.

"You got the flu." Ash's voice was tense, almost accusatory.

"I think you might be right." She sighed.

"But didn't you take the antivirals?"

"No, I didn't. I gave them to Hayes."

She looked at her feet.

"Goddammit!"

Ash ran out of the room. In a few minutes, he returned with Hayes.

"Yes, you most definitely got the flu." Hayes frowned. "That might be a problem. You have no spleen now, so your immune system is already compromised. Do you have any more antivirals left? You need those like yesterday."

"I have them." Ash opened his travel bag and pulled out the medicine that Celeste had given him.

"You were supposed to take those." She knit her brows.

"I had the feeling that you'd do something like that, so I saved my dose for you."

He shrugged.

"I won't take your medication," Celeste said stubbornly.

"I'll be okay. I've never had the flu in my life. I believe I'm naturally resistant. I'll be okay."

"Okay, you win." Celeste lay back down. "I feel like shit."

"Let me take care of you now. I owe you," Hayes said, handing her the medication.

"I swear, Celeste, if something happens to you because of this biological attack, I'll burn the Alliance's entire headquarters."

Ash ran his fingers through Celeste's hair.

"Thank you, guys! I love you both."

Celeste smiled and fell back to sleep.

Chapter 26

For the next several days, Ash sat by Celeste's bed, not taking his eyes away from her. He held her hand or ran his hand through her hair. He wanted her to know that he was there for her.

She no longer had a fever. The antivirals were working. Her cough, however, seemed to be especially stubborn.

"Don't worry, Ash, it'll go away," she said with a smile.

Hayes, on the other hand, had a different opinion. He had started giving her antibiotics.

"You are at a high risk of pneumonia," he said.

"You're exaggerating as always," she laughed.

"You should know better than that." Hayes frowned. "Don't make me feel guilty for removing your spleen."

"Fine, Dave, I'll take the antibiotics."

Even though Celeste downplayed her symptoms, Ash was worried. Every time he heard her cough, he felt on edge. He could clearly see her pale face and her fatigue. She slept for most of the day, and that wasn't like her at all. It had been a week since she got sick, and he was sure the flu was gone. She must be suffering complications from not having a spleen.

I hope those antibiotics work.

Celeste opened her eyes and saw Ash sitting on a chair by her bed, typing on his laptop.

"What are you doing, Ash?"

Her voice was soft, but he knew it was from fatigue.

"I'm just posting on Amnestic." He shrugged. "How are you feeling?"

"I still don't have much energy, but my breathing is getting better. Dave might be a jerk, but he's a good physician. I trust him with my health completely."

"I'm glad you are feeling better." Ash smiled. "I was worried about you."

"I know you were. Come, sit by me." Celeste propped herself up on the pillows. "I'd like to see how your forum is going. That is, if you don't mind, of course."

"Why would I mind?"

He sat by her on the bed and wrapped his arm around her shoulders, so she could lean on his chest and see the screen.

Celeste gazed at the forum board. There were so many posters, all offering different opinions about the Alliance and America. She smiled. The world was waking up. That was exactly the name of Ash's thread, "Wake Up."

She looked at the forum board again.

Amnestic Forums>>Memory Holes>>Thread: Wake Up.

Started by Ash on Oct 16, 2040, @ 00:00

Another day under the boot of the Alliance.

Once we were free.

We had dreams.

We had choices.

Now we are reduced to slaves. If we dare to protest, we die. It's time to wake up and reclaim our identity and our lives.

#6703 Rider1. Jan 20, 2041, @14:00

Subject: Wake up

I've been saying that. It's time to stand up against the machine. Let's go!

#6704 Reply

Posted by Ash on Jan 20, 2041 14:10

Quote from Rider1 on Jan 20, 2041 14:00

I've been saying that. It's time to stand up against the machine. Let's go!

Rider1, spread the word. We are still alive here, under the snow. We are ready to fight. They haven't managed to exterminate us yet.

They tried everything:

Executions.

Prison.

Disappearances.

Kidnappings.

Now biological warfare.

Yes, they just hit all American strongholds with mutated and highly virulent Influenza, killing tens of elderly people and children. Pass this on so everybody knows.

#6705 Reply

Posted by Zerochill on Jan 20, 2041 14:20

Quote from Ash

They tried everything:

Executions.

Prison.

Disappearances.

Kidnappings.

Now biological warfare.

Yes, they just hit all American strongholds with mutated and highly virulent Influenza, killing tens of elderly people and children. Pass this on so everybody knows.

We are ready. We are gathering volunteers. Just say the word.

#6706 Reply

Posted by Ash on Jan 20, 2041 14:30

Quote from Zerochill

We are ready. We are gathering volunteers. Just say the word."

We will tell you when it's time.

#6707 Reply

Posted by Napoleon

Quote from Ash

They tried everything:

Executions.

Prison.

Disappearances.

Kidnappings.

Now biological warfare.

Yes, they just hit all American strongholds with mutated and highly virulent Influenza, killing tens of elderly people and children. Pass this on so everybody knows.

Famous last words! Your days are numbered, Ash!

Celeste snatched the laptop from Ash's hands.

She stared at the forum board. Her face became a few shades paler.

"Celeste, I get threats every day. That's nothing."

"Log off, now. I know who Napoleon is. He's with the Alliance. They might be trying to track you."

Ash quickly logged off, powered down the laptop, and took the battery out.

"Stay inside. I'll make sure no one is creeping up on us."

Ash grabbed his rifle and his bow and walked out the door.

He found Hayes at the hospital.

"I believe we are about to be attacked by Alliance patrolmen. I need a few men to come with me to scout the area."

"How do you know that?" Hayes narrowed his eyes.

"Someone just threatened me on my online forum. Celeste said he was from the Alliance. They can't trace my forum, but they might have traced Celeste and me when we came here."

"Okay, I'll send my team with you. Well, whatever's left of it. While you're checking the perimeter, I'll move the women and children to the caves up the mountain."

"Please, take care of Celeste!"

"Don't worry about Celeste, Ash. I will make sure she's safe."

Ash and five more men took up positions down the road leading to the camp.

Minutes passed. Ash felt his nerves straining to the limit. If they weren't able to stop the Alliance, everybody in the camp, including Celeste, would die.

He took a deep breath. Now he heard the rhythmic sound of an engine. An armored vehicle turned around the bend and sped toward them. As soon as it came within range, Ash and his men sent several rounds at it. The soldiers inside the vehicle returned fire.

Ash looked at the road.

Only one vehicle...

There was something wrong.

This is a decoy!

"They will approach the camp from a different direction. You stay here and deal with these patrolmen. I'm going back to camp to make sure everybody is safe."

Ash waved at the men and retreated, taking cover behind the trees. Once far enough from the road, he ran, his heart beating in his head.

If something happened to Celeste...

Celeste was sitting at the edge of her bed with her stomach in knots. If the Alliance had sent an assault team to their camp, no one would have a chance of survival.

Especially Ash...

He and his men would get hit first. Now she heard the gunshots. She stood up and, with trembling hands, opened the door.

She found herself face-to-face with Hayes.

"Come on, let's go to the caves."

He grabbed her elbow and pulled her out of the room.

"Dave," she said with hesitation. "What about Ash?"

"He can handle himself. Let's go."

Celeste looked out of the window and pulled Hayes back.

"It's too late. There are Alliance patrolmen in the camp."

"Shit!" Hayes pulled his revolver from the holster. "Stay in here. I will draw their attention and buy you time to sneak out and run to the caves. Everybody is already there. It's just you and me in the camp. I won't let them touch you."

"No. You're not getting yourself killed for me."

"I'm your superior. You do what I order you to do."

"Okay, just let me grab my bag."

She quickly slipped her wedding rings from her finger and put them in her pocket, then took her handbag from the hook on the wall.

"Before you go and get yourself killed for nothing, look out of the window to make sure that I have a way out."

Hayes looked at her, narrowing his eyes as if he tried to figure her out, but then he lifted the curtain and peeked outside.

Suddenly, he felt sharp pain on the side of his neck.

"What the hell, Celeste!"

Holding the side of his neck, he looked at her with wide eyes.

"I told you, you ain't getting yourself killed for me. It's a powerful tranquilizer. Have a nice nap."

She pulled her revolver out and fired a shot at him, grazing his temple.

"'You do what I order you to do.' Asshole!" she said mockingly, watching him crumple to the ground.

Then she knelt and ran her fingers through his hair.

"Sorry, Dave! You'll thank me later."

She still had her revolver in her hand when the door flew open. Celeste turned around and gasped. In front of her was a well-built, tall man with black hair, sprinkled with silver, and dark eyes. His expression was cold and cynical.

"Celeste!" he exclaimed. "I thought I might find you here, but I wasn't sure this was your camp."

She swallowed hard but forced a smile on her face.

"What are you doing here, Gabriel?"

"Gabriel? Is this how you address your father? Never mind. Who do we have here? He pointed at Hayes. "Is this Ash?"

"Yes, it's Ash," she quickly lied.

"Did you kill him?" He nudged Hayes's body with his foot.

"I had to. You threatened him on his forum, so he was coming to ambush you. I tried to talk him out of it, but he got suspicious of my alliance with the Resistance, so I shot him. I can handle myself. I don't need your help."

"I can see that. We've been looking for that terrorist high and low, and look at you. You just popped him like nothing."

"Why are you here?" Celeste asked coldly.

"We got a tip that you might have arrived at this camp with him. I came to eliminate him. I see that it was unnecessary. Is this his laptop?" Gabriel pointed at Ash's computer. "Let me have it."

"No, leave it here. I'll impersonate Ash on the forum. If I come across people who are an actual threat, I'll let you know."

"That's my girl!" He patted her on the shoulder.

Celeste lost her balance, but Gabriel grabbed her elbow and held her up. She almost recoiled from the sensation of his touch, but stopped herself.

"What's wrong with you? Are you sick?"

"Yes, I got the damn flu like everybody else. Now you all are exposed as well."

"Don't worry about us. We are vaccinated."

"Vaccinated..." Celeste gritted her teeth. "So, the epidemic was..."

"My genius idea, yes. We developed this amazing designer strain just for the terrorists. After this, the Resistance would be pretty much done."

Celeste saw the face of every patient she had lost to the contagion and felt her blood boil. She was tempted to pull her revolver out and empty it into Gabriel's face.

"Smart move," she said with a forced smile.

"You should've never come into this hellhole."

"I had to. I can't allow them to suspect my allegiance."

"I understand. Are you going to be all right?" Gabriel looked at her the way a merchant looks at damaged goods. "Do I need to take you with us?"

"No. Do you want to blow my cover? I need you to get out of here now. I'll tell them that you killed Ash. Now you need to leave. Unless you want them to send someone else to negotiate with Canada and Mexico. I have to maintain my cover long enough to tank the negotiations. In order to do that, I need all of you to stay away from this camp. Do you understand that?"

"And that's why you're my daughter." He smiled coldly. "Now I don't regret saving your life."

Celeste tilted her head and looked at him with narrowed eyes.

"What? Who do you think spared your life when you got arrested last year? I sacrificed one of my agents, so you don't blow your cover."

"Well, your other agent almost blew my brains out and caused me to roll down a ravine, so your help wasn't great."

"I know, and trust me, that incompetent agent was dealt with accordingly."

Celeste took a deep breath.

Gabriel's revelations were like a parade of cruelty served on a freezing-cold platter.

"You need to hurry before their armed group returns to the camp," Celeste grumbled. "If that happens, I'll shoot you just to remain in character."

"I wouldn't expect anything less. But just to make sure I don't get shot..."

He grabbed her and put the barrel of his revolver to her head, pulling her outside.

Ash reached the camp and hid in the tree line to survey the area. He saw a group of Alliance patrolmen. Then he saw another one pulling Celeste out of Hayes's office, holding a gun to her head. He felt the rage hit his head.

Ash took an arrow and pulled back the bowstring. He observed Celeste's body language and realized that she wasn't frightened. She must be working the patrolmen. Ash lowered the bow.

The man holding Celeste, obviously convinced that there was no one in the camp, pushed her away and disappeared into the bushes. His men followed him.

Chapter 27

Ash watched Celeste quickly run inside the building. As soon as the Alliance's soldiers left, he followed her.

Ash found Celeste sitting on the floor, holding Hayes in her arms, pressing a cloth to his bloodied head.

"They shot Hayes?" Ash's eyes widened. "Is he dead?"

His heart tightened. Ash had never thought that he'd care for Hayes, but now he felt rage fill his chest.

"I shot Hayes, and no, he's not dead." Celeste raised her eyes and looked at Ash.

"He looks dead." Ash frowned.

"That's the point. Anyway, can you run to the hospital and bring me a suture kit? I'll explain everything to you later."

When Ash returned, she asked him to put Hayes on the bed. Then, she sutured the wound on Hayes's head.

"He'll be okay." Celeste went outside and waved for Ash to follow her.

"Why did you shoot him?" Ash asked with a bewildered look in his eyes. "Why is he still unconscious?"

"I injected him with a tranquilizer, and shot him."

"What did he do to deserve that?"

"He ordered me to run, while he attempted to distract them and get himself shot in the process. So, I made him look dead. That was the only way I could save him. I have an excellent aim and a steady hand. His life was never in danger. I know he'll kill me when he wakes up, but oh well."

"Remind me never to get on your bad side," Ash said, laughing. "You are one dangerous woman, you know that?"

"I also told them that Hayes is you, so now they think you're dead."

"Are you for real?"

"The person who threatened you on the forum wasn't bluffing. He is dangerous. He came here to execute you. Trust me, this is the best way. They will no longer look for you. You can continue to run Amnestic. I told them that I would impersonate you and look for terrorists."

"So, what exactly went on between you and those goons?"

"I told them to leave and never return to this camp, or they will blow my cover. I think we'll all be safe here for now. At least until we negotiate with Mexico and Canada."

"I had almost forgotten that you're a spy." Ash smiled. "Now I realize that you are scary good at your job."

"Let's go check on Hayes."

Celeste returned to the room and sat on the edge of the bed.

"Dave, do you hear me?"

She gently shook his shoulder.

He stirred in the bed and mumbled something unintelligible. Then his eyelids flickered.

"What the hell, Celeste!" He sat up and grabbed his head. "You shot me!"

"Yes, I did, right after I drugged you."

"I know you're insane, but I don't understand..."

"You don't understand? Why would you think I'd run away and let you get yourself killed?"

"Because I ordered you to?"

"Well, you can write me up for insubordination."

"You are truly insane." Hayes shook his head.

"Well, I chose the better option. I do apologize for the assault."

"Anybody else I'd kill."

"Oh, I'm sure. I didn't even know if I'd survive your wrath."

"You officially scare me. I really thought that you shot me in the head."

"I practically did. But I stitched you up if that's any consolation."

"I guess I owe you for saving my life, and for the PTSD."

"I'm sorry, Dave, I didn't want to do that to you, but there was no other way."

"I'm joking, Celeste. I'm grateful and jealous of the fact that you pulled that off so flawlessly."

"Okay, you should stay in bed for the rest of the day. Do you need anything?"

"If Ash doesn't mind, he can go and tell the people that the danger is gone, and they can return."

"I don't mind."

Ash stood up.

"I'll come with you." Celeste grabbed his hand and pulled herself up.

"You should probably stay. You're still sick."

"I think I'll be okay."

She followed Ash outside.

After they notified the women and children that the camp was safe, Celeste and Ash slowly walked back.

"I needed some fresh air."

Celeste took a deep breath.

"How do you know that the poster named Napoleon is dangerous?"

Ash stopped and looked at Celeste.

"I know who he is," she said.

He looked at her, waiting for the answer.

"His name is Gabriel Clement."

"Gabriel Clement!" Ash's eyes widened. "This is the Godfather of the Alliance. He was the one who instigated the invasion of America. Do you think he's here?"

"Yes, he was the one who held a gun to my head."

"You know him?"

"Ash, I have to tell you something."

She covered her face with her hands.

"What's wrong, Tink?"

He lifted her chin with his fingers and looked into her eyes. She was shivering, unable to meet his gaze.

"Tink..."

Celeste took a deep breath. "Gabriel Clement is my father."

"What?" Ash stepped back and stared at her. "But your name is Beaumont."

"You wanted to know about my mother..."

"Yes?"

"My mother left Gabriel, and we moved to the States. We lived in a suburb of New Orleans, Louisiana. About two years after we settled there, Gabriel showed up one night with a loaded gun and shot and killed my mother in front of me. I was only twelve years old. I was terrified. I saw my mom bleed out. He tried to take me, but I ran. Then he tried to shoot me, but he missed. I hid at my aunt's in the bayou. She raised me. I took my mom's maiden name, Beaumont. My aunt adopted me."

"I am so sorry!" Ash wrapped his arms around Celeste.

"I didn't hear from my father until after the war. He recruited me to work for him and installed me on Amnestic. I was your spy."

"Wait, what?" Ash's eyes widened.

"Yes, I was there to spy on you. Ravenville wasn't the first time; however, I had no intentions of spying for Gabriel. You wanted to know why I left Amnestic without telling you."

Ash looked at her with a question in his eyes.

"I had to leave Amnestic." Celeste sighed heavily. "Gabriel pressured me to give him information about you. I told him that you suspect me, so I can no longer log into Amnestic. I disappeared to protect you. I'm sorry, Ash! I know that hurt you."

Without saying a word, Ash wrapped his arms around her and pulled her to his chest.

"After I met you on Amnestic, I was inspired to join the Resistance." Celeste continued. "I wanted to cause true damage to the Alliance. I had the perfect opportunity as Gabriel thought I was his spy. In order to maintain my cover, I had to pretend that I cared about Gabriel. I pretended that I didn't remember what he did to my mom. My final act as an Alliance spy will be to kill him. He took my mom from me. I will avenge her death one way or another."

"Why didn't you tell me that before?"

"Ash, I feel responsible for everything that happened here. I carry that monster's blood. I was ashamed. I didn't want you to hate me. You probably hate me now, but I understand."

"No, don't talk like that." Ash kissed her on the top of the head. "He hurt you just as much. I will never blame you for anything he's done."

"Thank you! I was afraid that you'd never look at me again."

"How can I ever hate my Tink?" Ash smiled.

"I love you, Ash!" Celeste rose on her toes and kissed him. "Now I have to go and tell that to Hayes as well. I don't know if he'd forgive me as easily as you did."

"Let's go together."

Ash took her hand in his and led her back to camp.

Celeste sat next to Hayes.

"There is something you need to know. I am Gabriel Clement's daughter."

"What?" Hayes sat up with wide-open eyes.

"You have to know that my father recruited me to infiltrate the Resistance. If that was my intention, bringing me in would've been a huge mistake. However, spying for them was never my plan. I fully intended to hurt the Alliance, and specifically Gabriel, from the very beginning. I feel guilty for not being honest with you up front. I'd understand if you never want to look at me again," she whispered. "I came to you under a false pretense."

Hayes stayed silent for a long time after Celeste was done talking.

"I wouldn't call it 'false pretense'," he said slowly. "I realize that our history blinded me, and I could've compromised everybody by bringing you here. However, you always planned to be on our side. As far as Clement is concerned, none of what he did was your fault." Hayes shook his head. "I was just trying to figure out how we got so lucky that you are on our side. Your narcissistic father would do anything to hold on to you. You have the upper hand."

"Don't be fooled," Celeste laughed bitterly. "He would kill me the minute he realizes I'm a double agent. However, I'm planning to kill him first."

"Oh, I believe it, especially after what you did to me today," Hayes laughed.

"You'll never let that go, will you?"

"Absolutely not. I admire you, and I'm proud of you. You are now in my personal hall of fame."

"Have you two always been childish and murdery like that?" Ash raised his eyebrows.

"You can say that." Hayes shrugged. "Anyway, we should assess our situation after the flu epidemic. Right now, we are vulnerable. Celeste is protecting us for now, but we don't know how long that will last."

"I agree." Celeste rubbed her forehead. "I wouldn't trust Gabriel. He's a psychopath. We should have a good plan for defense and evacuation. There are children in this camp. We have to make sure they are safe."

"I'll take care of that as soon as my headache eases," Hayes said, getting out of bed. "I'm going to my room now. You and Ash can have yours."

"You can go back to posting on Amnestic now," Celeste told Ash. "They'll think it's me."

"I understand that. However, right now, I want to hold you in my arms. You gave me a good scare today."

"That sounds good to me." Celeste smiled.

Then she collapsed in bed. Now the exhaustion hit her fully.

"Are you okay?" Ash looked at her with concern.

"I'm tired," she sighed. "Today was too much for me. My plans didn't include shooting my friend and getting a social call from my mother's murderer."

"I'm sorry, Tink. I wish I could help you."

"You can. Lie by me." Celeste tapped the bed with her hand.

Ash changed his clothes and relaxed in bed with Celeste. She laid her head on his shoulder.

He wrapped his arm around her and held her while she drifted to sleep.

What she told him today had shaken him up. The horror she lived through when she was just a child, and the knowledge of what her father had done, was a heavy burden. No wonder she had dedicated her life to the Resistance. After all that, she had still remained a wonderful, caring woman. That was his Tink. He never expected less of her. She thought he'd hate her, but instead, he loved her more than he ever did.

Chapter 28

Ash woke up early in the morning with Celeste still sleeping in his arms. He smiled and kissed her on the forehead. She moved around and mumbled something unintelligible. He slowly pulled his arm out from underneath her and got up. He had to go hunting. Food supplies were almost completely depleted. The flu epidemic and road blockades had cut them off from all merchants.

Celeste opened her eyes and stretched in bed. She looked over, but Ash was gone. She figured she had slept in. She thought she should go to the hospital and help Hayes, but she felt weak after the exertion from the previous day. She sighed. Staying in bed was her only option because Hayes wouldn't let her work anyway.

In the following days, Celeste slowly started to regain her strength. Hayes's medications and resting in bed were working. No one else in the camp fell ill either. The virus had started to die off. Celeste was expecting it. Like any biological weapon, the infectious agent had a built-in self-limitation to prevent a pandemic after it had served its purpose. Essentially, the virus stopped multiplying and infecting new hosts.

Celeste headed to the hospital. She found Hayes in the doctor's office.

"Where's Ash?" she asked.

"He's up the hills hunting with the other men."

"Dave, we have something to discuss."

Celeste sat in a chair next to him.

Hayes raised his eyebrows, waiting for her.

"We can't go back to Dubois," she sighed. "Gabriel thinks Ash is dead. Even if I go alone, he will put me under heavy surveillance. We have to come up with a different plan on how to set up the meeting with Canada and Mexico."

"What do you suggest?"

"Let me think about it. I'll figure something out."

"I know you will." Hayes smiled. "You always do."

"For now, I can work alternate shifts at the hospital so you can rest."

She stood up and headed to the door.

"Celeste," his voice stopped her. "Thank you for everything you did for me."

"Dave," she turned to face him, "you've saved my life many times. You don't owe me anything. You removed my spleen in a cabin, for God's sake. No other surgeon would've attempted that."

"I wouldn't either," he sighed. "But you would've died within minutes if I didn't. It was the only option. It was a miracle that you survived. I still have nightmares about it."

"See, I don't owe you anything."

"It's not that." Hayes frowned. "I thought that since you married Ash, you'd forget about me. You didn't. That's what I'm grateful for."

"Dave, I've told you before, you are my brother. You have been for a while. I'd do anything for you."

"Including shooting me in the head. I know," he laughed.

"Sorry about that, but it was the only option that ended with you being alive."

"And I'm grateful to you."

When Celeste left the hospital, she saw that the hunters had returned and hurried home. Ash was probably tired and hungry. She was surprised not to find him in the room. Where could he have gone?

An hour passed, and he was still gone. Celeste was just getting up to go ask around when Hayes knocked on her door.

"Where's Ash?" Her face turned pale.

"The men ran into Alliance patrols and had to split up. Not everybody has returned yet. We just have to wait."

Celeste covered her face with her hands and sagged onto the bed.

"I guess when Gabriel promised not to come into the camp, he didn't include the area around it. We are pretty much prisoners here. I have to fix that."

"What are you intending to do?" Hayes knitted his brow.

"I have to talk to Gabriel. I'm going back to Dubois."

"Celeste." Hayes squeezed her wrist. "It's too dangerous."

"There is no other way. Please, don't let Ash follow me. Once I straighten things out, I'll come back. I'll also think about our negotiating options."

She quickly packed her bag.

"I need to use one of your vehicles. Don't worry, I'll keep in touch."

Driving back to Dubois, Celeste wondered if Gabriel had believed her.

I guess I'll find out soon enough.

All blockades on the road were lifted. Apparently, the Alliance knew the epidemic was over.

As soon as she arrived at her house, she called the Alliance headquarters in Denver.

"Is Gabriel Clement available?" she asked.

"Celeste! What a surprise. I didn't expect you to call," he said, hearing her voice.

"Gabriel, why are you patrolling the woods around the camp? Didn't I tell you to stay away?"

"Well, you said the camp."

"Listen carefully. If you don't pull back, they will set up the negotiations with Mexico and Canada elsewhere, and I wouldn't know anything. They are very jumpy after what you pulled the last time. You are about to ruin my entire work for the last year."

"I see. I will order my patrols out of the area, even though I might miss out on capturing some key Resistance members."

"You need to look at the bigger picture."

"I'm proud of you, Celeste. You're a good daughter."

Celeste barely restrained herself from smashing the phone on the table. She hated that man from the bottom of her heart. Hearing him call her "daughter" was like a dagger plunging into her chest.

She winced. The encrypted phone that Hayes had given her was vibrating.

"Celeste, what are you doing in Dubois?"

It was Ash.

"Ash, you are back." She sighed. "I was worried to death about you. I had to return to Dubois and talk to Gabriel. He will pull the patrols out of your area. You can no longer stay here with me. I know that isn't what I wanted, but it has to be that way for now. I'll call you, and I'll visit. I promise."

"I understand," he grumbled.

"Please, take care of yourself. I'll be worried." Celeste's voice trembled.

"You'll be worried? I'm fine. You are the one all alone there."

"Ash, don't worry about me. I've done this for years."

"The memories of you almost being executed are still fresh in my mind... Okay, but you have to visit at least every other week."

"Deal." Celeste smiled and disconnected the call.

She hated this new arrangement, but it was the safest choice. Being in Dubois gave her a chance to monitor the Alliance activities and, if needed, warn Hayes. She'd done this kind of work for years and felt comfortable. The only thing that was bothering her was Ash's absence. Being separated from him was eating her up inside. She barely slept or ate. Sometimes, she cried soundlessly alone in her bed.

She continued working at the ER, but the only thing that mattered was visiting the camp and spending time with Ash.

Celeste was driving toward the camp, thinking about the past several months. Being away from Ash was difficult, but they had adapted to the new situation. She kept telling herself that it was a temporary arrangement for the safety of everyone. Ash was more difficult to appease, but he had stopped threatening to come to Dubois. He still ran Amnestic, and this time there was no Napoleon.

Celeste pulled into camp and parked in front of Hayes's building. She stepped out of the truck and took a deep breath. It was the end of June, and the air was saturated with a scent of wild thyme and pine resin. She smiled and knocked on the door.

"There she is," Hayes said, hugging her.

"Where's Ash?" She looked around.

"He just returned from hunting, so he's probably at the creek washing up. Go put your bags in your room."

"It's nice of you to keep it available."

"Of course I would. It's your room."

"Thanks, Dave!"

Celeste went to change her clothes, then returned to Hayes's office.

"We have to talk."

"I'm listening."

He gestured for her to sit.

When Ash returned from the creek, the first thing he noticed was Celeste's truck. He smiled and ran to her room. She wasn't there, so he assumed that she was with Hayes. He just shrugged and went to prepare dinner.

The dusk was falling when Celeste and Hayes came out of his office.

"Let's eat." Ash pointed to the table he had set up.

"What a surprise! I'm starved."

Celeste ran and hugged Ash.

"I missed you, Ash!"

"Same, Tink." He kissed her, holding her tight.

"This is good," Celeste said while emptying her bowl. "I haven't had your elk pot roast for a while. You are an excellent cook."

"I'm glad you like it." Ash smiled. "Watching you eat this is the best compliment for me."

"Yeah, he can cook," Hayes said with his mouth full. "He's been feeding me, while you play doctor in the city."

"I'm glad you guys are getting along."

Celeste ran her hand through Ash's hair.

"I still don't like that city boy," Ash grumbled, "but he's okay."

After dinner, Celeste sat on the bed by Ash and rested her head on his shoulder.

"I'm going away on an assignment." She lifted her gaze.

"What do you mean by 'away'?" Ash frowned. "I don't think so."

"Stop being such an insufferable grump." Celeste laughed. "You are coming with me."

"Now you're talking. Where are we going?"

"We're going to the end of the world."

"The end of the world?" He gave her a bewildered look.

"We are going to my auntie Marie's house in Delacroix, Louisiana, otherwise known as 'the end of the world'."

"We are going to the Louisiana bayous?"

"Yes. We will meet the Southern Resistance. That is where we'll negotiate with Canada and Mexico. We can't do it here. Gabriel's watching. He's probably bugged every building. The Alliance doesn't dare to approach Delacroix. They don't even know the Resistance operates there. To them, my people are just some backwater rednecks with a French background. For some reason, they think Cajuns sympathize with the Alliance. They couldn't be more wrong. So, what do you say?"

"I've never imagined myself in alligator country, but I'm excited. I'd like to see where my Tink grew up. Yep, I can't wait."

Chapter 29

In the following days, Celeste spent time talking to Hayes and planning their trip to Louisiana. It was a complicated process as they had to remain undetected by the Alliance.

"I have spoken to the other Resistance cells from here to Louisiana." Hayes pointed at the map. "You will drive all the way down to Pointe à la Hache in Southern Louisiana, where the local Resistance will pick you up with a boat and take you to Delacroix. Expect travel time between two and three weeks if there are no complications. I will give you a detailed map with directions and safe houses to stop at on your way down. One thing I don't know is, once there, if you'd be able to return."

"Don't worry, Dave," Celeste patted him on the shoulder. "I'll come back. Gabriel is not going to escape his fate. My family will make sure of it."

"I believe you'll do everything possible to complete your assignment. Just please don't die!"

Celeste looked at him. There was no humor in his eyes. He was worried.

"It has to be done, Dave. You know that," she said.

"I know." He sighed heavily.Celeste and Ash spent several days studying the route and running several scenarios.

"I think we are ready to go," Celeste said while packing their bags. It will be a dangerous trip, but our only chance of negotiating assistance from Mexico and Canada is to do it away from Gabriel and his goons. I know that he wouldn't let me negotiate anything. As soon as we attempt the meeting, he will arrest everybody."

"You don't have to tell me twice," Ash muttered. "Your father is a cold-hearted murderer."

"Don't call him my father," Celeste snapped at him. "Hand me the ammo."

"I'm sorry, Tink. I promise to never make this mistake again."

"I apologize." Celeste bit her lip. "I just hate him so much."

Ash was handing her the box of ammo when he bumped into the bed and dropped it on the floor. The bullets spilled out. Ash began gathering them up, but then something caught his eye. Every single round was engraved with the initials "G. C."

Gabriel Clement...

Ash ran his finger along the bullet and looked at Celeste.

"What?" She shrugged. "I don't know which one will be the lucky one, so I mark them all."

Ash looked away, thinking that Celeste's trauma ran deeper than he had imagined. He wanted to wrap his arms around her and protect her against everything, but instead, he was following her on a dangerous journey.

"I know, you probably think I'm insane." Celeste pursed her lips.

"Don't worry, love." Ash smiled. "That's my kind of insane. I'm all in."

"I love you, Ash!"

Celeste cuddled up to his chest and kissed him.

"I love you too." He returned her kiss. "In fact, I'd go to the end of the world with you. Pun intended."

They left before sunrise.

"I'll be waiting for you," Hayes said, hugging Celeste. "Please come back!"

"I promise, I will." Celeste patted him on the back.

"Ash, please, protect her."

"That goes without saying, Hayes."

Ash sat behind the steering wheel and started the engine.

"I put several cans of gasoline in the back, so you don't have to stop to refuel too often," Hayes said.

"Thanks, Dave." Celeste waved goodbye as Ash pulled out of camp.

"With the extra gasoline, we can probably drive for twenty-four hours without having to stop at a gas station." Ash looked at the map. "You can relax."

"I'm okay," Celeste said, taking the map and spreading it on her knees. "I'll relax when we're out of Wyoming. I don't trust Gabriel."

Ash nodded in agreement.

Toward the evening, Celeste dug out some elk jerky from her bag.

"Eat something." She handed it to Ash.

He ate the jerky without taking his eyes away from the road.

"If you're tired, I'll drive."

"I'm fine." Ash glanced at her. "If I start feeling fatigued, I'll let you know. Don't worry, I've been trained to stay awake without losing my edge."

"If we hit the highway, we'll be faster," Ash suggested.

"No." Celeste shook her head. "Stay away from the main roads. There are too many Alliance checkpoints. We should avoid Cheyenne and Casper. It would be better to go through Lander and Torrington instead." Celeste looked at the map. "I don't want Gabriel to know I'm going to Louisiana. If he finds out where my family is, he'll kill us all."

"I see. Point taken, no main roads."

Ash only stopped a few times to refuel and then continued driving.

When the night fell, Celeste dozed off for a second but jolted herself awake.

Ash looked at her and shook his head. He realized that her heartbreak was worse than he'd thought. The memory of the engraved bullets flashed in his mind, and his jaw tightened. If he ever came across Gabriel Clement, he'd make sure that bastard paid for everything he did to her.

I should've loosed that arrow while I had him in my sight at the Camp.

They crossed into Nebraska through Scottsbluff about noon the next day.

"There should be a safe house about two hours away. We should stop there to get some rest." Celeste tapped the map with her finger.

Once in the safehouse, Ash dropped into bed and immediately fell asleep. Celeste stayed up to keep watch. She didn't want any surprises.

She woke up Ash at dusk.

"Did I fall asleep?" Startled, he jumped out of bed.

"That was the point, Ash. I let you sleep. You needed rest, so you could drive. Let's go."

They refueled and then continued driving southeast.

Celeste relaxed her head on the seat and drifted off to sleep.

She was awakened by Ash, who shook her shoulder.

"What...what's going on?" She looked around.

"We need to lay low here for a bit," he whispered.

Celeste gave him a questioning look.

"There was a checkpoint on the road. I managed to veer off and park over here."

She looked out of the window. They were off the road between some trees.

"Let me look at the map."

Celeste studied the route for a minute.

"We can go around the checkpoint." She pointed to the road.

"Okay, let's go." Ash started the engine. "You can go back to sleep."

She shook her head. There was no way she could relax. All her fears came back.

For the rest of the night, they drove without any complications. Ash insisted on driving through until they reached Kansas. It was around noon when they arrived at the safe house. For the rest of the trip, they had no problems. Celeste slept while Ash drove, and stayed up while he slept when they were at the safe houses.

Celeste was grateful for running water and soap in those places. The farther south they traveled, the hotter the weather got.

One would think that I'm used to that.

She shook her head. It had been almost fifteen years since she had gone down south. Celeste looked over at Ash. That poor mountain man was going to *fry* in Delacroix.

They had traveled for three weeks and were currently in a safe house in Mississippi. Normally, a trip like that wouldn't have lasted that long, but the need to use secondary roads and avoid checkpoints doubled the travel time. Tomorrow, they would enter Louisiana. Celeste felt a flutter in her heart. She wondered how her family was. Were they even still alive? Her stomach knotted up. She had always hoped that the Alliance had left them alone because of their French heritage, but what if Gabriel had gone after them because of a personal vendetta against her mother's American family?

I'm losing my mind. Gabriel never knew where my mother's family lived.

Celeste tried to calm herself, but the fear lingered.

At sunset, she woke up Ash, and they continued their trip.

"What's wrong, Tink?" Ash looked at her. "You look nervous."

"I'm just unsure whether my family survived the war. I never called, so Gabriel couldn't figure out our connection."

"I understand," Ash sighed. "Let's just hope for the best."

"I am. But either way, I'm going to Delacroix to do a job, so I will deal with any situation I find there."

"I know you're a strong woman, but don't forget that you have me. I'll be there for you."

"Thank you, Ash!"

She leaned over and kissed him.

They entered Louisiana early in the morning, but Ash didn't stop.

"I'll push through to Pointe à la Hache on the Southern coast. Then we can get some rest before we get picked up in the morning."

They reached the pickup point around midnight. Ash parked the truck in a public parking lot at a large shopping center.

"There is a safe house here. Hayes arranged it, so we don't have to wander the streets while waiting for the boat."

"Why don't you get some rest?" Ash said after they had taken a shower. "I'm no longer driving, so I can keep watch."

"How about we both relax for once? The boat is coming in the morning. You don't have to sleep. Just lie by me."

Ash smiled and relaxed beside her. Celeste cuddled up to him.

"I love you, Tink," he whispered.

She reached for him, and they kissed.

She was worried about her family and the future, but as long as Ash held her in his arms, she could face any obstacle that life had to offer.

Chapter 30

Celeste spent the night cuddling with Ash, but she was unable to fall asleep. Her anxiety was unbearable. She ached to go back home to her family, but not knowing what was waiting there for her was terrifying. She got out of bed early in the morning.

Ash immediately woke up and sat on the side of the bed.

"Here, put on a pair of shorts and a T-shirt." Celeste handed him clothes from the bag. "I packed hats here somewhere."

She continued to dig through the travel bags.

"I haven't lived here for a long time, and you've never been here, so we'll get sunstroke if we don't cover our heads. Aha, there they are."

She tossed a baseball cap at Ash.

Soon, dressed in light summer clothes, they were ready to go.

"We look like tourists," Ash said, laughing.

"You don't say." Celeste put her hair in a messy bun and put on the hat.

"You look amazing." Ash gazed at her.

"Tie your hair up or you're gonna sweat bullets."

He followed her suggestion and put his hair up.

"Now we are ready."

Celeste slung her bag over her shoulder and headed to the door.

They walked to the marina and sat on a concrete slab to wait for the boat.

Exactly at sunrise, a man approached them.

"Are you the northern visitors?" he asked.

That was the code phrase. Celeste looked at him and stared. They gazed at each other for a long minute.

"Titine?" the man whispered.

"Cousin, Pierre!" She jumped to her feet and threw her arms around his neck. "Please, tell me that Tante Marie is okay!"

"We're all good. We thought you were dead. I can't believe you're my cargo. Maman will be ecstatic. Let's go."

Celeste and Ash followed him to a small motorboat.

"Who's he?" Pierre gestured with his head toward Ash. "Can I trust him?"

"This is Tahoma Jensen, my husband. Before you talk about him, you should know that he speaks French."

"You're married?" Pierre's eyes widened. "Well, well, we will have some celebrating to do. I'm Celeste's cousin." He extended his hand to Ash. "Welcome to the family!"

Ash smiled and shook his hand.

Pierre carefully navigated the boat out of the marina and sailed through the bayous.

Celeste felt the warm breeze on her face, inhaled the familiar scent of the bayou, a mixture of earth and salt, and smiled. She was home.

Ash gazed at her for a second. He had never seen her so happy and at peace with herself.

They had traveled for about fifteen minutes when Ash suddenly grabbed Celeste's arm.

"Look," he pointed to the marshes.

Celeste followed his hand.

"It's an alligator," Ash exclaimed.

"Ah, le cocodrie du bayou," she laughed. "Welcome to my world."

Ash smiled and continued to stare at the alligator. He was seeing Celeste in a completely different light, and he felt like he was falling in love with her all over again.

The trip lasted about an hour. Pierre maintained a medium speed, so he wouldn't draw attention. Of course, there was not a living soul in sight, but he wasn't taking any chances.

"We had prepared a safehouse for you," Pierre muttered, "but I doubt that Maman would allow it. You're staying at our house. Finally, our family will be whole again, even though your man scares me."

"Him?" Celeste laughed. "He might look scary, but trust me, if things go south, you want him on your side."

Ash just shook his head, but smiled. Celeste's cousin was definitely a comedian.

When they arrived at Delacroix, Pierre steered the motorboat to a small dock. They were immediately greeted by a group of armed men.

"State your names," a short elderly woman ordered, pointing a rifle at them.

"Tante Marie!" Celeste exclaimed.

"Titine!" The woman slung her rifle across her back and ran to the boat.

Celeste stepped onto the concrete slab and embraced the woman.

"*'Ti Titine, toi, j'e croyais perdue, hanh!'* (I thought you were lost!)." The woman wiped a few tears from her face. "We all thought you were dead."

"No, Tante Marie, I'm okay."

"Who's that?" Marie looked at Ash with suspicion.

"This is Tahoma Jensen, my husband."

"A husband?" Marie's eyes widened. "Come on, let's go inside. You have a lot to tell me."

Marie led them to a house at the edge of the city. The old wooden house was built on stilts, like the rest of the homes on the island.

Ash looked at the moss-draped cypress trees and the endless marshes.

"The road literally ends here."

Amused, he looked at Celeste.

"I told you that I'm taking you to the end of the world," she laughed.

"I reckon."

"Everything is so different," Celeste sighed, looking around. "The whole town looks worn out and forgotten. There was a sign right there." She pointed toward the docks. "It said 'The End of the World,' but that's gone now too. Every summer, tourists crowd the island. It was noisy, people laughing, listening to music. Gabriel destroyed all that."

Celeste covered her face with her hands.

"Please, Tink, don't blame yourself for something a psychopathic fascist did."

"I carry his poisonous blood."

"I don't think so. You are exactly like your family here. You are full of light. No one can tell me different."

"Thank you, Ash!" Celeste wiped her tears and smiled.

"So, Titine, tell me everything," Marie said after they settled in the living room with a glass of sweet tea. "What did you do all those years?"

"I was spying for the Resistance pretty much."

"And how about Tahoma Jensen?" Marie nodded toward him.

"You can call him Ash."

"Ash?" Marie's eyes widened. "This is the famous Ash from the Northern Resistance?"

"You've heard of him?" Celeste raised her eyebrows.

"Of course we have. He is a legend around here. You married well." Marie nodded approvingly.

"Hayes doesn't think so," Ash muttered.

"Oh, Hayes," Marie laughed. "How's that city boy?"

"You know, he hasn't changed at all." Celeste shrugged.

"Of course he hasn't. Anyway, you must be exhausted and hungry. I'll have the boys bring some water for you to wash up. It's different here since *the connard* laid waste to our homes. No electric or anything..."

Celeste's face tensed. Her aunt always referred to Gabriel as "the connard (bastard)."

"I'm sorry, Titine!" Marie put her arm around Celeste's shoulders. "I didn't mean to bring ghosts back."

"He's no ghost, Tante." Celeste frowned. "He's very much real, but his day is coming. I promise."

Marie sighed without saying anything.

"I'll fix you something to eat." She hurried to the kitchen.

Ash went with Celeste's cousins outside to bring bath water.

In an hour, washed up and in clean clothes, Ash and Celeste were back in the living room.

"Come on to the kitchen," Marie called from the door. "We have Cocodrie en brochette and Maque Choux."

Ash looked at Celeste just to see her quickly licking her lips. He looked at the table and saw meat skewers and a dish of corn.

"Are we eating alligator?" He raised his eyebrows.

"Uhum," She was already reaching for the skewers.

Ash hesitated for a second but picked up one of the skewers and took a bite.

"This is really good," he admitted and took another bite.

"Yup." Celeste smiled and wiped her lips with a cloth napkin. "We'll make a Cajun out of you yet."

"Your aunt is an amazing cook," Ash said later, while taking a sip of sweet tea. "And this tea... It's delicious. What's in it?"

"Auntie Marie likes to put a hint of peaches in her tea."

"It's great." Ash took another sip. "Your family is trying to lull us into forgetting about the war. No wonder Hayes was afraid that you'd never go back. Hell, I don't even want to go back."

"Enjoy it while it lasts."

"Thank you for the dinner, Tante Marie," Celeste said, looking at her aunt. "We were starved."

"I thought so."

"How did you even get ice for the tea?"

"We have a generator for our ice maker. You know I'd never drink warm tea."

"I'm happy to be home."

"Why did you come?" Marie asked. "I love that you're here, but you were sent by the Resistance, which means this isn't just a social call."

"We have to negotiate a joint offensive with Mexico and Canada against the Alliance. We were going to do that up north, but Gabriel figured it out. So, Dave and I decided to organize the meeting down here. Of course, if you don't want to be involved in the negotiations, I'll call it off."

"Are you kidding me?" Marie shook her head. "I'd do anything to hurt the *connard*, who murdered my sister. I'm glad he hasn't hurt you."

"He thinks I'm on his side, but I have a bullet with his name on it."

Marie raised her eyebrows.

"She's not kidding," Ash muttered. "All her rounds are engraved with his initials."

"I expect no less from my Titine." Marie looked at Celeste, her eyes sparkling with pride. "I've also engraved on the stock of my rifle the initials of all Alliance operatives I've taken down."

"Your family officially scares me. I'm a huge fan now." Ash smiled.

"I like your husband." Marie patted him on the shoulder. "He looks scary, but I like him."

"Why does everyone in your family think I'm scary?" Ash asked later when they went to bed.

"It's probably because you're very tall and muscular. You also don't smile too much. You scared me too, when I saw you at first."

"Really?" He raised his eyebrow.

"Only briefly. Now I want you to hold me all the time."

Celeste cuddled up to him.

Ash smiled and buried his face in her hair. He loved Celeste's southern family. They were all friendly and supportive. They had accepted him as if he were one of them. Today was the most he had enjoyed himself in years.

Ash realized it was a false sense of security, but he didn't care. As Celeste had said earlier, they should enjoy it while it lasts—but even here, at the end of the world, the shadow of the Alliance was hanging over them.

Chapter 31

Ash opened his eyes. It was morning. He saw Celeste standing motionless, with her back to the bed. He stood up and wrapped his arms around her shoulders.

Now he noticed that she was looking at a photo on the stand.

"Your mother," Ash whispered. "You look just like her. What was her name?"

Celeste looked at him, her face wet from tears.

"Her name was Celestine." Tears rolled down her cheeks. "I miss her so much."

"I'm sorry, Tink!"

Ash pulled her closer to his chest.

"You probably think I'm selfish," she said. "You've lost everyone, and I still have a family left."

"No, my love, no grief is selfish. I want you to know that I'm here for you no matter what."

"Thank you!" She tiptoed and kissed him.

Now, he noticed that she was holding a little perfume bottle in her hand.

"It was my mom's," Celeste said, noticing his look.

She opened the bottle, inhaled the scent, and closed her eyes. Then, she put the bottle to Ash's nose so that he could smell it too.

"Jasmin!" he murmured. "This is how you smell."

"Yes, I use the same perfume. It's like I have my mom with me."

Ash sighed heavily. He wished she could wipe away all her past suffering.

"This is my room, you know." Celeste waved her arm, pointing around the room. "Tante Marie saved everything the way I left it when I went to college."

"That's amazing." He looked around.

"Coming back feels bittersweet, but I'm happy to be here."

"I can see that. I have never seen you as happy. Now, should we get out of this room so that I can scare your family some more?"

"They aren't really scared of you."

"It's probably the scar on my face."

"Are you self-conscious about it, Ash?" Celeste's eyes widened.

"Well, I'm aware that my face is maimed."

"To me, you are perfect just the way you are. I love you exactly like that. I don't want anything changed about you." She reached and ran her fingers along the scar on the side of his face. "This is your badge of honor. You've spilled your blood for us, and I admire you with my whole heart. Besides, I have scars on my face too." She touched the scars on her temples. "Except that mine aren't glorious. Both are a result of accidental mishaps."

"All I care about is how you see me, Tink." He pressed the side of his face against hers. "Should I start calling you Titine too?"

"No, I love when you call me Tink."

"Tink it is." He smiled.

Holding hands, they walked out of the bedroom.

Marie was in the living room waiting for them.

"Does your man want to go gator hunting with the boys?"

"You can talk to him, Tante Marie." Celeste laughed. "You can even speak French to him. Ash is fluent in both languages."

"Do you want to go with the boys?" Marie looked at Ash. "Pierre and Joseph can use a li'l help."

"I'd be honored to go hunting with your boys. Give me a minute."

He walked to the bedroom, pulled his rifle and his bow and arrows out of the traveling bag, and returned to the living room.

"You brought your weapons?" Celeste exclaimed.

"You didn't seriously think I'd go across the country unarmed?"

"Yeah, I should've known." She shook her head.

"Where did you find that man?" Marie asked after Ash left. "He's terrifying. Rumors say he's killed every foreigner who crossed his path. He looks like those Injuns from the movies."

"Please, Tante Marie, don't call him that! It's offensive."

"Oh, he's a real Native? Sorry!" She slapped her mouth with her hand.

"His father was Cheyenne."

"I'll watch my mouth. I promise. But how did you get together with him?"

Celeste told her about Amnestic and how she met Ash later.

"You're lucky he didn't kill you." Marie frowned.

"He tried several times, but he couldn't do it. Besides, he didn't know who I was. One of the times, Hayes ordered him to take me to the woods and shoot me."

"Hayes? What! '*Cuyon*' (Idiot)!"

"Yes, he is a damn idiot, but I love him anyway. Besides, he wasn't going to let Ash hurt me. Ash wasn't able to bring himself to do it either."

"You've all gone mad." Marie shook her head. "Do you love Ash?"

"Yes, Tante, I love him. He's my soulmate. I'd die for him."

"*Mais*! I never thought there would be a man good enough for you."

"Well, I found him."

"There's one thing I know." Marie nodded her head. "He loves you. I've been watching him. He has this darkness in his eyes, but when he looks at you, his face glows. I know that as long as he's breathing, he wouldn't let anybody hurt you, especially that *connard*. That makes me happy. Well, let's talk about something better."

"What do you have in mind?" Celeste gazed at her aunt's smiling face.

"I want to give you and Ash a real Cajun wedding."

"You're kidding."

"No, I'm serious. Unlike you up north, we have a good food supply here in the bayous. We have fruit, vegetables, meat, and no Alliance to steal it. None of them thieving bastards dares to come to the bayous. If they do, they never return. We make sure of it. *Les cocodries du bayou* take the blame as always."

"I missed you so much!" Celeste hugged her aunt.

"The day you left, our happiness left too. I feel blessed for this glimpse of the old days. I know it won't last, but I'm grateful."

"Don't tell Ash that you are throwing us a wedding. I want to surprise him. He surprised me when we got married up north."

"He sounds like a good man."

The rest of the day, Celeste helped her aunt prepare dinner. Being with her family was something she had dreamed of for the last ten years.

She thought of Ash and felt her heart tighten. He had lost his entire family, and it was her father's fault. She couldn't stop her tears. Ash should hate her, but he loved her anyway.

"What's wrong, Titine?" Marie put her hand on Celeste's shoulder.

"Tante, my father did this to our country... I carry his cursed blood. *J'suis maudite, moi* (I am cursed)."

"You are not cursed," Marie said sternly. "I don't want you to ever refer to that *connard* as your father. He's not, and he never was."

"I'm grateful for taking me in, Tante."

"Titine, you are my daughter. You are my precious legacy from my sister. I love you as much as my own boys."

"Thank you!" Celeste was crying on Marie's shoulder.

"Just promise me never to call that bastard your father. He was an abuser and a murderer first, and an invading fascist second."

"I don't consider him my father. I just wish I could cut his genes out of my body."

"You're a spitting image of your mother. I see nothing of his in you."

Celeste winced. Someone had entered the kitchen. She looked over and saw Ash.

"Are you okay, Tink?" he asked.

"We were just reminiscing." Celeste wiped her eyes. "Did you catch something?"

"Yes, we got a gator. We're about to clean it. Pierre and Joseph will show me how. I just wanted to let you know we're back."

They followed Ash outside to see the catch. It was a good-sized alligator. They had put it on a table, preparing to clean and skin it.

As soon as they saw Marie, Pierre and Joseph started talking over each other.

"You should've been there, Maman! Ash shot it with his arrow through the eye. One shot and done."

"I hate to be the Northern Alliance," Marrie muttered, but looked at Ash with open admiration.

Then she looked at Celeste and nodded approvingly.

Celeste smiled. Ash was winning over her family. Marie didn't take to outsiders easily, but Ash seemed to be an exception.

While the men were cutting up the meat, Celeste and Marie prepared bath water for them to clean up.

Later, Celeste lay in Ash's arms in bed, enjoying the warmth of his body.

"I heard what Marie said about Gabriel. He abused you?" Ash said. "You don't have to tell me if you don't want to."

"That was the reason we left him. I was young, so I didn't know at first that he was beating my mom. She kept it from me. One night, he came home and started insulting her because the dinner wasn't French enough."

Celeste took a deep breath to collect herself.

"He hit her in the face so hard that she fell to the floor," she continued. "Then he started kicking her. He wasn't drunk. He never drank. That was the first time he did that in front of me. I ran and tried to pull him away from her. He turned around, grabbed me by the neck, and started choking me, cursing and saying that I was an abomination who had injected peasant Cajun blood into his gene pool. I thought I was going to die."

Celeste squeezed Ash's hand.

"I was starting to black out when he threw me to the floor and ran out of the house. My mom quickly packed a bag, grabbed me, and took a cab to the airport. She must've been planning to leave him because she had money saved. Luckily, there was a plane departing for the United States. We boarded and left. We lived in a suburb of New Orleans. After Gabriel shot my mother, I ran out of the house and called my aunt, screaming for help. She immediately sent her brother, Uncle Marcel, to pick me up. That's my story. No matter how far I run, it catches up."

Ash sat silently, with his hands clenched into fists. He didn't speak. He couldn't.

Clement was a monster long before he destroyed America.

Ash vowed to put a bullet in him, even if it meant losing his own life.

"I should've told you all that a long time ago, but I try not to think about it." Celeste closed her eyes.

"I'm sorry, Tink." Ash wrapped his arms around her, and she leaned against his chest. "My heart hurts knowing the horrors you've lived through. Remember that if you ever feel sad, I'm here for you."

"Thank you, Ash." She kissed him. "No matter how upset I am, being in your arms calms me down. I love you more than I ever thought I was able to."

"You are my little miracle, Tink." Ash smiled and ran his fingers through her hair.

Celeste relaxed in his arms, and they made love, like two halves of the same soul. Then they held each other for hours, listening to the chirping of the crickets, the frog calls, and the alligator bellows from the bayou.

Chapter 32

Celeste opened her eyes and smiled. Ash's arm was wrapped around her shoulders, holding her to his chest. She laid a kiss on his lips. He stirred under the covers.

"It's hot," Ash mumbled and kicked the blankets off.

"*Mais*, get up now." She shook his shoulder.

"What?!" Ash jumped out of bed. "What happened?"

"We gon' drag some shrimp, sha?" She laughed and got out of bed.

"It's still dark outside."

"It's going to be a hot day. We have to move fast before a storm hits in the afternoon."

"I've always wanted to be jolted awake in Cajun lingo." He shook his head. "I was about to grab my rifle. I thought we were being attacked."

"Sorry." Celeste looked at her feet. "Sometimes I forget that you're a northerner."

"Titine, Tink," he wrapped his arms around her, "I'm just kidding. You, speaking like that, is the cutest thing. I love it. Let's get ready for shrimping."

They quickly put their clothes on and walked down to the road. Pierre and Joseph were already there, waiting for them. Pierre fired up his motorboat and steered it toward open water.

"Show Ash how to throw the trawl net," Celeste suggested.

"This is the net." Pierre pointed to a dark mass at the bottom of the boat. "First, we throw that."

They picked up the net and tossed it in. Then they lowered two boards (one on each side).

"This will spread the net evenly," Pierre explained. "There is a chain tied to the net that will drag it close to the bottom to scoop up the shrimp."

Once they had prepared the net, they sped up the boat a little.

Ash watched their every movement carefully.

This is how life is supposed to be, working together, without fear for our lives.

For a moment, the war and the Alliance seemed like a thing from another world, far away behind the northern veil.

"We'll trawl for about half an hour, and then we'll pull out the net to see what we've got." Celeste leaned against Ash.

"This is amazing!" He smiled. "No wonder you have such a free spirit."

"It's time." Pierre waved at Ash.

The men started pulling the net out.

"It's heavy," Joseph said, his voice beaming with satisfaction.

Celeste joined them. When the net emerged from the water, it was full of flipping shrimp and little fish. They opened it and emptied it into a big wooden box.

"Let's get pickin'." Celeste sat down and quickly started separating the shrimp from the small fish and crab.

Pierre and Joseph quickly joined her. They only kept the shrimp. The rest was thrown back into the water.

"You can help too, if you know what shrimp looks like." Celeste waved at Ash.

"Of course I know," he mumbled and joined them.

"We have time to trawl again." Pierre looked at the sun. "It's not too hot yet, and we can catch more to give some to the widows in town."

"We absolutely will." Ash jumped in to help with the net.

They returned to Delacroix close to noon.

Marie and a group of people met them at the pier. After the shrimp was distributed among the townspeople, Celeste and Marie took their share in the house.

"Are you ready to get cooking for your wedding?" Marie winked at her. "The boys will keep Ash busy, so he won't get wind of our plans."

"Are we doing this tonight?" Celeste's eyes widened.

"Yes. It's going to storm, so it's the perfect time. No one will come to bother us. Besides, I don't want to delay it anymore. Who knows when the Resistance will put you to work or send you back north?"

Toward mid-afternoon, it started thundering. Soon, the rain started pouring, lightning tearing through the sky.

Celeste's eyes sparkled, and she ran outside barefoot. She spread her arms and danced in the rain, laughing. The raindrops splashed against her skin with a refreshing coolness. She felt the warm ground under her feet almost pulsating like a heartbeat. Celeste twirled around engulfed by raindrops and steam that was raising from the ground.

She was home!

"What the hell are you doing?"

She felt Ash's arms around her. He scooped her up and ran with her into the house. He didn't put her down until he entered their bedroom.

"You could've been struck by lightning," he grumbled while taking off his wet clothes.

"Oh, come on." She laughed. "I missed all that up north. It was cute that you worried about me enough to kidnap me from the road."

"Celeste, you are insane!"

Ash shook his head but was unable to contain his smile. His wife was something else.

Celeste changed her clothes, sat next to him by the window, and together, they watched the storm rage.

"I haven't felt so relaxed in many years." Ash ran his fingers through Celeste's hair. "Your family knows how to have a good time."

"That they do. Why don't you go and see what the boys are doing? I'll help Tante Marie in the kitchen."

"Sorry, Tante!" Celeste looked at Marie with guilty eyes. "I got distracted."

"Uhum," Marie muttered. "If I had a loving man like you, I'd be distracted just the same. Seriously, it's strange how an intimidating man like him changes when he's around you. I'm grateful that you ended up with a good man."

Celeste blushed and looked at her feet.

"Come help me make the groom's cake."

"You have chocolate?" Celeste's eyes lit up.

"I've saved some for special occasions."

"I haven't tasted chocolate for almost ten years now."

"But didn't you say you pretended to be one of them? Surely, they have chocolate."

"I refuse to take anything from the Alliance, and I will never indulge in food that my people didn't have." Celeste frowned.

"You're an idealist, just like your mother." Marie smiled.

Finally, late in the evening, the dinner was ready.

Celeste took a bath. When she went back to her bedroom, she was surprised to see Marie sitting in there. Next to her, on the bed, was a beautiful white lace wedding dress and a veil.

"It was meant to be your mother's wedding dress," Marie sighed. "But she went off to France, and it just stayed unused. I want you to wear that dress tonight. Would you?"

Celeste ran her hand over the beautiful fabric. She felt her throat tighten.

"Yes, Tante Marie, I will wear it."

Her aunt helped her get dressed and put her hair up. Then she pinned the veil on her head.

Celeste looked in the mirror and gazed for a long time. It seemed as if she was playing dress-up in the middle of a disaster.

Damn the Alliance!

She shook her head. She was going to enjoy this night with her family despite everything.

Ash was standing outside by the beautifully arranged tables with food. He had no idea what was happening. Celeste's cousins had given him a decent-looking suit and told him to look presentable because an important celebration was taking place tonight.

The area was surrounded by lit up torches. People had gathered: relatives, friends, neighbors.

There was so much food! Marie had made a stuffed alligator loin with vegetables and potatoes as a side. There were shrimp and a pie that seemed to have crawfish inside. Several older men started playing cheerful music on guitars and an accordion, and then everybody started cheering.

Ash raised his eyes and saw Celeste coming down the stairs, with Marie on one side and an elderly man on the other.

Ash stared.

Celeste was dressed in a beautiful wedding dress that outlined every curve of her figure. A white veil cascaded down her back.

Suddenly, he understood. They were giving them a wedding.

Ash gazed at Celeste as if he were seeing her for the first time. She looked so beautiful and fragile. She was the only light in his existence. He had lost everything until she walked back into his life and revived his spirit. He smiled.

"You're already officially married, so we'll just have you jump the broom. Sauter le balai!" Marie announced.

Everybody applauded.

Marie took a hand-made broom with flowers tied to it, swept in front of Ash and Celeste, and threw the broom on the ground.

"Sauter!" She waved her hand at them.

Celeste put her hand in Ash's, and together, they jumped over the broom.

"Meet my Uncle Marcel." She pointed at the old gentleman, who had walked her down the stairs.

"Tahoma Jensen," Ash introduced himself and shook his hand.

After the main course, Marie brought out the chocolate cake.

"*Chocolate?*" Ash blinked at Celeste in disbelief.

"Yes, my aunt was saving chocolate for something special. I guess it was us."

Uncle Marcel cut the cake, and everybody took a piece. Marie wasn't done with the surprises. She had brewed a pot of chicory coffee.

"I'm in heaven!" Celeste's face glowed with happiness.

"I'm truly blown away. Thank you, Tante Marie," Ash said with gratitude. "Thank you for reminding me what it feels like to have family again."

"It's my pleasure." Marie nodded.

Celeste wrapped her arms around Ash with tears welling in her eyes. She could only imagine how he felt after having no one for years.

"Now, let's dance." Marie clapped her hands. "First, Le Bal de Noces (Wedding March)."

Holding hands, Ash and Celeste walked around the lighted area with all the guests joining. Then a slow dance played.

Ash held Celeste in his arms and danced under the southern stars. They gazed into each other's eyes, taking in the beauty of the night.

The next dance was for the parents. Ash danced with Auntie Marie, and Celeste danced with Uncle Marcel.

Despite Celeste's protests, Marie insisted that they have the money dance.

While Ash and Celeste danced, everybody approached them and pinned American dollar bills to their clothes. Celeste cried, seeing the symbolism. American money was nonexistent, but people kept the old paper bills as a reminder of the freedom they were fighting for. All her relatives and friends had lost loved ones. Now they were giving her the symbolic money, hoping for a change. She knew she would fight to her last breath to change their reality and bring back the old days.

"Your family is some of the nicest people I have ever met," Ash said later, while they lay in bed. "This night would be one of the best moments in my life."

"It was exciting marrying you again," Celeste whispered, then kissed him.

"I'd marry you every day if I could."

He pulled her to his chest.

They fell asleep tangled up with each other as if that was their first and last time together, two souls lost in borrowed time under the southern skies.

Chapter 33

Celeste was standing on the balcony, watching the sunrise. She took a deep breath. The scent of earth and sea had been her memory of home for years, and now she could feel it again. She didn't realize how much she'd missed home until they arrived in Delacroix.

She smiled.

Celeste knew it was a fragile peace, but for now, she let herself savor every fleeting second of it.

It was great that Ash had fit in just as if he were born there. He and the boys had gone out crawfishing, and she could already taste the boil they'd have for dinner.

Celeste shook her head. Better go and see if Marie needed help.

Her aunt was already up, preparing breakfast.

"What are you cooking?" Celeste asked, breathing in the sweet scent from the kitchen.

"I'm makin' some *'gâteaux aux figues and omelette aux shrimp, and café à la chicorée. T'aimes ça?'* (I'm making fig cookies, shrimp omelet, and chicory coffee. You like that?).

"'*Mais, sha*!' (You know I do!)" Celeste clapped her hands. "Do you need help, Tante Marie?"

"Well, sure. You can help me roll the *gâteaux aux figues*."

Celeste washed her hands and got to work.

Breakfast was ready right before the men returned mid-morning. They were tired and hungry, so the food disappeared quickly.

"Thank you for the delicious breakfast, especially the fig cookies. They were excellent." Ash looked at Marie.

"Oh, no, your femme made dem, sha," she said with a smirk.

Ash gave Celeste a small nod.

After breakfast, Celeste took Ash's hand and led him to the end of the road. She wrapped her arm around his waist and stood there, taking in the view from the bayou.

"You have to promise me," she looked at Ash, "that after the Alliance is gone, we'll come to visit here at least once a year."

"Absolutely!" Ash smiled. "I love it here."

"Titine!"

Celeste turned around and saw Pierre energetically waving his hand at her.

"What's up?" She quickly ran back to the house. "Something wrong?"

"No, the delegates are here. I just got the message. We have to move quickly with the meeting before the Alliance gets a sniff of it. Do you have any ideas?"

"Yes." She looked at the sky. "It's a hot day, so most likely it will come up with a storm in the afternoon. Bring the delegates to the wooded area at the Delacroix Preserve right when the storm is dwindling. I'll have someone else bring me there. The Alliance will expect us to meet early in the morning before the storms hit. That's why we'll do the opposite. The trees will shield us from drones. After the meeting is over, we'll split up. I don't want anyone to follow us to town."

"Mon Dieu, you ben smart, sha! That's perfect!" Pierre exclaimed. "That's exactly what I'll do."

Celeste nervously paced on the balcony, watching the thunderstorm rage.

"Are you going to be okay, alone with those people? "Ash gripped the stock of his rifle.

"I won't be alone. You and Joseph will take me there, and patrol the area with Pierre while I negotiate. I'm confident that the meeting will go smoothly. I will carry my revolver with me so that I won't be helpless."

"I trust you." Ash exhaled.

As soon as the lightning started to die off, Celeste, Ash, and Joseph climbed into the boat and headed to the wooded swampland. There, they met Pierre, who had already delivered the Mexican and Canadian delegates to the place of the meeting. Celeste went with him, while Ash and Joseph left to patrol the area.

Celeste looked at the two people sitting on a couple of bait buckets under the trees.

"My name is Tina Jensen," she introduced herself and sat down beside them. "I am the representative of the American Resistance. What is your language of choice for this negotiation?"

"We can talk in English. I am Miguel Castillo, representative of the Secretariat of Defense of Mexico."

"My name is Antoine Belanger, representative of the Canadian Department of National Defence."

"Thank you for coming here to speak with me. We greatly appreciate your willingness to ally with us in our efforts to remove the Alliance from our continent."

"Delegations from our countries had already met and discussed the matter. We have reached a mutual agreement. We are here today to officially deliver this message to our American counterparts," Miguel Castillo said. "I will be speaking on behalf of both countries."

Celeste looked at him, waiting for the verdict. Her stomach was in knots.

"For the last ten years, we attempted to be neutral," Castillo continued. "However, the Alliance is becoming increasingly aggressive in its annexation policies. That behavior forced us to reconsider our policies. We have decided to declare war on the Alliance. We will need your help from the inside to achieve a swift victory."

"We will assist you in any way. What do you need us to do?"

Castillo looked around, then leaned toward her and lowered his voice.

"Before we take any action, we will need you to eliminate their leader, Gabriel Clement. Our sources tell us that he is in America at the moment. This is the perfect time. Do you think your operative will be able to assassinate him?"

"Yes, it will be done. It has already been planned." Celeste felt her heart in her throat.

"Great," Castillo nodded. "As soon as that is done, and we receive the news, we will initiate our offensive. Eliminating Clement will shock the Alliance long enough not to figure out our actions. So, it is decided. This concludes our meeting. Thank you for the cooperation."

Celeste shook hands with the delegates, and they separated.

"How was it?" Ash asked.

"We'll talk later," Celeste said flatly.

Ash understood and didn't press further.

"How did the delegates manage to arrive undetected?" Celeste asked after Pierre returned.

"They sailed the Gulf of Mexico under the Mexican flag. The Canadian's French name probably helped him avoid detection when traveling to Mexico."

"Pretty smart. They sounded like they meant business." Celeste sighed. "We have to go back north soon. There's work to do."

"I wish you could stay," Pierre pouted.

"I know, cousin, I wish I could stay too. But I promise, after we're free, we'll visit often."

"Can't wait!"

For dinner, Marie had made a crawfish boil from their earlier catch. Celeste savored every bite, knowing that it would be a long time before she got a taste of home again.

"Titine, what you *tracassin'* (worrying) about?" Marie asked.

"Nothing, Tante." Celeste sighed. "Just thinking that we'll be leaving soon."

"Don't I know that?" Marie sighed. "Make sure you eat real good, sha."

Celeste ate quietly, soaking in every smile, every laugh, trying to seal them in her memory.

Ash watched her closely. Since returning from the meeting, something about her had shifted. A dark cloud seemed to hang over her. He felt his stomach knot up. What had they told her?

"Are you able to tell me about today?" he asked later, when they lay in bed.

"Yes, I can tell you." Celeste pressed her lips together. "Before they take action against the Alliance, they want us to eliminate Gabriel."

"Well, I'm sure Hayes will send a team."

"You know that's not how it will go." Celeste shook her head. "If someone's going to do it, it's going to be me. I have the best chance; besides, I have an old score to settle with him."

"Tink... please reconsider. He'll kill you."

"He can try."

"I don't want you to put yourself in danger."

"I might have no choice. You know that the safety of the entire Resistance camp is at stake. I just hope Hayes had the sense to move the camp. But either way, if I attempt to hide, Gabriel will lay waste to every Resistance camp he knows about."

"Tink, there has to be another way."

"Ash, I was damned from the very beginning. That's why I never told you about Gabriel. Ever since I joined the Resistance, the plan was to eliminate Gabriel as my final act."

"No, I won't accept that! I won't let you walk into his trap alone." Ash shook his head sharply and got out of bed. He clenched his hands while pacing restlessly back and forth. "I won't allow you to sacrifice your life. I can't lose you."

Celeste gazed at Ash. His breathing was ragged, his chest rising rapidly.

She closed her eyes. Celeste never wanted to hurt him, but she could see no other option.

"Ash, come here."

He sat by her and wrapped his arms around her.

"Don't be upset." She laid her head on his chest. "We still have time. Maybe we can figure something out."

"We will figure something else," he said sharply. "I'd be damned if I allow that fascist to take your life."

"I know you won't." Celeste smiled. "Ash, you are the best thing that has happened to me. I don't deserve you."

"You deserve the best, Tink." Ash kissed her. "You are an amazing woman. I wish you could see it too."

Celeste didn't say anything. She just cuddled up to him. She decided not to bring up Gabriel in front of Ash. She was afraid he'd do something stupid in his typical Ash way. The plan had to be executed perfectly as the entire offensive against the Alliance relied on it. Celeste knew that she was the only person who could achieve that. However, that moment belonged to the north, and here they were under the southern skies of Louisiana.

"I love you, Ash!" She pulled him into bed next to her. "I just want you tonight. Let's forget everything else."

"You read my mind, love."

He pulled her close to his chest.

Chapter 34

Celeste woke up at sunrise. She decided that they had to leave for Wyoming as soon as possible, so she packed their things. Again, to prevent them from being spotted by the Alliance, they were going to depart at the tail end of the storm.

Ash had left with Pierre and Joseph for one last shrimp drag, and Celeste decided to spend her last hours in Delacroix with her aunt.

"I'll miss you, Titine." Marie squeezed her hand. "You coming here was like sunlight breaking through an afternoon storm."

"I have never been as happy as I was in the last few days." Celeste smiled. "I had forgotten how it feels to be back home. I want to spend the last of my time here with you."

"Would you like to come with me to our garden to pick some tomatoes and peaches for the tea?"

"Of course, I'd like that. I remember your garden being on the side of your house."

"Now we have all our produce growing into the wetlands beyond the limits of our town. That way, Alliance drones can't pick up on what we have. What the Alliance doesn't know, it doesn't want."

Marie led Celeste out of town into the uninhabited areas of the island between marshes and cypress trees.

"My cousins and I used to come down here to play." Celeste smiled.

"I know you did, even though I told you not to. Little children are perfect snacks for the cocodries."

Soon, they reached a clearing. Celeste's eyes widened. There was a large garden with tomatoes and other vegetables. Several peach trees were strategically placed at the edges of the garden.

The women quickly began filling their baskets.

"How many of those gardens are around here?" Celeste asked and took a bite from a juicy peach.

"Almost every family has its own garden, except for the elderly. We feed them. There's plenty to go around. We take care of one another. *'Tu sais, hein, sha?'* (You know, right?)"

"I missed our Creole tomatoes." Celeste picked out the ripest ones and filled a basket. "You can't get those up north."

"I could never understand why you wanted to go to school all the way in Boston?" Marie stopped picking peaches and sat on the ground.

"I was young and stupid." Celeste sighed. "I just wanted to see the big cities. I wish I had stayed here. On the other hand, if I did, I would've never met Dave or Ash. I guess everything happens for a reason."

"I didn't think you'd remain friends with Hayes. He's very strange."

"Dave's a good guy. He saved my life many times. He's like a brother to me."

"I'm grateful there are people who care about you. All those years, I cried every time I thought of you. I believed that there was no chance you survived the war. Especially the thought of the connard out there, probably looking for you."

"Once the war started, he found me fast. The fool actually thought that I'd go back to the man who murdered my mother. It's hard, Tante Marie. I've used him to our interests, but every time I talk to him, I want to empty my revolver in his face. One of these days, probably soon, I will."

"Please, be careful!" Marie's eyes darkened. "I don't want to lose you."

"Let's hope for the best, but you must know that I will ensure Gabriel dies, even at the cost of my life."

Marie just dropped her head.

"I'm sorry, Tante," Celeste whispered. "I couldn't lie to you."

"I know, Titine. I'm just hoping for a miracle."

"Okay, let's hurry up before the boys come back." Celeste stood up.

Soon, they returned to town with baskets full of tomatoes, vegetables, and peaches.

Celeste helped Marie make breakfast and tea.

The men returned mid-morning. After they finished eating, Celeste and Ash went to their bedroom to finish packing.

"Whatever happened with your aunt's husband?" Ash asked.

"Her husband?" Celeste gave him a bewildered look. "Tante Marie was never married. She lived with a man, Pierre and Joseph's father, but they weren't married. His name was Benoit. One day, he went fishing and never came back. They found his boat abandoned in the bayou the next day. Officially, everybody believes that he fell over and was probably eaten by the *cocodries*. However, the whispered rumors are that he was tired of being a father and ran off to New Orleans."

"What do you believe?"

"Honestly, Uncle Benoit loved tipping the bottle. He definitely fell over and got eaten by the *cocodries*. Tante Marie loved him very much, so she never took another man in. Believe me, she had plenty of suitors."

"Oh, I believe that." Ash laughed. "Your aunt is something else."

"That she is."

Celeste winced. Someone was pounding on the door.

She opened it and saw Pierre.

"There are two Alliance speedboats on their way to the island," he said quickly. "I wanted to see if Ash would join us to hunt them down."

"I'll be right down."

Ash quickly grabbed his rifle and his bow.

"I'll come with you." Celeste snapped her revolver's holster around her thigh.

"No, you should stay here. Don't leave your aunt alone."

"You know what? You're right. Be careful."

She kissed him and went to find her aunt.

Ash met Pierre and Joseph by the dock. Most of the men in the village were already armed and boarding their boats.

Ash raised his eyebrows. He'd had the impression that the people here were mostly anglers and gardeners. Now he realized that every single one of them was a member of the Resistance.

He felt a tiny jolt of jealousy in his heart. People up north weren't as united. Now he knew where Celeste got her courage. He felt overjoyed with pride in being married to her.

"So, what's the plan?" Ash asked.

"Most of our men will hide in the swamplands. We and a couple of other boats will trick the Alliance patrols into following us to the swamps, where the rest of our people will ambush them. They'll be trapped, and we'll take them out."

"Good plan." Ash checked his rifle.

Pierre continued to steer the boat toward open water. They were just coming around a bend in the marsh when they saw the two Alliance boats.

As soon as they saw the small motorboat, the patrolmen sent several rounds of automatic fire their way.

"Get down!" Joseph yelled at Ash while Pierre steered the boat back into the marshes.

Pierre continued to swerve, trying to keep cover, so they wouldn't get riddled with bullets.

When they entered the swamplands, they hid between the trees and watched the two boats slowly pass them. The patrol was searching for their motorboat.

As soon as the Alliance boats were deep enough in the swamps, suddenly, the rest of the vessels appeared as if out of thin air and surrounded them.

Pierre and the other bait boat moved to cut their way out.

Ash pulled back his bow.

Pierre shook his head and gestured for him to lower the bow. Bewildered, Ash followed his order.

He looked back at the Alliance boats and saw several smoking glass bottles streak through the air and explode on the boats. Within minutes, the Alliance patrol boats were engulfed in fire. To escape the smoke and heat, the soldiers jumped overboard, and the alligators immediately charged at them.

Ash saw one of the soldiers trying to swim to Pierre's boat. He reached down, grabbed him by the shirt, and pulled him into the boat.

"What the hell are you doing?" Pierre hissed. "We don't take prisoners."

"We'll interrogate him. Then... well, you know."

The soldier looked at them, blinking at the sound of their conversation in French.

"He doesn't speak French?" Ash asked.

"No, most Alliance soldiers around here speak German."

"Well, that's interesting," Ash muttered.

Then he looked back at the soldier.

"Hey, hey! '*Schau mich an.*' (Look at me)." Ash snapped his fingers and asked in German.

"'*Bitte, hab Gnade!*' (Please, have mercy!)" The soldier clasped his hands.

"What are you doing here? Talk or I'll cut your throat." Ash pulled out his knife and put it against the soldier's neck.

"We're just a decoy. We weren't going to hurt anyone."

"Decoy for what?" Ash felt his heart tighten.

"We were told to draw you out of the village and give you a runaround just long enough for the drones to arrive."

Gabriel Clement!

Ash suddenly remembered how Clement had threatened him on Amnestic to draw the armed men out of the Resistance camp. He felt his blood run cold. Somehow, Clement must've learned about Celeste's family. The Alliance was going to lay waste to Delacroix.

"Piece of shit!"

Ash grabbed the soldier's head, twisted sharply, and snapped his neck. Then, he pushed the body into the water.

"Bon Dieu! Ash, what the hell?" Pierre jumped back away from Ash.

"The bastards are going to bomb the town. They lured us out and left the town defenseless, with no boats to escape. He said the drones are already en route."

As soon as he said that, they saw the drones fly over their heads toward Delacroix. The mechanical hum of the machines echoed through the silence of the bayou.

"Hurry up, let's go!"

Ash felt like someone's hand had locked around his throat. Celeste was there, not suspecting a thing.

Pierre set a course toward the island at maximum speed. They were only halfway there when the explosions echoed.

Ash fell to his knees and gripped the rifle with his heart beating out of his chest.

Hurry up!

He was at the nose of the boat, scanning the horizon. He wasn't sure what to hope for, but he was hoping.

She wanted to come with me, and I made her stay.

When the village came into view, Ash felt as if someone had kicked him in the chest. Delacroix lay in ruins. He jumped out of the boat onto the dock and ran toward Marie's house.

"Celeste!"

He cried out her name, his voice hoarse and desperate.

No one answered.

He remembered how he had argued with her over putting herself in danger, trying to eliminate Clement. If he had just known this would happen today...

It felt like a cruel joke of fate.

Chapter 35

sh ran into the rubble and started digging with his bare hands. Pierre and Joseph followed him.

Please, Tink, be all right!

His breath caught in his throat, and he felt hot tears rolling down his face.

I should've known!

"Mais, stop diggin'!"

Ash snapped his head around and saw Celeste, Marie, and the rest of the townspeople emerging from the swamplands.

He jumped to his feet, ran to Celeste, and grabbed her in his arms.

"I thought you were dead!"

"We would've all been dead, but I remembered what Gabriel pulled at our camp and told Marie to take everybody out of town."

"She's our hero." Marie patted her on the back. "She saved us all."

"No, Tante Marie. Because of me, everyone's homes were destroyed."

"Stop tracassin' yourself. We have temporary tree houses out in the wilderness. We'll stay there until we rebuild. Won't be the first time, won't be the last."

"We have to leave now." Celeste looked at Ash.

"It's going to be hard." Ash sighed. "The Alliance will probably be right on us. They must've found out we're here."

"I have an idea." Pierre scratched the back of his head. "I'll take you down to Hopedale. One of ours has a small plane that we captured from the Alliance. It won't raise alarms. He can fly you to Oklahoma. I will arrange someone to wait for you there and fly you to Wyoming."

"That's great. We can make good time." Ash nodded his head.

"Don't tell anyone that we survived the bombing." Celeste looked at Pierre. "Let them think we're all dead. If they think the job's done, they won't come back to finish it."

"What about Hayes?"

"He'll be alright."

"What are we going to do with your truck?" Pierre asked.

"It seems that you have an extra truck." Ash laughed. "I guess Hayes has to get over it."

"I saved our bags." Celeste pointed to their travel bags.

"I guess you thought of everything."

"Tante Marie," Celeste said, looking at her aunt. "Can I take my mom's picture with me? I promise, next time I come down here I'll bring it back."

"Yes, Titine, you can have it. It's yours."

"I'm also taking my mom's wedding dress."

"It actually is your wedding dress." Marie laughed.

"Okay, we have to go before we cause any more trouble."

"Titine." Marie embraced her. "Please, take care of yourself."

"I promise."

Celeste hesitated for a second, gazing at her aunt. This was probably the last time they'd see each other. She took a deep breath and, holding back tears, picked up her bag. Then she headed to Pierre's boat.

"Can I talk to you?" Marie put her hand on Ash's shoulder.

"Anything, Tante Marie."

"Please, promise me you will keep Celeste safe. I can't lose her the way I lost my sister. I still remember Titine screaming on the phone 'Daddy killed mommy. Help me!' Please, don't let that monster take my little girl away from me." Marie couldn't stop her tears.

"I promise to protect her with my life." Ash put his hands on her shoulders. "You have my word."

As he was walking away, Ash turned his head and gave Marie a nod, reinforcing his promise.

Pierre set a course for Hopedale.

They arrived about forty minutes later.

A man was already waiting for them.

Celeste hugged Pierre and waved goodbye to him.

Once the plane took off, Celeste rested her head on Ash's shoulder and closed her eyes. The guilt weighed on her chest. They had caused the destruction of an entire town. The people didn't seem upset about it, or at least didn't show it. They must've considered the negotiations important enough to risk their homes and lives.

Celeste had to admit, the Southern Resistance was stronger than the groups up north.

"What are you thinking about?" Ash wrapped his arm around her shoulders.

"Everybody around me is in danger. I think Gabriel is keeping tabs on me."

"Tink, you scared me today," Ash whispered. "I thought you were dead."

"I'm sorry."

"You don't have to apologize. Also, stop blaming yourself for that psychopath stalking you."

"I'll try. Please, hold me. All my troubles go away when I'm in your arms."

Ash kissed her on the top of the head and pulled her closer to his body.

She relaxed and slowly fell asleep.

Celeste woke up when they landed in Oklahoma. Another Resistance member was already waiting for them at the airstrip.

Celeste stood for a minute on the concrete airstrip and took a deep breath. Her heart was breaking from leaving her family, but at the same time, she couldn't wait to return to the Resistance camp in the mountains and Hayes. He was probably worried sick after hearing about the bombing in Delacroix.

On the new plane, Celeste was unable to go back to sleep. The closer to Wyoming they got, the more anxious she felt. They arrived just before sunrise. The pilot landed on a small airstrip outside Dubois. A truck was already parked there for them.

"Let's go to my cabin for now," Ash said as he sat behind the wheel. "Tomorrow we'll find Hayes."

Celeste nodded. She was exhausted.

Ash parked off the main path and slung his rifle and bow across his back. Then they picked up all their luggage and hiked up the mountain.

When they were close to the cabin, Ash told Celeste to sit down, and he went to scout the area.

"No one has found my cabin yet. Let's go."

He patted Celeste on the shoulder.

Once inside the cabin, she sagged down in bed and immediately fell asleep. Ash lay beside her but remained awake. He didn't want to risk getting ambushed in his sleep.

Celeste opened her eyes. She had no idea what time it was. She looked around, but Ash wasn't inside.

She got out of bed, washed her face, and stepped outside.

Celeste took a deep breath. The air was so sweet, saturated with the scent of herbs, pine resin, and moss. She loved her family in Delacroix, but this cabin was home. Here she felt safe and at peace.

Now she saw Ash coming out from between the trees.

"Everything seems calm around us. Do you like mushrooms?" He set a bagful of mushrooms on the deck.

"Yes, I eat mushrooms." She shrugged. "Are you cooking for me?"

"I sure am. Come on, I'll teach you my recipe."

He cleaned the mushrooms and some greens he had picked.

"I like to put stinging nettle and some rice in my mushroom soup," Ash explained, while chopping the onion. "I hope you like it."

"It smells good," Celeste said, breathing in the steam, when the soup started simmering.

"I think it's ready." Ash took the pot off the stove.

"That was really good," she said, finishing her bowl in no time. "How can you cook so well?"

"I've lived alone for ten years. I've learned how to feed myself. However, cooking for you makes it a hundred times more enjoyable."

"Your soup tastes like the mountains. I love it. I'm glad to be home."

"I'm glad you think of my little shack as home." Ash laughed. "Even though I don't have all the amenities your aunt did."

"I like your bath better. It will be a while before my people down south rebuild their homes. I cost them their comfort."

"This was a Resistance assignment. We were all invested."

"I guess you have a point, but I can't help it."

"Look, my aunt let me keep my mom's picture." Celeste took the photo out of her travel bag and set it on the table.

"You should have it." Ash nodded.

"I also brought my wedding dress. You can hang it up next to your fancy suit."

Ash laughed and shook his head.

"I can go for a warm bath. What do you say?"

Celeste grabbed Ash by the hand and pulled him up.

Later, they lay in bed, cuddled up to each other.

"For everything we went through... I think this trip was worth it," Celeste said. "The negotiations were a success. Gaining our freedom never seemed so realistic."

"I don't know." Ash sighed. "If the price for it is your life, I don't think I want anything to do with it."

"Ash." Celeste sat up in bed. "We aren't fighting for us. We are fighting for everybody. Just think about all those children in the camp, freezing in tents during winter and dying from weaponized flu. Those are the people I'm fighting for. I want to be a family with you for a long time, but if giving my life is what it takes for everybody to live theirs, I'm willing to."

"I love you, Tink!" Ash took her in his arms. "I admire you for everything you are."

"I will make every minute with you count."

She caressed his face.

Ash found her lips and kissed her, absorbing every trace of jasmine scent radiating from her.

Then they made love under the dim light of the oil lamp.

Ash took Celeste in his arms, feeling the warmth of her body and the soft sensation of her skin pressing against his. Her breath brushed against his chest. She had told him that she was ready to give her life for their cause, but he knew one thing: if someone wanted to take her, they'd have to go through Ash first. He had promised so to Tante Marie, and he was going to keep his word.

Chapter 36

Celeste woke up in the morning with the feeling of Ash's arms around her. She smiled. Being held by him always felt like home. His love was all she needed in her life to be happy.

She ran her fingers along the side of his face and kissed him.

Ash opened his eyes and gazed into hers.

"I love you, Tink," he whispered and kissed her back.

"We have to go back to camp and let Dave know that we are alive. He's probably going insane. I also have to brief him on the negotiations."

"Okay, we'll get going as soon as I fully wake up."

"Can I leave my things in your cabin?"

"Celeste," Ash laughed, "you're my wife. This is our cabin. Of course, you can leave your stuff here."

"Sorry," she said with a guilty smile. "I still have to get used to the fact that we are married."

"You mean two weddings didn't do the trick?"

Laughing, Ash got out of bed.

Celeste dressed and sat in the chair at the table.

"What's wrong, Tink?" Ash gazed at her. "You look like something's bothering you."

"I'm worried about my family. We left them in ruins."

"I know," Ash sighed. "I promise, once we put everything in motion here, we'll go back to Delacroix to help them."

"Promise me," Celeste grabbed his hand, "that if something happens to me, you wouldn't forget about them."

"Nothing will happen to you," Ash said curtly.

Celeste started to object, but she stopped herself and just sighed.

The best thing was not to argue with Ash.

In an hour, they left the cabin and hiked down the mountain. They moved carefully, looking for a possible ambush by Alliance patrols. The mountain was quiet, no soul in sight.

The air was heating up. It was going to be a hot summer day.

Celeste took a deep breath of the familiar scent of herbs and pine resin. She equally loved the bayou and the mountains, so different and at the same time so close to her heart.

She thought about what it would've been if the war had never happened. She would definitely still be living in New York City, working as a surgeon, and she would've never met Ash.

Celeste bitterly smiled. She would gladly go through all her hardships and suffering, all over again, just to have Ash in her life.

She gritted her teeth. Gabriel was going to ruin everything. She hated him! He was the cause of everybody's suffering. She had always suspected that he led the invasion of America as revenge for his American wife escaping his torture.

Celeste swallowed hard. She had to kill him. She owed that much to her people for carrying his cursed blood.

Ash frowned. He could feel Celeste's torment with every fiber in his body. He wished he could just absorb her pain, but all he could do was protect her from physical harm.

"I'm here for you, Tink." He found her hand and took it in his.

"Thank you, Ash."

She looked at him and smiled.

Ash drove carefully, choosing back roads to avoid checkpoints.

When they entered the camp, Celeste gasped.

The entire camp was destroyed. All buildings and tents were torched.

Celeste jumped out of the truck and ran to the middle of camp. Helplessly, she stood, watching the wind twirl the ashes.

Her breath caught in her throat. She felt suffocation. Had Gabriel killed everybody out of spite?

"There are no bodies."

She heard Ash's voice.

"They must've left before the camp was torched. We have to find them."

"I don't know where they might've gone."

"I do." Ash rubbed his forehead. "There is a contingency plan in case this location is compromised. Hayes must've moved camp immediately after we left. These ruins look old. This didn't just happen."

"Let's go." Celeste headed to the truck. "I have to talk to Dave."

When they approached the new location, Ash parked about a mile away.

"Let's approach on foot," he suggested.

"I don't know what I'm walking into, so we've got to be careful."

Ash saw the guards and crouched down. He signaled Celeste to circle the posts so no one would see them.

Now, they saw the tents. It looked like everybody was fine.

"I don't see any Alliance soldiers," Ash muttered.

"Okay, let's find Hayes."

As soon as they entered the camp, everybody surrounded them. Celeste spotted Rose and her son. She noticed something in the woman's eyes that resembled fear.

"We thought you were dead," Rose said, wringing her hands.

"Where's Hayes?" Celeste asked.

"We don't know. He vanished yesterday."

"What do you mean?" Celeste felt her stomach wrench.

"He went to the old camp to look for something and never came back. We think he was ambushed by an Alliance patrol." Mary looked away.

Celeste closed her eyes and took a deep breath.

"Where's his tent?" she asked.

Rose directed them to the tent Hayes was staying in.

“I need to talk to you,” Celeste said, pulling Ash by the hand. “Let’s go outside camp.”

Wondering what she had in mind, he followed her.

Celeste walked about half a mile into the woods and sat on the ground.

Ash sat next to her, waiting patiently for her explanation.

“We have a mole in the camp,” she whispered.

“How do you know?”

“Gabriel knew we went to Delacroix. There was no way the Alliance just randomly bombed the town. And now, all of a sudden, Dave is captured. Someone must’ve given him up. He is careful. He would’ve never carelessly exposed himself. Someone sent him to the old camp, where an Alliance patrol was already waiting.”

“Shit!” Ash swore. “How are we going to find out who’s the mole?”

“I already know who it is.”

“Who?” Ash raised his eyebrows.

“It’s Rose.”

“Mountain dweller, Rose? Why would you suspect her?”

“I don’t suspect her. I know. She’s been the one constant in every mishap. First, we got ambushed at her house in the mountains. That was probably Gabriel’s strategy to embed her within our camp. We took her there ourselves. Then she was here when we left for Louisiana. And again, she was still in the camp when Hayes disappeared. I watched her while talking a little bit ago. Her body language screamed guilt and fear.”

“We have to eliminate her, but how? She has a little child.” Ash frowned.

"We aren't killing Rose." Celeste shook her head. "She was probably blackmailed to spy for them. Gabriel is ruthless. He most likely threatened the life of her son."

"So, what do you suggest we do?"

"I will remove her from the camp. I'll take her to Ravenville. Hopefully, they're holding Hayes there. I have to free him."

"No way. I can't let you do that. That moron Rognon's going to kill you. You bashed his head with a bottle."

"I can handle him."

"I'm coming with you."

"You can't. I have to go alone."

"Celeste, please!"

"You have to trust me, Ash. There is no other way."

"What if Clement is there?"

"Well, if that's the case, I guess it's a win-win," Celeste said with a faint smile.

Ash closed his eyes, trying to slow down his pounding heart. There was no way he'd let Celeste go into that lion's den alone.

"You're going to follow me, aren't you?" She frowned.

"You know it."

"Okay, you can follow me, but make sure Rose doesn't see you. I'll use all my Alliance credentials to save Dave, and you will blow my cover."

"What credentials are you talking about?"

"I have an Alliance-issued passport under the name Celestine Clement."

"How come I didn't find it when I searched your documents the day I met you?"

"I didn't have it on me. It was in my stuff at camp. I carried it with me when we left for Louisiana. It's my strongest Ace, but I've never used it before. I will now."

"I understand." He nodded. "I'll stay invisible. I'm good at it. I won't interfere unless you're in danger. Deal?"

"Deal." Celeste stood up and shook the grass off her clothes. "Let's go get that done before they ship Hayes off to Denver."

When they returned to camp, Celeste pretended that she was completely unaware of Rose's involvement.

Celeste went to check out the new hospital.

Hayes had done a good job of moving everything. They had made a large dugout for the new hospital, similar to the one in the old camp.

She felt her heart tighten.

I hope Dave is okay.

If something happened to him, she'd never forgive herself. It was Ash and she who brought Rose to camp. On the other hand, that was the only reasonable option at the time.

Gabriel is an evil genius, but not for long.

Celeste returned to Hayes's tent and packed her travel bag. Then she went to find Rose.

The woman was in the kitchenette, heating water to make noodles for her son.

Celeste patiently waited for the child to finish eating, pretending she was making lunch for herself.

When the child finished eating, Celeste approached them.

"Walk with me," she whispered to Rose.

The woman immediately knew. Her face drained of color.

"Please," she mouthed.

Her eyes darted to her son, like she could shield him from what was coming.

Tears ran down her face.

"Let's go. Say one word, and the whole camp will know what you are."

Trembling, Rose followed her to one of Hayes's trucks.

Celeste had the woman and her son buckle in, then she left camp and drove to Ravenville.

Ash looked at Celeste's truck vanishing down the road with his stomach in a painful spasm.

"No way she's going there alone." He shook his head, waited a few minutes, grabbed his rifle and bow, and followed them in his truck.

Chapter 37

Celeste drove in silence for most of the way.

Rose was quietly crying.

Celeste snapped her head around and looked at her.

"Please, don't hurt us!" the woman whispered, clutching her son's hand. "I didn't have a choice. They threatened to kill my son and me both if I didn't cooperate."

"How long have you been an informant?" Celeste asked coldly.

"For several years now. I'm sorry."

Celeste took a deep breath. She was angry with Rose but understood her situation. She probably would've done the same if her child's life were at stake.

"Your cover is compromised. You weren't careful."

"You're going to kill me," Rose whispered. "Okay, I get it. I deserve to die. Just, please, spare my son!"

"I'm not going to kill you. I'm taking you to Ravenville. You can no longer stay at camp. If anyone else found out, you'd be history."

"How come you're so merciful? You're Hayes's closest, if not only, friend, and I betrayed him. I also gave up your family's location in Louisiana."

"Just count your lucky stars that I was the one who found you out," Celeste muttered, trying to collect herself.

The thought that Rose almost got her family killed was making her blood boil.

When they reached the checkpoint, Celeste switched off the engine.

As soon as the soldier saw her face, he promptly drew his revolver and pointed it at her.

Celeste put her hands on the steering wheel and let them cuff her hands.

"Who are they?" The soldier pointed at Rose and her son.

"Those are your spies. I was returning them to you. Better put them up before someone arrives to execute them."

"You allowed us to capture you to save our spies?" The soldier gave her a bewildered look. "I don't understand."

"You don't need to," Celeste said coldly.

The soldier just shook his head and dragged her to one of their vehicles.

When they arrived in Ravenville, they walked her to the jailhouse and pushed her into the cell.

Celeste found herself face-to-face with Hayes.

"Celeste!" he exclaimed. "You are alive. Thank God! I thought you and Ash were both killed in Delacroix."

"Well, we weren't. Glad to see you're alive too."

Celeste stepped back and gazed at Hayes. His face was bruised and bloodied.

"Why did they beat you?"

"No reason. Anyway... why did you get yourself captured? Miss me that much?" He playfully winked at her.

"You thought I'd just let them execute you?"

"That's the protocol. You know that. If one of us is captured, we have to let them go."

"Was that why you and Ash chased the Devil to find me when I was captured?"

"Touché!" he laughed. "So what now?"

"Now we try not to get killed."

Celeste turned her head toward the door. Rognon had just walked in. She could see the scars from glass laceration on the side of his head.

"I knew I'd put my hands on you again," he sneered at Celeste.

"Play dead," Celeste whispered to Hayes, grabbed him by the hair, and slammed his head against the metal bars of the cell.

He dropped to the floor.

"Why the hell did you beat up your coconspirator?" Rognon's eyes widened. "You're insane."

"Watch your mouth when you're talking to me, you pervert."

She looked at him with contempt.

"This time, I'll have the upper hand."

Rognon drew his revolver and pointed it at her. Then he opened the cell door and yanked her out by the arm.

"I can shoot you right now. Give me one good reason not to do it."

"How about looking in my bag?"

"Interesting." He took her travel bag from the side of the chair where the soldiers had hung it and unzipped it.

"What exactly am I supposed to find in here?"

"A passport."

Rognon found the document, opened it, and immediately dropped it on the floor as if it burned his hands.

Celeste just smiled and raised an eyebrow.

"You're... his daughter?" he stuttered.

"Uhum, I'm Gabriel's daughter dearest."

"Why... why did you hit me in the head then? I don't get it."

"I'm in deep cover within the Resistance. You morons are repeatedly trying to blow my cover, including Gabriel. My patience is wearing thin. I brought you back your store-brand spy. If it wasn't for the child, I would've blown her brains out, but I understand you blackmailed her. This is very irresponsible of you. You almost compromised my cover."

"I'm sorry." Rognon was visibly shaken. "Please, don't tell your father."

"You're all morons." Celeste narrowed her eyes. "You didn't even question whether my passport is real. I could be lying to you."

"I know you're Clement's daughter. I can see the resemblance in your eyes."

Celeste felt his words like a freezing slap across her face.

My eyes resemble Gabriel's?

She took a deep breath.

"Fine. I expect you to set up my escape and his." She gestured toward Hayes.

"You want us to let him go?" Rognon's eyes widened. "He's one of the Resistance's leaders."

"Precisely. I've been working him for years. He'd die for me. I need him as an asset. You almost ruined several years of my work. My father will be furious."

"Please, I'll fix it, just don't tell him."

"Okay, I won't, but he still might find out. One of yours will eventually blab. Then I can't protect you. Gabriel doesn't tolerate incompetence."

"Thank you! Thank you so much! I'll make sure no one talks. It will be like this never happened."

"Okay. And stay away from the camp. If Hayes feels he's being watched, he'll delegate assignments elsewhere, and we'll end up with no intel."

"Understood, Mademoiselle Clement." Rognon bowed his head. "So, how do we do that?"

"Take us out in the woods as if you are going to execute us. There is one of the Rebels trailing me. He will start shooting. Try to escape without being killed. This is the best option. Don't brief your soldiers. It must look legit. However, it's your job to make sure your people don't shoot us."

"Yes, madam. I'll get everything ready." The officer left the room.

"Goddamn it, Celeste!" Hayes sat up, rubbing his head. "You are ridiculous...That's a compliment by the way."

"Sorry for hitting your head." She smiled while quickly checking his head.

"With you, that's just another Tuesday," he muttered with a half-smile.

In a couple of hours, the officer and a small patrol group pulled Celeste and Hayes out of their cell and cuffed their hands.

Without explanation, they loaded them in one of their vehicles and drove them out of town. Then they forced them to hike to a clearing in the woods.

"To your knees!" Rognon commanded.

As she knelt, Celeste noticed that the officer took cover behind his soldiers.

They pointed their rifles at Celeste and Hayes. She took a deep breath to slow down her heart. If one of those soldiers was impatient...

Suddenly, several quick shots echoed. Half of the soldiers fell to the ground. Rognon gave a command to retreat, and the rest of the patrol disappeared between the trees.

Celeste grabbed her bag that Rognon had left on the ground and ran in the opposite direction. Hayes followed right behind her. They ran into Ash.

"Hurry!" he waved his hand. "The truck is not far from here."

They all jumped in the vehicle, and Ash peeled out.

Celeste unzipped her bag and found the keys for the cuffs, left there by Rognon. She uncuffed herself and threw the keys to Hayes.

"What?" Ash's eyes widened.

"Rognon brought his people into your ambush willingly." Celeste laughed. "It was all a fake. He peed a little when he saw my passport.

He's terrified of Gabriel. I told him that Clement will be furious about their incompetence. I'm sure he'll keep his mouth shut."

"You're something else." Ash looked at her with a sparkle in his eye.

"By the way," Celeste glanced at Hayes. "You had a mole in camp. It was Rose that we brought with us from the mountains. Sorry about that."

"What did you do with her?"

"I removed her. She's back to Ravenville, safe with her son."

"You didn't kill her?" Hayes raised his eyebrows.

"I'm not a monster, Dave. She was forced to do it. They threatened her child's life."

"You're a better person than I am," he muttered. "I would've eliminated her."

"Sometimes, sparing a life is better. If I were in her place, I probably would've done the same."

"We have to move camp again." Hayes frowned.

"Yes, we do." Celeste nodded.

"We have to scout for a location."

"I know a perfect place," Ash interrupted them. "I know the area. There is a secluded valley not too far from my cabin. It's accessible by road, but it's tucked between two ravines, so there's only one road leading in. It will be easy to protect and difficult to find."

"Perfect!" Hayes rubbed his hands together. "We can start moving immediately. Thank you both. You saved my life."

"Of course we did." Celeste turned around and punched him in the shoulder. "Tante Marie says hi. She called you a 'cuyon' for telling Ash to shoot me."

"Of course she did." Hayes smiled. "Your auntie's the best."

"You've met her family?" Ash turned his head and looked at Hayes, narrowing his eyes.

Hayes smirked, clearly enjoying himself. "Oh, don't get jealous now. It was a long time ago, before the war. One summer, Celeste took me with her to Delacroix. I don't think her family ever fully accepted me, but they were a lot of fun and fed me very well. It was an eternity ago, anyway."

"I'm not jealous," Ash grumbled.

Hayes just shook his head, chuckling. Ash would never change. And thank God for that.

Chapter 38

As soon as they arrived at the camp, Hayes hugged Celeste and Ash.

"I'm so damn glad you are alive!" he blurted out. "My heart was broken when I heard that Delacroix was destroyed. Probably, that was the reason I let my guard down and got ambushed. Of course, you'd come through and save me. I don't care what you have to say. I love you both."

"Okay." Ash huffed. "I can't say I love you, but if you died, I'd be furious."

Ash turned around and walked away.

"I'm shocked!" Hayes blinked. "I thought he hated me."

"He'd never admit it, but he cares about you. Now that we're married, you're his brother too."

Hayes smiled. He considered himself blessed.

It took them two weeks to move the entire camp. They worked mostly at night to ensure that no one was monitoring their movements.

"It will take us a while to rebuild everything." Hayes frowned.

"I'll lead your building team," Ash suggested.

"Are you sure you can handle it?"

"Hayes, I'm an engineer, I can build a few shacks."

"You're an engineer?" Hayes's eyes widened.

"My MOS was 12N and 17X, not to brag. You fix people; I fix structures. See, we are similar in a way, except that my mistakes lie above ground, while yours go under."

"Good one, Mister Jester." Hayes laughed. "Okay, you can lead the building crew."

"I guess marriage looks good on Ash," Hayes said later, while Celeste and he were working on the new hospital.

"What made you say that?" She tilted her head and smiled.

"He made a joke earlier, a good one at that. Besides, I had no idea that he was an engineer and a veteran. I thought he was only good at... ending people."

"He can do that too, professionally. He never told you he was a SEAL?"

"He was? No, he never told me anything. I thought he was just a local mountain man."

"No, he fought the war. He also speaks fluent French and German, as far as I know. I don't think he likes to brag much."

"I must say, he has my respect."

"Wow, you've evolved, Dave."

"Stop it, Celeste! You know I love you both."

"I know, sha. We love you too."

The dirt road leading to the camp split off from the main road. Once everything was moved from the old campsite, Ash built a wooden movable frame with bushes woven into it to serve as a gate. He installed the gate to camouflage the entrance. From the outside, it looked like a natural brush, so no one would suspect there was an accessible road beyond it.

Ash's crew built small wooden homes for all families. It took them most of the summer to finish the project, but everything was done before the cold months started.

"Finally, I don't have to share a house with Hayes," he grumbled. "I like privacy when lying in bed with my wife, without having to hear his snoring next door."

"What about him?"

"We built him an office with adjacent living quarters. I'm not going to leave him out in the cold. I even included a small fireplace in each one of the houses. I know you hate that people have to shiver all winter long."

"I love you, Ash!" Celeste threw her arms around him. "You're the best."

"I'm happy when you're happy." He smiled and kissed her.

Celeste took several trips to towns in the area to stock up on medical supplies. With all the moving of camps, their supplies were running thin. She avoided Dubois out of fear that Gabriel was monitoring her old house.

The camp was fully built by the end of September. This time, they had built the houses and the hospital between the trees to avoid drone detection. There were enough clearings in the area that people could go to enjoy the sunlight.

Celeste was satisfied with the outcome of their efforts. This camp was definitely an upgrade.

"We are within walking distance of my cabin now," Ash said, putting his arm around Celeste's shoulders. "That means, when we need some time alone, we can just walk up there."

"That's great," Celeste exclaimed. "You know that your cabin will always be my true home."

"How about Delacroix?"

"Louisiana is my home, but my true home is where you are."

Ash pulled her to his chest, burying his face in her hair. He inhaled the jasmine scent that always radiated from her.

"You know, Ash, Dave admires you."

"He does?"

"Yes, you have grown on him."

"Ugh, fine. I guess he doesn't annoy me as much."

"Then, officially, we are all family. That makes me happy. Anyway, let's go get some sun." Celeste pulled him by the hand. "Soon it will start snowing. Let's enjoy the last warm days of the year."

They climbed to the clearing and sat in the grass.

She turned her face to the sunlight and closed her eyes. The warmth on her face was like the last caress before the winter freeze.

"I have to talk to Hayes about the negotiations in Louisiana."

"So, you're going to ruin his day too. Great! He'll be ecstatic to hear about your suicidal plans."

"Nothing has been planned yet. He may have some good ideas. He's a good leader and has operatives everywhere. I might not have to be involved at all."

"That's more like it," Ash grumbled. "Maybe he can put some sense in your head. Obviously, I can't."

"Let's not talk about that. I'm thinking that we should spend a couple of days in the cabin. I miss it."

"That sounds like a great idea to me. I think we have enough time to walk up there before dark."

They walked back to camp and let Hayes know before they left.

As Ash had said, they made it to the cabin at dusk.

While he was stocking the stove, Celeste put down the blackout curtains and lit the kerosene lamp.

Then, she took potatoes and dry elk meat, onions, and garlic out of her bags. Celeste looked through the cabinets and pulled out the oil and flour.

Ash was out back hauling in firwood. As soon as he walked back into the cabin, he was hit in the face with the best southern scent he had ever experienced. It was like he had materialized in Tante Marie's kitchen.

"What are you making?" Curious, he walked to the stove.

"I'm making elk gumbo." She stirred the pot and scooped a little with the spoon. "Do you want to taste it?"

Ash slurped the juice from the spoon and smiled.

"I never thought that some Cajun taste in my kitchen would make me so happy, but there I am. How did you get all the products?"

"Tante Marie gave me some spices. I'm glad you like it. I was worried that it might be too southern for you."

"Your cuisine broadened my perspectives. I didn't know I was missing Cajun cooking until I entered your Auntie's kitchen. Now I'm a fan."

After they got done eating, Celeste cleaned the table and sat by Ash.

"Did you eat well?" she asked.

"Yes, very well. It's amazing how you can conjure a delicious meal out of almost nothing. I guess I lucked out with a wife. Now, tell me what I can do for you."

"I need a bath." She said with a playful smile. "Would you like to join me?"

Ash stood up and heated water. After taking a bath together, they lay in bed.

Celeste completely gave in to Ash's embrace, knowing their time together might run out soon. She said nothing, though she knew he probably thought the same.

Ash was awakened by the scent of fried pastry. He sat up in bed and saw Celeste dancing around the stove.

"Are you making breakfast again?"

"Yes, how about my Auntie's beignets recipe with some Chicory coffee?"

"You are going to spoil me."

"Dat's de point, sha." She smirked, slipping into her Cajun lilt just to make him smile.

Ash walked up to her.

"I love you so much, Tink!"

He picked her up and spun her around.

After they finished breakfast, Celeste walked outside and sat in the grass. Ash followed her.

"I love it here so much!"

Celeste took a deep breath. She could smell fall in the air, a mixture of crisp morning air, the earthy scent of the fallen leaves, and the spicy touch of the pine resin.

"Have I ever told you how beautiful you are?" Ash ran his fingers through her hair.

"Actually, no. You've never said it."

"I guess I was too busy taking it in. You are stunning."

"Now I'm blushing." She laughed. "How did you picture me when we were friends on Amnestic?"

"I thought you were a little blond thing, like Tinker Bell. Instead of that, I got a heartbreakingly beautiful southern woman. I still can't believe my luck."

Celeste chuckled.

"How about me?" Ash asked. "How did you picture me?"

"Actually, I pictured you exactly as you are, strong, carrying scars from battles, and being an insufferable grump."

"So, no surprises for you?"

"Oh, there was a surprise. It was your smile."

Ash and Celeste stayed in the cabin for another day and then returned to camp.

Chapter 39

The next morning, Celeste walked to Hayes's office.

"Do you still have your encrypted phone?" She closed the door behind her.

"Yes, but why do you need it?"

"I want to listen to the messages on my answering machine in Dubois. I don't want to get traced."

Without further question, Hayes handed her his phone.

Celeste dialed the number and listened. Her face darkened.

"Bad news?" Hayes asked after she hung up.

"I'm being recalled to Denver. My Alliance boss wants a meeting with me, at Gabriel's order, no doubt."

"You aren't considering this, are you?" Hayes frowned. "Celeste, have you lost your mind? He tried to murder you in Delacroix."

"Dave, I have to go."

Speechless, Hayes just raised his eyebrows.

"Before we continue this conversation, I have to brief you on my negotiations with Canada and Mexico."

"The negotiations. I didn't think you managed to set that up."

"We did; the meeting happened. Canada and Mexico are ready to declare war on the Alliance. There is only one condition. Gabriel Clement must die first. They won't attempt anything until that happens."

"I don't think our operatives can get to him. He's the best-guarded Alliance official. How do they expect us to achieve that?"

"That's where I come in. I'm the only one who can get close enough to him to do it."

"No!" Hayes shook his head. "I'm not letting you commit suicide. Absolutely not! This is out of question."

"Dave, you know this is our last chance at freedom. I'm ready. My blood is responsible for what happened to this country. My father murdered your family, Ash's family... I have to redeem myself, even if it costs me my life. I hope you can understand."

"There has to be another way. We can hire a professional assassin."

"Dave, we'll only have one shot at that. I am your best assassin."

Hayes closed his eyes, his breath ragged. He stayed silent for a long time.

"Okay," he finally said. "I know that you'd do it regardless of what I or Ash has to say. So, I will allow it with one condition. I'll arrange for my operatives in Denver to trail you. A few of them are embedded within the Alliance intelligence office. I'm willing to sacrifice their cover for this. Once you eliminate Clement, they will extract you."

"Yes, you can have it your way, Dave. Now, we have to sell that to Ash."

"Good luck with that. You'd be lucky if he doesn't tie you up and chain you to your bed. I can easily see him doing it. In fact, I'm hoping that he does."

"Dave..."

"Celeste, I don't care if Gabriel is your birth father. He didn't raise you. None of that's your fault. I can't lose you!"

"Let's hope your operatives can help then."

Hayes looked for a long time at the door after she left. Then he shook his head and started making calls.

After leaving Hayes's office, Celeste went looking for Ash. She found him getting ready to go hunting.

"I'll bring some meat for dinner." He slung his bow and arrows on his back. "Tonight, I'm cooking. Can I count on you to prepare some potatoes and carrots?"

"You got it." She smiled.

As soon as she turned around, her smile faded. She didn't have the heart to tell him before his hunt. She decided to talk to him when he returned to camp.

Celeste was peeling potatoes, thinking about Ash.

How am I going to say goodbye without saying it?

She felt her heart tighten. How would she leave Ash, knowing it will probably be forever? Tears rolled down her face. She was happier than she had ever been in her life, and it was coming to an end.

Celeste had told Hayes that she was ready, but she wasn't. She didn't want to leave Ash. Her heart was already breaking into pieces just thinking about it. She hated Gabriel. He had ruined her entire life, and now he was going to be the cause of her demise.

Celeste was scared and angry. She wished there was another way. A way that didn't end with losing Ash forever. Unfortunately, the only option was already laid out—it was her and no one else.

I guess Gabriel will be the end of me, as he was my mother's. That must be fate. 'Astre, ça!' (That's fate.)

Celeste took a deep breath. There was too much at stake to fall apart over personal heartbreak. The future of all children in this camp, in Delacroix, and the rest of the country was in her hands. There was no going back.

Ash came back in the afternoon with a deer. He cleaned the meat, gave most of it away to the people in camp, and, after washing up, cooked a pot roast.

"Probably my meal tastes bland to your Southern palate," he joked.

"Not at all. You are a great cook. I love when you feed me."

"I'm glad."

"I need to tell you something," Celeste said after they finished eating.

Ash's stomach dropped.

"I have to go to Denver."

"You're joking, right?"

He stood up.

"No, I was ordered to go to Denver for an important meeting."

"There's no way I'd let you go alone in the lion's den. If you do that, you'll never come back. I won't have that."

"I have to go, Ash. We both knew it would come to that."

"No. Just no."

"Ash, the fate of the entire country relies on this one thing. You know that. We've had this conversation before."

"Then I'm going with you."

"You can't. If you do, we will both die before I even manage to get anywhere near Gabriel."

"Tink, please! You don't understand. I can't..."

His hands gripped the edge of the table.

"I won't be alone. Dave is sending his Denver operatives to extract me once the deed is done."

Ash felt his world fall apart.

"Ash..." Celeste touched his knee.

"Tink..."

She saw pain that she had never seen before in his eyes.

She reached and ran her hand down the side of his face.

"I won't be alone, Ash." She repeated to reassure him.

"Okay, I'll let you go, but don't you dare to die!" Ash clenched his jaw.

"I'll do everything in my power to come back to you. I promise."

"I'll hold you to that."

That night, Celeste lay in Ash's arms, listening to the cracking of the wood in the fireplace. She closed her eyes and smiled. All she needed in her life were the mountains and Ash's embrace. She didn't know if she'd ever get to feel peace again, but this moment was all that mattered.

When they woke up in the morning, it was snowing. A thick layer had already accumulated on the ground.

Celeste started to pack her traveling bag. She slipped off her wedding rings and put them in the drawer of the stand by the bed.

"Is this the reason you wanted to go to the cabin the other day?" Ash asked while watching her.

"In part. I didn't know about the meeting in Denver, but I knew it was coming. I wanted us to spend time in the cabin one last time."

"That wasn't the last time, Celeste."

"I hope not, but if it was..."

"No!" Ash cut her off. "I don't want to hear that."

"If something does happen to me..." Celeste swallowed hard. "Promise me you'll keep fighting, for both of us. Please, don't give up!"

"How can you ask me?" Ash balled his hands in fists, so she wouldn't see them trembling. "I barely survived losing you once. I don't think I can do it a second time. Not after I got to know you. You are my life, Tink."

Celeste wrapped her arms around him, unable to stop her tears.

They held each other for a long time.

"I have to see Dave too."

Celeste headed to Hayes's office.

"I need a vehicle."

"You're leaving today?"

Hayes's face tensed up.

"Yes, I have to go before the snow closes the roads. Did you call your agents?"

"Yes, everything is set up. You can have my truck. Leave it at the airport in Dubois. You can bring it back when you return."

He stood up and hugged her.

"Please, be careful. If you die, you'll break my heart," he whispered.

"I promise. I'll be careful."

She took Hayes's keys and walked to his truck to load her luggage.

She found Ash at the same place she had left him. He looked helpless, defeated.

"Ash..." She touched his hand.

"Please, come back!" he pleaded.

"I'll do everything in my power to do so. Kiss me now!"

He took her in his arms, and their lips locked, each trying to absorb the other and remember every scent and sensation of their touch. For a moment, everybody else disappeared. It was just Ash and Celeste, holding each other in the middle of a whirlwind of snow.

Chapter 40

Celeste cried as she drove away from the camp. She felt as if she was forcefully ripped away from everything that mattered in her life. She visualized every bittersweet moment she had shared with Ash, his brooding nature, the warmth of his lips, and the strength of his arms...

Then she thought of Hayes and her Louisiana family, Tante Marie, Pierre, and Joseph. Celeste didn't hold any illusion that she'd ever see any of them again.

She felt the pain of that thought deep down in her soul.

Celeste took a deep breath.

I have to pull myself together. The future of everybody I love is in my hands.

She hoped that Gabriel wouldn't have her arrested before she could come face-to-face with him. Ash and Hayes were right. Going to Denver was a huge risk.

Celeste wondered if she was making a mistake going there. It was probably a setup. However, if she waited any longer, Mexico and Canada could reconsider. Yes, going to Denver was a risk, but it was the best option at the moment.

When Celeste arrived in Dubois, she bought a plane ticket to Denver. The first plane was scheduled to leave early in the morning. She spent the night at her and Ash's house.

She listened to the messages on her answering machine again. The order to return to Denver was coded, and it was her main Alliance handler who had called. It wasn't a suggestion. It was a direct order, straight from Gabriel Clement, no doubt. He had probably figured her out by now.

Either way, it didn't matter. All that mattered was meeting him face to face. She had a stealth razor-sharp dagger made of reinforced glass. It was undetectable by metal detectors. She knew she could deliver a deadly strike with surgical precision. All she needed was a minute of face-to-face with Gabriel. What happened to her afterwards didn't matter.

Celeste sighed heavily. Thinking that she would have no regrets was lying to herself. All she could do was think about Ash.

"I love you, Tink," his words echoed in her mind.

I love you, Ash!

She hoped Hayes would be there for him after...

She knew this moment was coming from the very beginning.

I should've never let that relationship breathe.

On the other hand, it was inevitable. Ash and she were both cursed to fall into a hopeless, all-consuming love that had no chance from the very beginning.

Celeste wiped her tears and lay in bed, staring into the darkness. She wanted to leave a farewell letter for Ash, but knew it was impossible. This house was most likely compromised, and the Alliance would probably search the entire place as soon as she left in the morning. She would never leave a trail that would compromise Ash or the Resistance.

Celeste got up early in the morning and took a shower. She stood in front of the mirror in the bedroom. On impulse, she took her bright red lipstick from her makeup drawer, painted her lips, and left a kiss on the glass. Then she drew a heart around the kiss.

She smiled. That childish message was all she could leave behind. It was enough. Ash would understand.

Celeste took a deep breath and walked out of the house. She boarded the plane with no issues. Obviously, Gabriel wanted her to make it to Denver. If he intended to arrest her, he would've already done it.

The flight was about an hour. Celeste spent that time trying to calm her wildly beating heart. She was scared. Telling herself it was righteous didn't help.

Once in Denver, Celeste went to her apartment there. She frowned, seeing the thick layer of dust covering everything. She hadn't been here for almost three years.

She walked into her office and opened the desk drawer. It was full of her evidence of searching for Ash. Celeste stepped back and looked at the desk. It was the only piece of furniture not covered in dust.

Gabriel!

Of course, he had gone through her things. He probably knew Hayes wasn't Ash.

Celeste pressed her lips together. Everything was about to come unraveled. Clement probably knew about her relationship with Ash. Of course, he knew! Rose had probably told him everything.

Celeste felt her heart tighten. She only hoped that Ash would stay in the camp. There, he was relatively safe. If he followed her, Gabriel would have him arrested and executed.

Please, Dave, don't let Ash leave!

Celeste took several deep breaths and called the Alliance headquarters.

"I'm in Denver. When do you want to see me?"

"Get some rest today," her handler said. "I want to see you in my office tomorrow morning at nine."

Celeste spent the day cleaning the apartment. She had to keep herself busy, or she would spiral. Gabriel was probably delaying the meeting to torment her. He most definitely knew.

She realized how close to losing their lives they had come in Louisiana. Clement had tried to wipe out her entire family without regard for whether her life was in danger. She had always known that he wouldn't spare her. He had always hated her. In his eyes, she was an abomination, a stain on his "pure" French blood. As soon as he had no use for her, he was going to destroy her. The strong resemblance to her mother was surely fueling Gabriel's hatred.

I guess that time has come.

Celeste felt her anxiety wane. The farther from her people she was, the safer for them.

Eliminating Clement was the only thing that mattered right now.

Celeste arrived at the Alliance Intelligence Headquarters at exactly nine o'clock the next morning. She sat in the lobby, waiting to be called in. Two hours passed, and she was still waiting.

Gabriel's a snake.

He knew how to play on her anxiety.

Celeste smiled coldly. She had cried all her tears and suffered all her fears the days before. Now, she was only concerned with her mission.

"Mademoiselle Beaumont."

She heard her name. Clement had instructed his staff not to address her by his last name. Not that she wanted him to accept her as a daughter. It was a sign that he had no intentions of doing so.

Celeste entered the office of the agency's director. She looked around the room. Clement wasn't there.

"Mademoiselle Beaumont, sit."

The director pointed to a chair.

"So, why am I here?" Celeste asked.

The director raised his finger, telling her to wait.

She took a deep breath. She was sick of Gabriel's games. If he wanted to talk to her, where was he?

Celeste felt the blade of her glass dagger poking against her skin in her sleeve.

All she needed was Clement to arrive.

"So, why did you want me to come all the way here?"

"I didn't call this meeting. It was ordered by Monsieur Clement."

"When is he coming?"

"I asked you to wait."

Celeste felt her nerves straining to the limit. Obviously, Gabriel was orchestrating this as a psyop to intimidate and scare her.

She wasn't going to allow him to have the satisfaction.

"Fine, I'll wait. It's not like I have anything better to do, like maintaining a cover with the Resistance."

Celeste leaned back in the chair and crossed her legs.

Another half hour passed.

Then the phone rang.

"It's for you." The director handed her the handset.

"Hello, Celeste." It was Clement.

"Gabriel!" She attempted to keep her voice steady. "I thought you'd be here."

"I didn't expect you to come, so I didn't."

"So, what's that all about?" Celeste tried unsuccessfully to hide her irritation.

So this was all for nothing. He wasn't even in Denver!

"You owe me an explanation," he said coldly.

"Explanation about what?"

"You need to explain why you lied to me."

"Since when do I owe you anything?"

"Drop the act! I know Ash is alive. Not only that, but you went to Ravenville, humiliated my soldiers, had some of them killed, and extracted one of the most wanted leaders of the Resistance. Explain yourself."

"I need those individuals as assets. My position in the Resistance relies on them. You are trying to kill my only means to keep my cover intact."

"Fine. There's the deal. I no longer need you embedded in the Resistance. I don't care about anything they do. They are helpless anyway. Your assignment there is over."

"So, that's it. You just want me to leave?"

"Oh, no. You aren't getting off that easy. You betrayed my trust. Now you need to prove your worth to me. That's if you want to continue breathing."

Celeste took a deep breath, feeling the rage rising in her head.

"What do you want me to do?"

"Kill Ash."

"What..." Celeste's breath caught in her throat, and she gripped the phone until her knuckles turned white.

"Do you think I don't know about your infatuation with him?" Clement laughed coldly. "I know everything, Tink."

Celeste felt her blood run cold.

"I should've arrested you as soon as you arrived in Denver," he continued, "but I will give you one more chance to redeem yourself. Eliminate your terrorist crush, and you can be my daughter again."

"How do you suppose I do that? I can't touch him in their stronghold. They will kill me."

"Don't worry, he made it easy for you. He's at your house in Dubois. I could've had him eliminated several times over, but I want you to do it. This is your last chance at redemption. So, your turn."

"Fine." Celeste clenched her jaw. "I'll do as you ask."

"Good. You will fly back with one of our jets. Once it's done, I'll meet you in Dubois for a debriefing."

He disconnected the call.

"Mademoiselle Beaumont," the agent who had called her in, waved at her from the door, "follow me. Your flight is waiting."

Celeste sat in her seat and closed her eyes.

I have to figure something out!

Clement had outmaneuvered her again. He had known everything all along!

The anger raged in her head, but she gathered all her strength to stop it from showing. She was sure he was watching.

She had lost the game. And this time she was out of moves.

The only option now was to find Ash and trick the Alliance long enough for them to escape.

It wasn't ideal, but it was the only move she had left.

Chapter 41

Celeste took a cab to her home in Dubois. She walked to the house, feeling her legs weakening as she stepped through the door. Ash was sitting on the sofa in the living room. As soon as she walked in, he jumped to his feet.

Celeste put her finger to her lips and quickly started looking for cameras. Ash understood and joined her efforts. Soon, they found the devices and destroyed them.

"You're back!" Ash grabbed Celeste and pulled her to his chest. "I was worried to death. I was hoping to get here before you left for Denver. I was planning to talk you out of it, or even stop you from leaving, or something, but I was too late. So, I just decided to wait for you here. Did you get Clement?"

Celeste just shook her head.

"Tink, what..." Ash's stomach dropped.

"He knows everything. He wasn't even in Denver. He ordered me to kill you to redeem myself."

She sagged down on the sofa. Her hands were trembling.

"If that would keep you alive, I'm ready for it." Ash looked into her eyes.

"What are you talking about? I'd never hurt you. I'd die before... Besides, killing you isn't going to fix anything. This is Gabriel's punishment for lying to him. He knows everything about you and me... Everything. He wants me to kill the man I love. He has no intentions of sparing my life. I can clearly see his scenario. If I kill you, the next will be to tell him where the new camp is so that he can destroy it. Once it's all done, he'll put a bullet in my head, like he did to my mom."

"So, what do you suggest?"

"Let me think for a second."

She laid her head on Ash's chest, and he wrapped his arms around her.

"I can only assume that there is an Alliance operative watching the house. If we try to run, they will shoot us. I'm also sure Gabriel knows that I'd never kill you."

"So, we'll go out, guns blazing." Ash smiled. "I have no intention of allowing them to arrest me."

"Gabriel doesn't want to arrest us. It's the endgame for him. Let me just enjoy you holding me for a few more minutes, and then we'll see."

Celeste looked up to meet his eyes.

"I found your love letter on the mirror." Ash smiled.

He put his hand behind her head and pulled her closer. They kissed and stayed pressed against each other for a long time.

Celeste breathed in his familiar scent, a faint mix of gasoline and machine oil. She smiled. Being in his arms again wasn't in her plans. Even if this was the last time, they held each other, she'd gladly take it.

"Ash, if we're unable to escape together, we'll die together." Celeste looked into his eyes and smiled.

"That's the worst-case scenario. I have a better idea. This is what we're going to do."

He moved her off his lap and reached for his rifle.

"I will walk you out of the house at gunpoint." Ash rubbed his forehead. "Let's test if Gabriel truly doesn't care for you. If you're right, and he doesn't, we'll try to shoot our way out. Make sure your revolver's safety is off."

Celeste quickly released the safety of her weapon and put it back in the holster on her thigh.

"This is the worst plan I've ever agreed to." She laughed. "I guess, when you're out of options, that'll have to do."

"The worst plan is always better than no plan."

"Well, let's not delay it then."

"I love you, Tink!" Ash pulled her close and kissed her one last time.

"I love you, Ash." She caressed his face. "Let's go shoot us some Alliance goons."

Celeste stepped out of the house and drew in the freezing winter air. She felt the muzzle of Ash's rifle pressed against her back. There was no way this plan was going to work.

She thought of everyone she loved and sighed. All her plans had failed. She should've stayed in camp as Hayes and Ash had suggested and baited Clement. Instead, she had walked straight into his trap.

She had only made a few steps toward Ash's truck when her eyes caught a movement on the side of the house.

"Both of you, stop!"

Gabriel!

Clement and one of his patrolmen were standing a few feet away from them. He had his revolver pointed at Ash.

"Don't move or I'll put a bullet in her." Ash pressed the muzzle of his rifle against her back.

"How about one better? If you don't lower your rifle, I'll put a bullet between her eyes." Clement laughed coldly and moved his aim to Celeste.

"You will shoot your own daughter in cold blood?" Ash narrowed his eyes.

"She's no daughter of mine. She was raised by backwater swamp trash. She's a disgrace to my bloodline. She was meant to die with her mother years ago. But better late than never."

"You're a monster!" Celeste could no longer contain her rage.

"I've been called that before. Not really a bad thing to be when dealing with social degenerates like you."

"Tell me, why did you kill my mother? She did nothing to you."

"Nothing? She embarrassed me by leaving with my child. I married her, even though she was undeserving. Instead of being grateful and making an effort to integrate into our society, she chose to show her American defiance. Well, that doesn't fly in my world. I had to discipline her. She had already poisoned you as well. After she ran off, I realized that it was your dirty southern blood that was the culprit, and the only way to deal with it was to erase it out of existence."

"You deserve to die!" Celeste gritted out.

"Enough chit chat." Clement waved his gun. "Come on, lower your weapon before I shoot your sweetheart. I know you aren't going to hurt her."

At that moment, Ash knew that Clement wasn't going to spare Celeste. There was only one option left.

He started lowering his rifle to the ground. As he did that, he simultaneously pulled Celeste's revolver out of her holster, stepped in front of her, and pushed her to the ground, while firing simultaneously.

Celeste lost her bearings and fell. She saw Ash's bullet strike Clement between the eyes. With a shocked expression on his face, Gabriel crumpled to the ground.

A split second later, Celeste saw Ash fall. Her heart sank. She quickly grabbed the revolver from his hand and shot the second Alliance soldier.

Then she hovered over Ash. There was a bullet wound above his heart. He was breathing fast; his jacket was soaked in dark blood. Clement must've fired at the same time as Ash did.

"Shit! Ash, can you walk?" Celeste felt her mind spiral.

"Leave me," he said, gritting his teeth. "I'll only slow...slow you down."

"No!" Celeste shook her head. "If I can't get you in the truck, I'm staying. I will never leave you behind."

"Help me then," he whispered in a breathless voice.

She lifted him from the ground and walked him to the truck. Once he sat in the passenger's seat, she jumped behind the wheel and peeled out.

"Please, hold on!" She pushed with her hand on his chest, trying to put pressure on his wound, even though she knew it was pointless.

He continued to bleed from the exit wound on his back.

"Stay with me, Ash!"

Celeste looked at him. Bright blood was dripping from his lips. She reached over and wiped his mouth with her sleeve.

"Spit that blood. It will help you breathe easier.

He didn't answer.

"Are you still with me? Ash!"

She found his hand and squeezed it.

Celeste pressed her lips together. Ash was fading out fast. She didn't even know if he could hear her, but his chest still rose and fell. She felt her panic spiral out of control.

Calm down! Pull yourself together.

She pressed the accelerator to the limit.

Hold on, Ash, we are almost there!

As soon as she reached the dirt road leading to camp, Celeste exited the vehicle and opened the gate. She drove through and closed it behind the truck.

She looked at Ash. He seemed unconscious. Celeste put her fingers on his neck. She could feel the weak, thready pulsation under her fingertips. With a sigh of relief, she pressed the accelerator.

Ash felt his mind slip.

He saw himself sitting in the grass behind his cabin. Celeste was across, smiling with the sunlight reflecting from her shiny, dark hair.

"I live for your smile." Celeste's eyes sparkled. "I will remember you as you are right now, sitting by me on the spring grass, smiling like you own the world..."

Ash took a ragged breath and opened his eyes.

"I love you, Tink!"

He reached for her, but his arm fell to the seat, and his head lolled.

"No! No, no, no!"

Celeste slammed on the brakes. The truck came to a screeching stop, snow flying from underneath the wheels.

"Mais, don't be doing dat! C'mawn, sha!"

She put her fingers on the side of Ash's neck.

Nothing!

He was still, too still. She jumped out, opened the passenger's door, and pulled Ash to the ground. Then she started doing chest compressions.

"Come on, Ash, don't give up now!"

She blew air into his mouth and started compressions again.

She took Ash's phone out of his pocket and dialed Hayes's number.

No answer!

"Dave, please, help me," she screamed once the voicemail kicked on. "Ash got shot in the chest. He went into cardiac arrest. I'm doing CPR on the road. We're about a mile away from you. Please, help me!"

"Come on, Ash, you can't leave me... not like that. Please!"

Crying, she continued to compress his chest frantically.

"Come on!"

Celeste's heart was beating in her head. She didn't care that it was too long. She continued to compress his chest. It started to snow. The snowflakes fell on Ash's face and didn't melt.

Celeste put her entire weight into the chest compressions, trying to push as fast and as hard as she could. Rage surged in her chest. No, Clement wasn't taking the only light in her life!

Celeste let out a helpless cry. "'*Què'qu'un…s'iouplaît…aidez-moi*!'(Please, someone help me!)."

Then she heard the rhythmic hum of an engine. The camp's medical van whipped along the bend, then swerved and turned around. A second later, Hayes exited the vehicle and knelt by her.

"I've been doing compressions and nothing…"

He stared at her. She was as pale as a ghost, Ash's blood on her hands, face, clothes… Her eyes were wide with despair.

"Hand me the tamponade syringe," Hayes shook his head and ordered. "I think he has a cardiac tamponade. It doesn't seem that he's lost a critical amount of blood."

Celeste quickly followed his directions.

Hayes exposed Ash's chest and inserted the long needle directly into his pericardium. He pulled back the plunger, and the syringe filled with dark blood.

While he was doing that, Celeste inserted an intravenous line into Ash's arm and an endotracheal tube in his airway.

Hayes pulled the needle out and started compressions.

"Bring the defibrillator."

Celeste ran to the medical van, grabbed the machine, and quickly attached the electrodes to Ash's chest.

"Asystole… Shit! Inject epi."

She followed his order while he continued compressing Ash's chest.

"Three minutes since I injected the epinephrine," she announced.

"Rhythm check." Hayes looked at the monitor. "Ventricular fibrillation. Thank God! Defibrillate now."

He removed his hands from Ash's chest and pulled back.

Celeste charged the machine and pressed the button. Ash's body jerked briefly under the electric current.

Hayes continued compressions. In two minutes, Celeste defibrillated again.

Hayes resumed compressions. After two minutes, he checked for a pulse.

"I have a pulse. Let's go. Help me put him on the stretcher."

Hayes ran to the van. They loaded Ash on the stretcher and then into the vehicle.

"Drive!" Hayes ordered. "I'll stay in the back with him."

Celeste hit the accelerator and drove straight to the hospital in the camp.

Chapter 42

Hayes and Celeste spent hours together, repairing the damage to Ash's chest. The bullet had missed his heart but torn the pericardium, causing blood to rush in and constrict the heartbeat, resulting in cardiac arrest.

"Well, his heart held," Hayes said after they closed Ash's chest. "Now it's one day at a time."

"Do you think he'll make it?" Celeste asked with a trembling voice.

"We just have to hope for the best." Hayes sighed. "He was down for a long time... Even if he wakes up, he might not be the same person."

"Don't say that!" Celeste cut him off. "Ash is a fighter. He'll pull through."

Hayes looked at her, feeling his chest clench. He didn't want to give her empty promises, but he also didn't want to take her hope away.

Celeste sat by Ash's bed for the next two days. His vitals held.

He had survived the surgery.

Now, it was a waiting game.

Hayes wanted to keep him sedated and on a ventilator, at least for a week, to give his brain time to recover. Then, he was going to attempt to wean him off the breathing machine.

He looked at Celeste. Her pale face and dark circles under the eyes made his heart tighten. It was a miracle she hadn't collapsed yet.

"Please, get some sleep. I'll sit with him." Hayes put his hand on Celeste's shoulder. "I promise, if something changes, I'll tell you right away."

She nodded and walked to the little home that Ash had built. She opened the drawer in the bedside stand, took her wedding rings, and put them on.

Then she sagged down on the bed and closed her eyes. She ran every moment from the previous day through her mind.

Suddenly, it dawned on her. Ash had planned everything. He had decided to sacrifice himself so she could live. Before they stepped out of their house in Dubois, he had asked her to remove the safety of her revolver. He knew exactly what he was doing. He didn't tell her, so she wouldn't stop him.

Celeste covered her head with the blanket and silently cried until she drifted into restless sleep.

She didn't know how long she'd been asleep when she suddenly woke.

Ash!

She jumped out of bed, washed up, and walked to the hospital.

Hayes was sitting on a chair next to Ash's bed as he promised.

"Did you get some sleep?" He looked at Celeste.

"Yes, I did. How is he?"

"He's alive. His vitals are holding. The tamponade was what did him in. How long was it before you realized he was in cardiac arrest?"

"I knew immediately. He was in the passenger seat. So, I parked right away, dragged him out of the truck, and started compressions."

"That's actually great news. His chances of full recovery just improved. Besides, the extremely low temperatures that day might have been in Ash's favor. His brain might not have suffered as much damage as I initially thought."

"He'll pull through. You'll see. My Ash will fight. I know it."

She reached to move a strand of hair away from Ash's face.

Hayes closed his eyes. His heart was breaking for Celeste. She had fallen apart right in front of his eyes. He prayed that Ash recovered, for Celeste's sake.

"So, are you going to tell me what happened, or is it too soon?" Hayes touched her shoulder. "You don't have to talk if you don't feel like it."

"Now is as good a time as ever." Celeste sighed. "Clement set a trap for us, and we walked right into it. Once I got to Denver, he ordered me to kill Ash. He wasn't even in Denver. He was waiting for us in Dubois. Why did you let Ash follow me?"

"He left without telling me anything. You know him."

"Yes, I do. Anyway, after I found Ash in the house, I knew we were doomed. Long story short, on our way out of the house, Gabriel showed up and threatened to shoot me if Ash didn't drop his rifle. Ash dropped the rifle but pulled my revolver, pushed me away, and shot Clement, absorbing his bullet as well."

Hayes's eyes widened.

"Yes, Gabriel is dead." Celeste nodded. "He died from a bullet with his name engraved on it. You can send the message to our allies."

"Phenomenal!" Hayes smiled.

"I always thought it would be me to sacrifice my life for the cause, but it was Ash who did. He took a bullet meant for me."

Celeste covered her face, unable to stop her tears.

"Have faith, Celeste." Hayes wrapped his arm around her shoulders. "He will recover. He survived the gunshot wound. We just have to correct the blood loss."

"Take my blood. I owe him."

"Are you sure?"

"Yes, I have fully recovered from my surgery. It's been a year since. You can use my blood."

"Okay, let's go to the lab."

Later, Celeste sat by Ash's bed watching the blood slowly drip into his veins.

"Now, you'll carry me in your heart too," she said, smiling. "'Mo t'aime, sha!' (I love you, dear!)"

She placed a kiss on his forehead.

Celeste sat next to Ash's bed day after day. She took care of him, repositioned and washed his body to ensure the integrity of his skin.

Hayes gave up trying to talk her into going home, so he brought one of the recliners from his office to the hospital for Celeste. He also made sure to bring food and water for her. He sat and watched her until she ate.

Celeste was grateful to him. She knew that without him, Ash would've died, and she would've lost her mind.

"Thank you, Dave!" She squeezed his hand. "I owe everything to you."

"You owe me nothing, Celeste. I'd give my life for you if I had to."

"I know. You got shot trying to do it." She smiled.

"I remember. I was there." He laughed.

Celeste had just finished with Ash's morning routine when Hayes walked in.

"Are you ready?" He looked at her. "I will attempt to wean him off the ventilator."

Celeste just nodded. She felt her heart wildly beating in her chest.

Hayes decreased the anesthetic and discontinued the paralytic agent.

"We will know shortly."

Celeste silently gripped the armrests of her chair.

Please, Ash, breathe!

"It's time."

Hayes disconnected the tubing of the ventilator.

Shaking, Celeste stared at Ash. Finally, his chest rose, and he took a breath.

"He's breathing on his own." Hayes deflated the balloon of the breathing tube and removed it from Ash's throat. "Now we have to wait for him to wake up."

"Yes," Celeste said through her teeth.

Hayes had said "...wait for him to wake up," but she knew he really meant to say: "to see if he'd wake up."

"C'mawn, sha!" she caressed Ash's face. "I'm waiting for you. Please, come back to me!"

He didn't react, but Celeste didn't give up. For the next several days, she continued talking to him about Amnestic, their moments together, the trip to Louisiana, and the cabin.

Hayes came several times. He tried to tell her that Ash can't hear her.

"I stopped the anesthetic yesterday." He sighed. "If he hasn't woken up yet, the chances are slim."

Celeste just shook her head and continued talking to Ash.

"I know you can hear me, love. Please, don't leave me!"

She took his hand in hers, then lowered her head and kissed him.

"If you die, I'll die too," she said through tears. "It was never meant to be just you or me. We were meant to be together. Always!"

Celeste felt her heart breaking into a thousand pieces. She covered her face with her hands, sobbing uncontrollably.

"Tink..."

The name fluttered in the air, quiet, barely audible.

Celeste gasped and looked at Ash. His eyes were open.

"Don't cry," he whispered in a raspy voice.

"Ash, thank God!"

Celeste knelt by his bed and threw her arms around him.

She cried, but those were happy tears.

She felt Ash's hand on the top of her head.

"Please, don't cry!" he said again.

Celeste quickly pulled back. "Am I hurting you?"

"You didn't hurt me."

"Thank you for coming back to me! I begged you for days." She smiled.

"I know; I heard you. Thank you for believing in me. I didn't think I'd make it. The bastard got me good. I thought I was going to die."

"Yes, you died. Your heart stopped en route to camp. The situation was bad, but you married into a family of surgeons. Dave and I fought for you."

"What about Clement?" Ash asked.

"You never have to worry about him again. You sent one of my signature bullets right between his eyes. He's gone."

"Are you okay?" Ash reached and touched her face. "He was your father."

"He was never my father. Tante Marie and Nonc Marcel were my parents. Gabriel was the monster in my closet... Ash, why did you take that bullet? It was meant for me."

"The day we left Delacroix, I promised Tante Marie to protect you with my life, so I did. I would've done it either way."

"You gave me such a scare!" Celeste rested her head on her hand, still crying.

"Don't worry about me. I'll be all right. That's not my first rodeo. During the war, I came close to death many times. That's why they call me Ash."

"I believed in you. Dave was skeptical, but I think he pretended to be hopeful just to make me feel better."

Celeste turned her head to a noise at the door and saw Hayes walking in.

"Oh, my God!" he exclaimed, seeing Ash awake. "Celeste was right that you'd pull through. You're one stubborn bastard, I tell you. I didn't think you'd make it."

"Well, you know me."

"I was coming to tell you that the news of Clement's demise is out. Things will start moving soon. We owe this to the two of you. America will be forever indebted to you."

Celeste just looked at him and raised an eyebrow.

"What? I'm saying the truth." Hayes defended himself.

Celeste shook her head.

"I swear, Celeste, you and your southern spice. All that was missing in your response was 'bless your heart.' You're something else."

He left the room, laughing.

"Get some rest." Celeste planted a kiss on Ash's lips. "I'll go take a shower. I'll be back later."

Ash smiled. Seeing her face again was something he didn't think would happen.

He closed his eyes and thanked fate for that miracle.

Chapter 43

Ash's recovery was slow and steady. Celeste spent most of her time in his room, helping him feed himself and perform exercises to recover his muscle strength.

Once he was able to talk without losing his breath, she called Hayes, and they both helped him out of bed.

"You have to walk. Just hold on to our shoulders."

Ash didn't protest. He did everything they asked him to. After a couple of weeks, Hayes allowed him to leave the hospital and go to his and Celeste's house.

That night, she tucked him in bed and pulled up a chair to sit next to him.

"What are you doing?" Ash gave her a bewildered look. "Lie in bed with me."

"I don't want to hurt you."

"I'm fine. The wound is healing. I'm not in any pain."

Celeste slipped under the covers and lay her head on his shoulder.

"That's it." He smiled. "You in my arms is all I need."

The following days flew by quickly. The news of Clement's demise spread around the world like wildfire. The countries in the Alliance rose and demanded a change in government. Simultaneously, Mexico and Canada amassed their military on the American borders.

Within months, the Alliance fell apart. In the face of the neighboring armies, the Alliance forces quickly left the continent, leaving everything behind without a shot being fired. Everything was over as fast as it had begun.

Hayes walked into Celeste's and Ash's house with a bottle of champagne.

"We won. We have our freedom again, and you guys are the reason for it. Celeste, we can party again."

"Dave, we're a little too old now, but yes, if we want to, we can party. I think I'd just buy a few pounds of coffee." She looked at Ash.

"That reminded me of that day, when I made that contraband coffee in Ravenville. Do you remember?" He smirked.

"Of course I do." Celeste laughed. "You were trying so hard to hate me that you didn't even drink your cup of coffee."

"Thinking back, I can't believe how stupid I was."

"You weren't stupid." She shook her head. "You didn't know who I was, and I didn't tell you. You had to protect your people."

"I almost killed you."

"But you didn't. Ash, I never blamed you for anything. However, I blame him for all of it." She pointed at Hayes.

"Guilty as charged." He raised his hands. "I'd better skedaddle before you decide to unleash your southern temper on me."

Laughing, he took his bottle of champagne and walked out.

"I must say that he's growing on me." Ash smiled.

"Dave is a weirdo, but he has a good heart. We both owe our lives to him."

"I know. I'll be grateful to him for life."

Ash was getting stronger every day. Once the Alliance left the towns, the people from the camp went back to their homes. Celeste and Ash moved to their house in Dubois.

Hayes immediately ordered Ash to the hospital so his heart could be properly examined. All tests came back normal. Ash's heart had not sustained any permanent damage, his blood loss had stabilized, and his shortness of breath had disappeared.

"Just take it easy for a few more months. Don't try to be the tough guy," Hayes ordered. "I'm going to DC to start working on our government reinstatement. Don't let me hear that you're sick."

In the following days, Celeste was busy cleaning the house, and Ash logged into Amnestic to thank all his followers and congratulate Americans for their newly gained freedom.

"So, what now?" Celeste asked while lying in Ash's arms on the sofa. "I have no idea how to lead a normal life. I barely remember how things were before the war."

"Tell me about it." Ash ran his fingers through her hair. "But don't worry. We'll figure it out."

"For starters, Dave removed my implant while we were at the hospital." Celeste pointed to the little mark on her upper arm. "I'm ready to start our family."

"So am I." He lowered his head and kissed her.

Celeste winced, startled by a knock at the door.

"I'll get that." Ash opened the door to see Hayes standing there.

"Dave, what are you doing here?" Celeste exclaimed. "I thought you'd gone to DC."

"I was. I was trusted with the honor of being the new acting President of the United States, until a democratic election is held. I came here for you, Celeste. I want you to be my vice president."

"No, Dave, I won't do that. You will be a good president. Find a vice president who actually knows politics. I just want to live my life in peace."

"I understand." Hayes nodded. "I'll honor your choice, but I want you both to know that I'll keep bothering you from time to time. You aren't getting rid of me that easily."

"Of course, Dave." Celeste hugged him. "You will always be my brother. You know that. You're welcome to our home any time. Now, go recover our country and try to live a little. If I ever find you passed out because you've run yourself down to the ground, I'll slap some sense into you."

"I get it. I'll take care of myself. I promise. And what are you planning to do?"

"I think for now we'll take a vacation in my cabin up the mountain." Ash shrugged.

"Well, I think you're well enough to hike the distance, so have fun."

"When you go to the big boy house in DC, don't forget us. Call us!" Celeste smacked Hayes on the arm.

"You bet." He smiled and walked out.

Celeste watched him get in his vehicle, surrounded by Secret Service officers.

"He'll be a good president," Celeste said, while watching them drive away. "He might be a jerk, but he will govern fairly. Of that I'm sure."

"I have to agree. Hayes is a good guy." Ash sat back on the sofa.

"Do you really want to go to the cabin?" Celeste asked.

"Yes, I was serious. When I was dying in the truck, I had that vision of us sitting in the grass behind the cabin. The time we spent there after I found my Tink was the first time I felt happiness in years. I want to go back to that. How about you?"

"Absolutely. We can pack tomorrow and go. We just have to take it easy up the mountain. I don't want you to rupture your insides like I did that one time."

"Oh, you had to remind me about that, didn't you?" Ash laughed. "I still haven't forgiven myself for what I did to you."

"Please, that's ancient history. You repaid me tenfold by almost dying when you took the bullet meant for me."

"Okay," Ash said, smiling. "I promise never to shoot you again. How's that?"

"Deal." Celeste laughed.

The next day, they packed food and clothes and drove to Ash's mountain.

Celeste made sure that Ash took his time hiking up the hill. It took them several hours, but they finally reached the cabin.

While Ash was resting, she cooked dinner.

"It feels amazing to relax in bed with you without the dread of danger," he muttered. "It's a strange feeling, one that I'd forgotten existed."

"It's the best feeling."

Celeste cuddled up to him and kissed him. Then they slowly made love without dreading tomorrow.

When she opened her eyes in the morning, Celeste realized that Ash had never let go of her. He was already awake, gazing at her.

"We slept in. We should probably get up." He moved the hair away from her face.

Celeste looked out of the window. "Looks like a nice day."

She dressed, walked outside, and sat in the grass.

Ash followed her.

Celeste leaned on him.

"When you left for Denver last year, my heart shattered," he whispered. "I didn't think I'd ever see you again. I couldn't stay in camp. I had to go to Dubois and wait for you."

"And that's how you got in trouble."

"Honestly, if I didn't do it, Clement would've probably killed you. I'm glad for all the mistakes I made. It all led to this moment right here."

Celeste turned her head and looked into his eyes.

"There it is. The smile I love."

She traced his lips with her thumb.

"And you are the reason for it, Tink."

He wrapped his arms around her.

"It was two years ago, almost to the day, when we sat right here for the first time." Ash ran his fingers through her hair.

"It was, wasn't it? The day I heard you say, 'I love you' for the first time." Celeste smiled.

"Back then, I was confused and didn't know what to do with myself. One thing I was sure of was that I loved you. That I never doubted."

He kissed her on the side of her neck.

Celeste looked at the cascading ridges in the distance. The mountains were blooming with spring flowers and herbs. She turned her face to the sunlight and took a deep breath. She had done that before, but now it was different. The sense of danger was gone. Now she could enjoy every minute without feeling tension or fear. They had gotten their lives back. Every loss, every hardship had led to this moment, her in Ash's arms, owning the world.

Epilogue

Celeste laughed and took a bite of the alligator skewer in her hand.

They had arrived in Delacroix a week ago.

It had been two years since the Alliance was defeated, and things were only getting better.

Shortly after all communications were restored, Celeste reconnected with her family in Louisiana.

While she worked at the hospital in Dubois, Ash spent several months alone in Delacroix. He simply said that Tante Marie had asked him for help.

Celeste figured that they needed him for the rebuilding, so she didn't mind.

Hayes also visited often.

"I miss you guys," he kept saying.

He also tried to talk them into moving to DC, but Celeste and Ash both refused.

Two years later, Hayes took a vacation and agreed to visit Delacroix with Ash and Celeste.

When they arrived, Celeste was surprised that the town was completely rebuilt. Now, tourists filled the streets, laughing and shopping.

"This is how I remember my town."

She looked at Ash and smiled.

Tante Marie had prepared a big dinner. She hugged everybody, including Hayes.

"'Mon couyon préféwé!' (My favorite idiot)." She patted him on the back.

"Tante Marie, he's the president now," Celeste said playfully.

"Euh!" Marie gasped, then laughed.

"Tante Marie can call me anything she likes. She's my honorary Auntie." Hayes shrugged.

"I raise a toast to my family." Marie lifted a glass of orange wine. "Yes, you too, my honorary son, Dave, le Président. Let's drink to our freedom."

Celeste reached for the pitcher to pour wine into her glass, but Marie slapped her hand. " *'Cép toé'* (not you)."

Celeste gave her a bewildered look.

"'T'es dans l'état, toé.' (You are in the state/pregnant.)"

"Wait... I'm pregnant?" Celeste stared at her aunt.

"C'mawn, sha, I know." Marie laughed.

Celeste blushed, glanced down, and then up at Ash.

He was staring at her with wide eyes.

"I guess I have to get a pregnancy test." She shrugged.

After dinner, Ash and Celeste walked outside, holding hands.

"Did you help rebuild all the houses?" She looked at the new buildings.

"Yes, I did."

"It looks like you built more. My aunt's house was the last one on the street. Now there's another one right by it."

"Yes, love, that's our house."

"You built a house for us?"

"Yes, I was going to ask you if you'd want to move to Delacroix. I learned that there is no physician in town. You could open your own practice. We can spend our summers in my cabin in Wyoming. Of course, if you want that."

"Yes, that's perfect! Our children will grow up knowing their family. I'd love that."

Celeste threw her arms around his neck and kissed him.

Finally, she would have the family she always wanted.

"Thank you, Ash!" She laid her head on his chest. "I've always known that we'd have to travel to the end of the world to find our true happiness."

www.ingramcontent.com/pod-product-compliance
Lightning Source LLC
LaVergne TN
LVHW041110080826
845145LV00007B/1758

* 9 7 8 1 9 7 1 8 4 1 0 0 7 *